The World Behin

Chapte

Sometimes I wish I could I escape, in fact most days I think about how I could get away from my boring, repetitive existence. This week I did escape from the dull village my family and I used to live in, but I'm still extremely bored without very much things for me to do. Mum, Dad and I have moved to a beautiful Victorian country mansion, it is spectacular. I still haven't seen every room just yet and we have been living here for the last three days. We have land as far as the eye can see with a forest in the distance and a river running through the grounds. It is a lovely view from my bedroom on the third floor and I am sure I could go and find Bertie, our fluffy Old English Sheepdog, and go for a long walk but I can't find the motivation to do anything. I am just sitting in the window seat of my bedroom watching the day go by.

I thought moving away would be exciting but it hasn't really turned out that way. Mum said I could have friends to stay as much as I like but that is not much good when they are one-hundred and fifty miles away and they have no way of getting here. I'm sixteen years old and I am stuck in the middle of nowhere with no friends. The nearest school is twenty miles away and I don't think anybody lives close enough to be referred to as a neighbour. Even if I did find our neighbour they probably don't have any kids my age, so, as you can imagine I am in a fantastic mood.

Mum and Dad had this theory that if we move to the country we will live longer, happier, healthier lives. Well, not if I die of boredom first! There is no point sitting around all day moping so I suppose I will have a look around the house and see what is in the other rooms. I head down the long corridor, with its old fashioned dark wood decor, to the top of the antique stairs which spiral down to the main entrance hall. Walking down the stairs I hold the long skirt I am wearing gently at the knees and lift it up about an inch. I could be a princess going to the ball as I tip-toe down the stairs my feet click against the light silver marble, I elegantly swish my hair from side-to-side as I make my way down.

Now, where to go next? I look to the left which is the large dark wooden door to the kitchen, but, I don't think there is anything particularly exciting in there. Off to the right is the lounge so I think I will go that way and have a look inside. I open the large door which is twice the size of me, it creepily creaks open like something out of a horror movie. The room is quite plain because Mum and Dad haven't done much decorating yet, if any. The wallpaper is floral with pink tones and the carpet is cream with patterned pink flowers. I can't imagine Dad likes it very much, I think they will be decorating sooner rather than later.

The view from the bay window is marvellous as I walk towards it to look at the scenery. I can see there is a huge grey cloud looming and the trees are blowing wildly. I'm glad I didn't go outside for that walk now when it would appear there is a storm brewing, not to mention the fact that Bertie is a nightmare to dry off if he gets wet with all his fluffy fur. As I turn around I see there is a door at the back of the lounge which I hadn't noticed previously. I think I will have to go and see what is behind this door.

This door is painted white and smaller than the entrance to the lounge and easier to open, letting out an eerie creak as I push it, then I flick the light switch on. The room is filled from floor to ceiling with books, and in the middle of the floor there is a table with four chairs. It isn't a huge room, it must have been used as some kind of small library with books that look old and dusty, like they have been there since the house was built. I go towards one of the shelves to have a closer look at some of the books. There is a whole range of old encyclopaedia's, story books and biographies, then, I see a whole section devoted to witchcraft, sorcery, magic, myths, legends and more! This really wasn't what I expected, a whole range of books based on all things magical seems a bit surreal, I am well and truly intrigued.

I pick up a thick leather bound book and take it over to the table, wiping of a thick layer of dust, it is dark blue coloured and in silver writing it reads: "The Magic of Our Time". Now this looks interesting, I turn to the first page and written in ink it reads: "Things are not always what they seem. Don't make judgements at a glance, look deeper and you will see what others cannot." I feel a shiver run down my spine and notice all the little hairs stand up on my arms. As I turn the page I hear a thunderous roar as the storm outside begins to worsen.

I shut the book fast and put it back on the shelf, now it really is like something from a horror movie! I take a deep breath and look around the room at all the books and realise that my mind is playing tricks on me. Then, all of a sudden, there is another loud rumble of thunder, the light goes out and I can't see anything. Now I'm getting really scared, I run towards the door and the light comes back on just as I am scrambling for the handle.

I'm not going back in that room for a while, that was far too creepy. I start shouting for Bertie. He doesn't come to me and I begin to feel extremely anxious. I go into the kitchen to see if he is there but he is nowhere to be seen. I notice a small door at the back of the kitchen is slightly ajar and head towards it.

"Bertie!" I shout again loudly through the door, looking down the steps into darkness is another part of the house that

I hadn't found yet. I wonder where it leads to, as the storm continues to rumble on outside I am too scared to go down there to investigate. "Bertie! It's Melody!" I called again but no reply. Suddenly, I hear a yelp and a thud coming from the bottom of the stairs. Despite being so afraid, I have to go down there and check what has happened because Bertie might have hurt himself.

I begin to tip-toe down the stairs, every noise and creak makes my heart feel like it is going to burst out of my chest. I can hear some shuffling noises and now my heart is racing. "Bertie? Is that you?" I ask in the hope of some kind of reply in the darkness but all I can hear is the battering of hailstones coming down outside. I see a flash of lighting through the tiny window in the middle of the room. It must be a basement or perhaps it was used as a wine cellar. I hear more shuffling noises and I see movement beside a door in the left corner of the room.

"Bertie!?" I shout out feeling much more panicked than before. Suddenly, he comes bounding towards me and jumps up with his paws on my chest almost pushing me over. "What's wrong Bertie? Did the thunder give you a scare?" I ask him more gently now as he is clearly shaken. I wrap my arms round him and give him the biggest cuddle ever. "You're okay Bertie, it will stop soon." I say soothingly trying to reassure him, whilst stroking his huge fluffy head.

I find myself overwhelmed with curiosity at what is behind the door to the left of us, there appears to be a blue tinged glow coming from the room. I feel a little less frightened now I have Bertie with me, I decide to have a look through the door. I move towards the door slowly and carefully, pushing it open tentatively. It begins to creak slowly as I peer into the room it looks quite big, it is very dark which I find a little odd considering there was a glow only moments ago. Bertie seemed to have calmed down now that I am with him and stays by my side whilst I try to find a light switch.

After a few minutes I find the switch and click it a few times, but nothing happens. "The light isn't working Bertie! Let's go back into the other room." I hear another rumble of thunder and Bertie yelps. "It's okay Bertie, it's getting further away." I say softly. I find a light switch in the first room of the basement and as I press it a dull light flickers on. "Well, this isn't going to help us see into the other room Bertie, do you know what's in there? Do you?" I say playfully as I pat him.

I find a chest of drawers beside the steps down to the room and decide to have a look to see what is inside. I open the top drawer and there is nothing but a few pens and paperclips. In the second drawer there is a notebook, I pick up the book to open it when I notice some matches in the drawer and then lay it back down. "Perfect!" I tell Bertie.

I take the matches with me and go back through the door into the other room. I light up a match and notice my reflection directly in front of me. I walk closer to my reflection and realise there is a huge mirror from the ceiling to the floor. I walk along to the left, the mirror stretches the length of the room on one side. "I wonder if this was some kind of dance studio. What do you think Bertie?" I ask him, but as usual he doesn't reply. He just looks up at me breathing heavily with his tongue hanging out.

I start to walk back towards the right of the room, looking in the mirror as I go but I can't see anything in the reflection, the room is so huge and dark. As I come to the right corner of the room the match fizzles out. I reach into my pocket to light another one and then notice that there is a glow coming from the mirror. I look around the room but I can't see any windows. *How is this possible?*

I look at the mirror trying to see if there is anything reflecting and then I see something, a figure, it looks like a person. "What the...Bertie can you see that?" I say quietly feeling panicked that somebody might be in the room with us. "Who is there?" I ask a little louder. Then Bertie starts to bark, which causes me to panic, run out of the room and up the stairs. I stop at the top for a moment, Bertie comes running towards me. "Is somebody down there? Why would someone be in our basement? I think we should tell Mum and Dad" I whisper as I stroke his furry head.

I close the door firmly, go back through the kitchen and up the stairs to my room, I let Bertie come in before shutting my door, then, I put a box of school books against it before sitting down on my window seat. I begin staring outside, going over and over what just happened in my head. I want to talk about it with somebody, but there is nobody around to talk to. I wish Mum and Dad would hurry up and come home. I can't even talk to Bertie because he has fallen fast asleep at the end of my bed after his ordeal. I play out what happened again and again. *How could somebody be down there? Why wouldn't they come up? Why would they just stay down there? I must have imagined it.*

I kept thinking about the books I read in the library, how mysterious and out of this world they were. Perhaps they had something to do with the person I saw in the basement and that's if I really did see someone. Maybe my eyes were just playing tricks on me. I thought about the words written in the book, I picked up something about 'looking deeper' and 'seeing what others cannot'. I can't remember exactly, but maybe it could have something to do with it. This house has a strange atmosphere and I don't normally get spooked that easily, but there is definitely some weird things happening.

I look at the clock and notice the time is 4:45 p.m., Mum and Dad should be home any minute. They have their own landscaping business and they usually are home by around 5 o'clock. I plan to tell Mum and Dad that I think there could be somebody down there so that they will go and check. I'm finding the idea that there might be another person in this house with me extremely creepy but at least I have Bertie with me. I think our housekeeper, Jemima, is around here somewhere but it is easy to lose somebody in this huge mansion and it definitely wasn't her that I saw in the basement.

Chapter 2

I hear the faint mumblings of voices coming from downstairs, realising Mum and Dad are home I move the box of school books, open my door and run to them, Bertie charges after me. I run up to Mum, she looks immaculate as always with her curled dark blonde hair and smart long pleated cream dress with matching cream shoes. I give her a hug, snuggling into her and inhaling her delicate perfume. Bertie runs towards Dad who is wearing a dark green jumper and black jeans with big black boots. Bertie bangs into him head first and then proceeds to circle him with his tongue hanging out, breathing heavily as he goes around his legs repeatedly.

"Mum, I know you will think this is really stupid but, can you check something downstairs for me please?" I ask her nervously, hoping she doesn't think I am being ridiculous. "What is it you want me to check sweetheart?" She asks stroking my hair gently. "Well, I know it sounds a bit strange but I think somebody is down there in the basement." I say timidly.

"Oh dear Melody! I think your mind must be playing tricks on you. What were you doing down there by yourself?" Mum asks in a concerned manner.

"Well, Bertie was scared of the thunder storm earlier. I went down there to get him because he was howling, and then I found another room." I explain.

"Hmmm, I will go down there and have a look Virginia. I didn't know there was another room. This all sounds a bit strange." Dad spoke seriously, before heading down the basement stairs. Mum and I decide to follow along behind him to see what he finds. "The light doesn't work Dad." I say to him before he tries the switch.

Dad has a look around the basement using the camera light on his mobile phone to help him see where he is going. "I can't see another room Melody sweetheart, are you sure you weren't imagining things?" Dad asks gently.

"No dad, it's over there, in the left corner of the room." I pointed to the corner so Dad knew where to go but there was no glow this time. Dad shone the light of his phone in the corner and noticed the door which was smaller than any other door in the house. Dad is six-foot-three and he has to crouch right down to get through the door. I feel nervous as he enters the room, I feel all the little hairs stand up on the back of my neck. I can hear him shuffling around the room for a moment and he comes back out looking surprised.

"Well, Virginia I think we will have to get the bulb fixed in there. That room is huge! I can't believe we didn't know it was there! It looks like it was used as some kind of a gym, perhaps. There are mirrors that go all the way from the floor to the ceiling. Don't worry Melody, I can't see anything scary in there, it must have been your mind playing tricks on you. Let's go upstairs for supper." So with that, we all head back upstairs as Dad put his arm around me giving me a reassuring squeeze.

Mum serves up a bowl of carrot and coriander soup that Jemima prepared for us earlier. As I tuck into the delicious soup I find my mind still wandering. As much as I believe Dad that there was nothing scary down there, I am sure that I saw somebody down there and I can't shake the feeling that something strange is going on. I decide that I will go back down to the basement later on at night despite feeling very nervous about doing so.

Mum and Dad are deep in conversation about work stuff and they don't seem to notice that I haven't even said one word since we sat down. I'm not bothered because sometimes it's better not to be noticed. Mum and Dad can worry too much, ask me too many questions, it can be extremely frustrating.

I finish my soup, go to the sink to rinse the bowl and put it in the dishwasher, all the time still thinking about what is going on downstairs in the basement. "Is it okay if I go upstairs to my room?" I ask quietly. "But you haven't had your main course, you will be starving." Mum replies sternly. "I'm not hungry. I feel a bit light headed. I think I need to lie down." I say in the hope Mum excuses me because I just don't have any appetite at all. All I can think about is going down to the basement later to see if I can find anything or more to the point... anyone.

"Okay Melody, maybe you're just upset because you gave yourself a fright earlier. Go and have a lie down. I will check on you after dinner." Mum speaks more calmly. I nod and then make my way back to my room. I decide to get changed out of my clothes and into my soft pink pyjamas before getting into bed and wrapping myself up in the blankets tightly. An hour must have passed whilst I keep thinking about what I saw. I tried to picture the face of who I saw but it all happened so fast, I was shocked at the time, I am still not entirely sure if I really did see a person at all. I have to get back down to the basement tonight.

I hear my door open and Mum comes in carrying a tray. "I know you said you didn't want anything but I brought you a cup of fruit tea and some grapes. I thought you might feel like a little something now you have had a rest" she whispers, lays the tray down and kisses me on the forehead.

"Thanks Mum. I will have that and then go to sleep." I whisper back. Mum tip-toes gently out of the room and blows me a kiss as she closes the door. I drink the tea and eat a few grapes all the time trying to decide when I can go down to the basement and investigate exactly what had happened. I finish the tea and get out of my bed heading over to my closet. There is a shoe box with some pens and pencils in it that I use for school, but I think I remember putting my torch in here as well.

After searching for a few minutes I find my torch and then I decide to get changed into some clothes. If there is somebody in the basement I don't want to be seen in my pyjamas! I pull on a pair of black jeans and a red t-shirt, I don't suppose I look very smart but it's better than pyjamas. I walk over to my door and stand with my ear against it. I can't hear anything, I feel my heartbeat quicken as I start contemplate the trip back down to the basement.

I check my torch to make sure it's working, switching it on and off a couple of times. I get two batteries from my desk drawer and put them in my pocket to be on the safe side. I open my door and look left, then right to make sure nobody is around and begin to make my way down stairs towards the kitchen. As I walk slowly and gently down the staircase trying to make as little noise as possible every creak and movement sounds louder than ever before. I look around me, then across to the entrance hall, the coast is still clear and I get a free run straight into the kitchen. Moving more quickly I dash across to the kitchen door, I open it slowly and peak inside, my heart is racing. Luckily nobody is in the kitchen so I close the door lightly behind me. I dart across the room to the basement door putting my hand on the door knob, I turn it but the door does not open, to my surprise somebody must have locked it.

I look around the kitchen but cannot see a key anywhere. Mum or Dad must have hidden it somewhere but where would they put it? I open the drawer nearest the basement door which is filled with all sorts of bits and bobs ranging from a penknife to a tube of glue. I rummage around hurriedly but the key doesn't seem to be in this drawer and I am becoming aware that I could be making too much noise.

Suddenly, I hear footsteps coming down the corridor beginning to feel panicked. I look around for somewhere to hide but there is no time. I move a chair and get underneath the dining table hoping that nobody will see me, pulling the chair back in towards me. The door opens, Mum comes into the room filling the kettle with water and puts in on to boil. Thankfully, she has no idea I am under the table I just hope it stays that way. She takes a teaspoon from the drawer and it slips out her hand, dropping onto the floor. My breathing becomes quicker and I close my eyes, praying she doesn't see me because she will definitely know I'm up to something now.

Just as she bends down Bertie comes bounding into the room barking. "What's wrong Bertie?" Mum sounds a little concerned, probably because Bertie doesn't bark very often. I hope he doesn't see me hiding under the table, I open one eye to look and then close it again, clasping my hands together praying for a miracle. They both go out of the room and I hear Mum shouting at Dad to come quickly.

How long am I going to be stuck under here? I couldn't move out from underneath the table for fear they might see me and wonder what I was doing. Mum might come back in for the cup of tea she was making. Bertie might run back in to the kitchen and see me! *What have I got myself into?*

I hear the front door open and unusual voices, there must be people outside. I hear my Mum say, "Yes, come in officer." It must be the police. I hope there is nothing wrong. Then I hear them walking down the long corridor, they must be going through to the lounge. I should have some time now to find that key and get down to the basement. I push the chair out gently so as not to make a noise, my heart racing more than before and try to think where the key might be. I look around the room but realise it could be anywhere and that this may take a while. I am aware that I might not have a great deal of time to do this. I look at the fridge and for some reason I can't explain I get an urge to look on top of it. I move the chair over to the fridge and stand on it and sure enough there is a key on top of it.

I try the key in the lock and it opens but I hear voices in the hall and realise I have to lock the door behind me to avoid raising suspicion. I am very apprehensive about doing this but I have no choice so I lock the door quietly, switch on my torch and head down the stairs. I still feel quite nervous about what I might find once I get down to the room but it's too late to go back.

I see the same glow coming from underneath the door and wonder whether I should turn off my torch. I switch it off but the darkness scares me and I decide to leave it on whilst I investigate what is on the other side of the door. As I enter the room it is in darkness again. *Maybe I should switch off the torch.* I flash the torch around the room, but can't see anything and I decide there is no reason why I can't switch off the torch. As I turn it off I realise just how dark the room is, I can't even see my hand in front of my face.

I walk towards the mirror and put my hand on it, feeling the cold glass against my skin. I walk along the mirrored wall looking closely into the darkness but I see nothing. I remember the words from the book about 'looking deeper' but I'm staring as deeply as I can and all I see is blackness. "Ouch!" I shout as I bump my head against the mirror, I suppose I was trying to look too deeply.

I remember the notepad in the drawer in the other room and decide to go and have a look at it. I switch the torch back on so I can see where I am going and catch sight of my reflection in the mirror. I walk back towards the mirror and look at my face, it's so pale, I look so plain and boring. Maybe, I should start wearing make-up and put my hair up, glam myself up a bit. I twirl my hair round my finger and smile at myself and then I start to giggle out loud and shut my eyes.

When I open them again I can't believe what I see in front of me. It was the same face I had seen when I was here earlier. It seems to be a reflection in the mirror. "Oh my!" I say out loud. I flash the torch behind me and look but there is nobody there. *Is it a ghost?*

My first instinct is to run out the door because I am so frightened I can hardly catch my breath. I feel my heart beating so hard, it's like it will pop out of my chest any minute. My hands and legs are shaking, my knees are trembling, I feel myself backing away but somehow I am mesmerised and I don't want to leave.

The person is clearly a young man, about the same age as me I think but he looks quite unusual. His hair is bright red like a post box and his skin is white and pale, he's looking down towards the ground. His clothes are certainly not what boys usually wear. He is wearing some kind of black robes with a white cord round his waist. *What is he looking at?*

I don't think he can see me but I decide to try and talk to him. "Hello! Can you see me?" I ask bravely. He doesn't reply or look up. I get the feeling that he is very far away. I notice how beautiful his skin is and how handsome he is despite him looking so different to the boys at my school. I walk closer to the mirror trying to see him more closely. I raise my hand up and place it on the mirror feeling a strange energy, it is almost electric, I notice a blue glow filling up the room. I tap the glass and suddenly he looks up. I don't know what to do or whether he can see me but he must have heard me. I tap again and he appears to come closer to the glass, I notice my reflection has disappeared and I am looking at a night sky filled with stars and the face of the young man.

Unsure of what to do I decide to wave at him to see if he responds and with that, he waves back and smiles. I notice he has the most gorgeous green eyes, like emeralds looking right back at me. I mouth the word 'Hello' to him but he just squints back at me, like he doesn't understand. I try placing my hands on the mirror to see if he presses his hands against mine but he just shrugs his shoulders. I am running out of ideas of what to do, I don't know how we can communicate or why he is there. I don't know if he is a ghost or, if he is stuck in the glass somehow or, if he is somewhere else in the world or, he could be in another world. I don't want to give up on him though, so I try thinking of ways we could communicate with each other.

I can't think of anything and I have an uncomfortable feeling, like I might get caught any minute, I need to come up with something fast. I want to go and get the notebook but I'm scared if I leave he will disappear again. He's still looking through and smiling at me, I am sure he can see me but he has an expression on his face that looks as though he is struggling to look at me which is strange because I can see him perfectly. Suddenly I have an idea, I stick my tongue out at him and put my hand over my mouth almost instantly afterwards with embarrassment. To my delight he sticks his tongue out back and then covers his mouth also, then, I begin to laugh and he starts laughing too. He has the loveliest smile, I think I am starting to get a crush on him. I don't even know his name and we haven't even spoken a word to each other. I don't even know how to get to him or if he is part of another world. *How is it possible that I can have a crush on him?*

Looking into his perfect emerald green eyes it is hard to imagine not having a crush on him. I press my nose to the glass to get as close as I possibly can and start to wonder if he thinks I'm slightly crazy. He starts to move closer, I feel so excited and then all of a sudden he disappears. I jump back from the mirror "Oh no!" I shout, but then he reappears looking like he has been splashed with water and I feel a little relieved, then, I realise that he is not looking at me through a mirror, he is looking into water and somehow he can see me. Now, I am sure he must be in another world, a world behind the mirror! *This has got to be the most bizarre event of my life so far!*

He shakes his head, smiles at me and then points behind him, he's looking down again. I wave to him and he waves back, then he walks away. He must have had to go away, maybe his Mum and Dad are looking for him. I hope my parents aren't looking for me since I have been down here for ages. I start to think about finding a way to speak to the boy on the other side of the mirror. I wonder if we could write to each other but perhaps we don't speak the same language. I decide to go and get the notebook from the chest of drawers in the hope that it may have some explanation of these extraordinary happenings, and what I can do to explore them further.

The room is dark and I can no longer see the night sky in the mirror. I switch the torch back on, retrieve the notebook and tip-toe back upstairs, when I reach the top I push my ear close to the door to make sure nobody is there so I can sneak back up to my room without being noticed. I can't hear anything on the other side and decide it's safe to unlock the door. As I turn the lock I hear a rattling sound above my head that makes me tense up with fear. I take a deep breath and struggle to open the door. When I push the door open a cloud of dust falls on my head and I am absolutely covered. I start to sneeze uncontrollably and wipe my face hastily and hope that I stop because somebody might hear.

As I'm dusting myself down I can hear the sound of Bertie charging down the corridor. I realise I have no awareness of what the time is because I have been down in the basement for so long. I hope Mum and Dad are in bed because they are less likely to hear me and come to investigate. The kitchen door is shut and I know Bertie will bark if I don't let him in so I go over to open the door. He comes bounding in and starts sniffing me, but luckily he doesn't make any loud noises. I notice a trail of dust from the basement door to the kitchen door. I will have to clean that up or Mum and Dad will definitely know I was up to something.

I grab the brush and sweep all the dust back onto the stairs as fast as I possibly can. Then I put the brush back and place the key back on top of the fridge. Some of the dust is still in my hair but if any falls off I will just have to hope Mum and Dad blame Bertie. I sprint upstairs, back into my room clutching the notebook the whole time, I put it into my top drawer, give my head a rub with a towel that was sitting on my radiator. I shake the last of the dust out of my hair before I climb into bed.

Chapter 3

I had some very peculiar dreams last night about the boy I saw in the mirror. I dreamt about walking with him hand in hand on the beach and talking to him all the time, but he didn't say anything he just smiled at me. I felt a warm, fuzzy, happy feeling inside. Then, all of a sudden the sky becomes very dark, I look up and see a terrifyingly huge tidal wave. I feel utterly petrified and helpless as it comes down on top of us and at that point he is gone. Somehow I was left alive sitting on a rock but he had been taken away from me and there was nothing I could do, then I just woke up.

I get out of bed and go down the corridor to the bathroom, it's the summer holidays and I don't have to do anything today which is perfect so I can try and find out more about the boy inside the mirror. I quickly jump in the shower and get scrubbed and washed as fast as possible so I can get back to my investigations. I grab my robe from the hook on the back of the door and wrap my hair in a towel before running back down the corridor to my bedroom.

I grab the notebook from my top drawer, along with my hairbrush and sit on my bed. I look at the front cover of the notebook, feeling slightly nervous at what I might find out if I open it, but there is no going back now. I feel like I must open the book, especially now that I know I wasn't imagining things yesterday and there definitely was something very unusual about this house, and especially with seeing the boy in the mirror in the basement. I couldn't stop thinking about him and I had to find a way to communicate with him so that at least I can understand why he is there. All of that aside, I cannot help but feel completely and utterly drawn to the boy, he was the most handsome person I have ever seen in my life.

I open the notebook to the first page, which has drawings all over it. The pictures are in black ink and some are of flowers, one is of what appears to be an old witch and another is of stars and planets. I wonder if the pictures have anything to do with what is going on in the basement but it is difficult to tell. I turn to the second page which has writing on it, it's clearly a diary:

19th September 1966

There have been some very extraordinary events taking place in this house. I doubt anyone will believe me if I attempt to tell them. I believe there to be something on the other side of the mirror in the downstairs basement. I think it could be another world, not unlike the world I live in.

The lady appeared in the mirror again today, and finally after many months of studying my books I was able to speak to her. It was the most wonderful moment when we finally spoke to each other. Her name is beautiful and not like a name I have ever heard before, "Alazena".

She told me about her life there which is very different to mine here. I want to know more. I would love to go and see her world but I fear it would be an impossibility. I will study my books again to try and find a way to travel there, if it is possible.

Nobody will believe me, they would say I am going crazy but I know I'm not.

I find myself completely intrigued by the diary insert I have just read and almost feel a little bit guilty about what I am reading because perhaps nobody was meant to read these notes. But, if nobody is meant to see it then why would they leave it lying around for people to find?

I decide the person who wrote this must have wanted it to be read. I flick through the book quickly only to discover there to be hundreds of pages of notes. This could take ages to read and I want to get back down to the basement to see if the boy is there again. As I flick through the pages I try to find out if there is any way to communicate with him, but, I can't see anything.

I put the book down for now and walk over to my dressing table to dry my hair. I look at my pale face in the mirror and my long dark hair, I finish off brushing my hair whilst trying to straighten out the curls. Sometimes I think I look ugly but I don't suppose I am. I think my pale skin with my dark hair makes me look a bit like a witch. Sometimes I think I should cut it short but I don't have the courage, I prefer having long hair, I am scared I would miss having my long hair if I cut it all off.

I open the door to my wardrobe and try to pick something to wear, but I don't have much in the way of fashionable clothes. I am never really sure what is trendy and although Mum takes me shopping every now and again I still seem to always buy the same things. A couple of pairs of jeans, a few tops and frilly dresses because Mum likes it when I'm dressed like her 'little lady' as she calls me.

I pick out a flowery lavender blue and white dress that comes to my knees, it is fitted at the waist so it doesn't look quite as dowdy as some of the outfits I have in there. I begin to take notice that I am concerned about how I look, which is a first for me. I must really like this boy if I want to look pretty for him. I have never liked any of the boys at school like this, it is a new experience for me.

I put on a pretty, purple, tanzanite pendant my Mum gave me for my birthday and whilst I am looking in the mirror, I decide I need to do something about my pale face. Mum isn't very keen on me having make-up on, all I have is lip gloss and a few pots of nail varnish. I open my door and look down the corridor to see if anyone is there, the coast is clear, I begin to make my way upstairs to the top floor where the master bedroom is.

Looking out of the large window, which is directly over the staircase overlooking the front lawn I can see it is a beautiful, crisp, clear day outside. The thunder storm must have cleared the air, it is a perfect day for a walk but I couldn't drag myself away from the task I have set myself. I walk across the landing into the master bedroom and notice Mum has left her make-up bag and perfume sitting out on her dressing table.

"Perfect!" I say to myself as I run over to look through her make-up bag. I realise that I don't really know how to put make-up on, and as I look at my face in the mirror I can't imagine what I should do. I try and picture what Mum does when she is getting ready in the morning, many times I have sat on the bed and watched her apply her make-up gently and carefully. I always thought she was beautiful without make-up.

She has some face powder so I decide to dab some round my face using the sponge inside the lid. I look like I have a bit more colour and even smile at my reflection. I take out the blusher which I know goes on your cheeks and dab some on with a brush. My cheeks look really rosy, maybe I put a little too much on but it probably doesn't matter. I look at her eye make-up but it looks too complicated to use apart from the mascara. I have seen adverts on television where they put mascara on. I apply a little to my eyelashes before putting all her make-up back in the bag.

I dart out the room, back downstairs and along the corridor to my room before anyone catches me in the act. I need to find shoes to match with the dress I am wearing. I open my closet and look in the bottom to try and find a pair of matching shoes. I have around thirty pairs of shoes, but I can't decide what pair will go with the outfit. I find a navy-blue pair of pumps with a flower off to the left side of the toe and decide they are a good enough match. I put them on and go over to my mirror to have a look. I think I look more grown up than usual, and then wonder whether I should put on a little heel. I am quite tall though at five foot seven and decide that pumps might be better, plus I don't normally wear high heels, I would struggle to walk in them.

I sit down at my dressing table and look in the notebook again to see if I can find any information which might help me communicate with the boy. I notice that there is one book in particular that is mentioned a few times. Maybe if that book is still in the library it might give me an idea for how the person that wrote it spoke to Alazena. I have never heard a name like this before and this little notebook makes the strange things happening in this house even more intriguing. There must be more people inside the mirror, living in another place that is different from the world I live in. It seems so surreal, so magical, I have to find out more.

I grab the notebook and head downstairs to the library, but just as I am about to go through the door I change my mind, I spin around on my heels and head to the kitchen instead, climbing up on the stool to get the key. I can't resist going down to the basement straight away to see if the boy is there. I unlock the door and rush down the stairs and through to the back room, closing the small door behind me.

I look around the dark room and wonder if I need some form of light to draw attention to my presence there. I don't have anything that lights up today, no matches and I left my phone in my bedroom. I go close towards the mirror and knock on it gently with both hands but there is no response. I knock a little harder and press my nose against the mirror, peering trying to see something but all I see is my squished face. Then I realise that I smudged my make up against the mirror, I stand back and try to fix the smudged bit on my face with one hand whilst wiping the mirror with the back of my other hand.

All of a sudden, I noticed the room beginning to glow, the blue light fills the room and the mirror comes to life. I can see treetops with sky breaking through which is a very deep blue. I notice it is much brighter than before, it must be during the day unlike last time which was much darker.

Then I see the boy from before looking straight at me, waving and smiling. I find myself looking at his beautiful green eyes for a moment and then notice his scarlet coloured hair again. It is very striking and unusual in colour, it looks like he must have used some hair dye, it looks amazing to me. I realise I have become entranced by what I can see and I am completely ignoring the boy who now has a blank expression on his face. I snap myself out of my trance and wave back at him, he smiles whilst pointing down. I can't see what he is pointing at, so I hold my hands up and shrug my shoulders in an over-exaggerated way to assist him with working out what I am trying to convey to him.

Then he lifts what looks like some kind of sparkly, colourful crystal up in front of him and shows it to me. It looks beautiful, glowing different colours from blues, fading into purples and then to a deep red, then pink, back to purple shades and back to blue continuously. It is the most beautiful crystal I have ever seen and both of us stare at it, in a state of wonder for a few moments. I notice he is pointing at it again and then he points at me. I motion to myself with both hands then, point to the crystal but shrug again feeling confused. I don't know what he wants me to do and it is difficult when he can't communicate with me by talking.

He points at me again and mouths what looks like "you need to get one". After a moment of thought I realise that I must need to get a crystal, but again I am not sure what the reasons are for this. I want to ask him, but he can't hear me unless he could make out the words I am saying from lip reading. It suddenly dawns on me that we have been speaking the same language, I work out asking him a question would be worth a try.

"Why do I need that crystal?" I ask very slowly. He mouths back a long sentence but he must be speaking quickly, because I can't work out what he is saying. I shrug my shoulders and hold my hands up again. Then he points to his eye and mouths what looks like "can" and then he shakes his ear lobe and points at me. "You can hear me?" I ask him. He nods and smiles in reply to my question. "But, I can't hear you" I say feeling slightly frustrated.

I think for a moment and then have a moment of realisation - I need a crystal similar to his one in order to hear him speak. "How do I get the crystal?" I ask him excitedly. He shakes his head and shrugs his shoulders, so I don't think he knows how I get a crystal like his one. I smile at him and decide to speak to him for a little while rather than go and investigate this crystal business. "How old are you?" I ask. He holds up his fingers to show me his age and then points towards me. "You're fifteen! I am fifteen, we are the same age." I reply cheerfully. "My name is Melody, what is your name?" I ask interestedly. He takes a moment as this is not so easy to mime for me, he appears to be getting something. Then he holds up what looks like a leaf with some colourful glowing writing. "You're name is Kala! It's a very nice name." I tell him.

Reluctantly, I decide I should attempt to go and find the crystal otherwise communicating with him will continue to be difficult with him miming a performance for me whilst I guess what he is saying. He seems as keen as I am to talk, I just hope he likes me because I really like him. "I will go now and try to find the crystal. Will you be here later?" I ask him hesitantly. Kala nods in reply to me and points to the crystal and then points to his ear. "Does it make a sound when I am here Kala?" I ask hopefully. He nods again with a huge grin across his face. I wonder what his voice will sound like. I wave to him and he waves back. I dash back upstairs to the kitchen, lock the door behind me, place the key back on top of the fridge and make my way to the library.

I look around the room and realise that it might be difficult to find the crystal. I put the notebook down on the table and open it to the page where I notice a book title was written, it is called, 'The Art of Ancient Mystical Magic'. I go back upstairs quickly, heading towards the library to the section that was filled with books on magic and witchcraft, where I found the book when I looked the day before. As I read all through the many titles I cannot see the book anywhere. I notice on a shelf below there is a rather strange looking metal box. I pick it up, it's quite heavy. It has swirly golden patterns and stars carved into it. I place it on the table and open it up and inside is the book I am looking for, it is a red leather bound cover with the writing in gold.

I look at the chapters in the book which are written in a beautiful antique style font:

Chapter 1: Origins of Mystical Magic

Chapter 2: Types of Spells

Chapter 3: Casting Spells

Chapter 4: Fortune Telling

Chapter 5: The Power of Crystals

Chapter 6: Healing

Chapter 7: Potions

This has to be the most interesting book I have ever seen, I am sure I could read this for hours, but there is only one chapter I am particularly interested in at this point and that would be chapter five. I turn to the page to find out more about the power of crystals and there is some fascinating information but it doesn't help me further into finding out where to get one. As I get to the end of the chapter I notice written in ink at the bottom of the page is the number thirty-four. I wonder what the number thirty-four could relate to, and with that thought I refer back to the notebook.

I flick through the pages of the notebook, but can't see the number thirty-four anywhere. Then I try counting thirty-four pages from the start of the book and find some very interesting information on that particular page. According to what the author has written, the crystal should be buried in the garden. There is even a map depicting where I have to go to get it. I grab the notebook and walk through to the lounge, looking out the window it is still bright and sunny outside – perfect weather for digging!

I head outside the front door and along the path to the left of our driveway, past the garage and around the corner to our shed. I rummage around in the shed for a moment and find a shovel which will be perfect for digging. I hear barking and see Bertie running towards me. "Hello Bertie!" I shout cheerfully, I am quite glad of the company. Bertie and I make our way along the route marked out inside the notebook.

The route leads to the bottom of the garden at the front of the house, in amongst the trees. As Bertie and I run down to the bottom of the garden, we can hear the trickle of water as we get closer to the trees. The river passes through the grounds, near to the trees. I am slightly concerned Bertie decides to go diving in. Mum will not be pleased if he gets himself soaked and muddy, dragging a mess through our immaculately clean house.

There is an 'X' clearly marked out on the map, which must be the spot where the crystal is buried so I work out the exact location and start to dig. It is really hard work, I must have been digging for about fifteen minutes when I hear a great big splash. I look around and see Bertie splashing around in the river. "Bertie! Get back here!" I yell at the top of my voice, wishing I had brought his lead, but it is too late now. Then I realise there is no point in shouting for him because he has already gone in and when he gets out he will get mud all over him.

As I get back to digging I find that I am quite far down and still no sign of the crystal. I check the map again feeling fearful that I could be digging in the wrong place. According to the map I am in the right place so I carry on digging. "Bertie!

You dopey dog! You could help with this! Dogs are designed for digging!" I shout at him but he ignores me, he's having a great time swimming about whilst I'm hard at work. Then as I am about to plunge the shovel in again I hit something solid like a rock, I tap it a couple of times and realise I will have to dig around it. As I get down deeper I notice it is some kind of small chest made out of metal. "This must be it!" I shout cheerfully.

I dust down the dirty old looking chest, realising I am now covered in mud and I can't get it to open. Then, I notice a lock on the front! "Oh no! I must need a key!" I say to myself before dropping the chest and running back over to the hole. I scramble around in the mud hoping for a key to be in there, but it is like looking for a needle in a haystack, impossible!

Bertie comes running towards me as I sit on the ground prodding at the box, thinking about how I could get into the crystal inside, and that's assuming it is in there. I shake it and something rattles so I'm guessing it is in there, I have to try and break in. I look at the notebook again but it doesn't say anything about a key or a chest. I get up, dust myself down pick the box up and shovel before I start making my way back to the house.

Bertie just stays still as I walk away, but I will have to do something about the state he is in, his beautiful white and grey coat is muddied and brown. Mum and Dad will know I took him outside without his lead and I will get into trouble. "Bertie! Come on let's hose you down!" I shout and he starts to run towards me so I begin walking again. I hear him getting closer to me and I slow up a little to try and grab his collar. Just as I turn around he jumps up on me with both paws and knocks me over and I drop the chest. "Bertie! For goodness sake!" I yell at him angrily. My dress is completely covered in mud now, I have grass all over me and twigs in my hair. I am so frustrated I get up and kick the chest hard. To my surprise it opens up! I slowly step towards it and timidly have a look inside. The crystal is there but it's not glowing, it looks rather plain, like glass, it's also smaller than I thought it would be. Perhaps it only glows when I am beside the mirror and Kala is there.

I pick up the chest and put the crystal in my pocket safely before I jog round to the back of the house and get the hose, I have Bertie by the collar now so he cannot escape. I lay down the chest out of harm's way, I turn the tap on, stand with my legs either side of Bertie and squeeze him in-between to make sure he can't run away. I give him a pat on the head whilst grabbing the nozzle, I turn it on but Bertie starts to wriggle. I grab his collar again and hop off him and start to hose him underneath. He gives up trying to wriggle free and stands looking melancholy whilst I get the worst of the mud off. "Mum is going to have to send you to the dog groomer Bertie boy!" I announce as I get the last of the dirt removed. "Good boy Bertie." I say whilst patting him on the head.

I lead Bertie back to the front of the house and into the vestibule. "Now you stay here Bertie! I need to get you a towel." I tell him as I shut the doors either side of him to stop him escaping.

I kick of my shoes and dash upstairs to my bedroom to put the crystal safely in my jewellery box. I take off my dirty clothes and grab a baggy old green jumper and blue jeans before hurrying along to the bathroom to get Bertie a towel. Just as I pick up a towel I hear him start to bark "Coming Bertie! Stay calm!" I yell as I sprint back down the corridor and downstairs.

I open the door only very slightly and push myself through the gap to stop him getting into the house. I start to rub him all over with the towel and get him dry enough to be let loose. "Ok Bertie you can go!" I say happily as I open the door and set him free. He trots straight into the kitchen, he must be thirsty. I follow him into the kitchen to find him slurping from his water bowl. "What should I do now Berite? Should I take the crystal down to the basement and see what happens?" I ask ever hopeful that he will give me some advice, but he never does for some unknown reason.

I decide to go back upstairs to my bedroom and take the crystal out of the drawer. I sit on the bed for a moment and stare at it. I don't know what I expect to see, it still looks like a simple piece of glass. I suppose I better pluck up the courage to go down to the basement with it. I might hear Kala's voice for the first time and it would be amazing. I wonder again what his voice will sound like and what his accent will be like. I think about whether he speaks another language although he understands English.

As I walk back into the house and towards my bedroom, I try to decide what to wear because my dress is far too mucky to wear now. I look through my clothes but I can't see anything that I think is good enough to impress Kala. I decide to pull on a pair of black leggings and a cream tunic that has a pattern of glittery beads around the edges. The sparkle is so pretty just like the beautiful world behind the mirror where Kala lives. I check my make-up and luckily it has stayed the same but my hair needs to be brushed again. After I am finished I stand and look at myself in the mirror, I hope he likes how I look.

Chapter 4

I stand at the bottom of the stairs looking at the entrance to the room but this time I am slightly apprehensive. This is the first time we will actually speak to each other and I want to impress him. I don't want to say anything stupid but I have no idea what I am going to say. I take in a deep breath and close my eyes, clasping the crystal tightly in my hand. When I open my eyes I can see the blue glow coming from under the door and I know it's time for us to meet again.

I slowly open the door and enter the room when I look down at the crystal it is glowing. I sit on the floor and cross my legs and as I hold the crystal in front of me, it changes colour, starting from blue, then changing to green and through every colour of the rainbow before going back to blue again. I watch the colours changing and become engrossed by the beauty of the crystal. I was so engrossed with the crystal that I stopped noticing the room around me, I didn't even look in the mirror for Kala. I just stared at the beautiful crystal enjoying the pretty colours, it was like I was in some kind of trance.

"Hi." A pleasant voice broke the silence and startled me a little. I look up from the beautiful crystal and was pleased to see Kala looking at me expectantly, waiting for me to speak.

"Hello! I found the crystal." I shout cheerfully. "I can talk to you now, it's brilliant!"

"Wow! It is amazing! I can talk to you now!" Kala responds with his sweet voice. I look at him and he looks back at me. Neither of us know what to say and I shy away, focusing my attention on the crystal. I can't help but look at him again and I see his beautiful eyes as he looks back into mine, sending a shiver down my spine.

"So, where do you live?" I ask desperate to know all about him.

"I live in Adia. The people who live here are called Adians. In my part of the land we live in villages. Each village has a different name, my village is called Honovi." He tells me joyfully, seemingly delighted that I am so interested in where he comes from.

"That is fascinating! Does everyone speak the same language?" I ask very interestedly.

"Mostly, apart from one of the large tribes. The Vultus-Saudades have their own language that they use, so outsiders cannot understand them. They can be quite scary, so most people try and stay away from them and hope they don't bother us." Kala explains.

Kala and I talk for hours about all sorts of things, like our families and how different our lives are. Eventually, it becomes late and my parents will be home soon. We decide to pick up where we left off, the next day because we can't get caught. We agree to meet the following morning. He can meet me anytime because he is not looking into a mirror like me. He is looking into a lake, in amongst the trees near the Honovi village. It is peaceful and usually nobody will be around, so he can speak freely.

I reluctantly go upstairs and hide the key, feeling a great deal of sadness that we couldn't continue our conversation into the evening. I was completely fascinated by his life in the land of Adia. I went upstairs to my bedroom and Bertie followed, to give me a well needed cuddle. As Bertie and I cuddle up on the bed, I think about all the information Kala gave me. Part of me believes it is some kind of elaborate trick and none of this can be true. It seems so far-fetched and impossible that there could be another world behind the mirror in my basement. However, I have seen it with my own eyes and the more I think about the wonderful world behind the mirror, the more I want to go there and see it for myself.

I find myself lost in a dream imagining the world Kala lives in and pretending I am there with him. I imagine the beautiful world he told me he lives in with the brightly coloured flowers, trees, beaches and turquoise seas. I dream we are walking together through the peaceful forest and once we are deep in the middle of the trees when nobody else is around that we kiss. The most long, loving, tender kiss.

"Melody! What are you doing in your bed at this time missy!" I hear the voice of my mum shout and I am angered at her spoiling the perfect daydream.

"Sorry mum, Bertie and I had a long walk today and we are tired." I explain to her apologetically.

"Well, supper will be ready soon! Maybe you should go to the bathroom and freshen up sweetheart." Mum suggests in a moderately forceful manner.

"Okay, I will do." I reply half-heartedly.

I head to the bathroom and wash my face and hands, in order to freshen up for dinner. I can't stop thinking about Kala now. I imagine being with him in his world. I don't feel like I want to be part of this world anymore. I look around the house as I walk downstairs to the kitchen and I feel detached from my surroundings, everything looks so plain and boring. All the images in my mind about Kala and his world are exciting, and light up my dull life. My daydream nearly causes me an injury as I walk right into Dad before entering the kitchen.

"Oh! Sorry Dad!" I shout.

"Be more careful will you, love. You are a bit dopey sometimes!" Dad bellows at me.

I shuffle embarrassedly into the kitchen, trying to pay more attention to where I am going. I smell the delicious aroma of food cooking. I didn't realise that I had been so busy speaking to Kala all day I had forgotten to eat anything since breakfast. I am so very hungry now and can't wait to eat. As I sit at the table, I feel like banging my cutlery and demanding something good to guzzle.

Mum serves up a scrumptious plate of bangers and mash and I tuck in before anyone else has a chance to sit down. As I scoff up all the delicious sausages, mash and gravy I can feel my Mothers' eyes piercing right through me. I lick my lips and look up, as I swallow another tasty mouthful.

"Well Melody, I didn't raise you to be quite so greedy!" Mum says sternly.

"Sorry Mum. I am really hungry today." I respond sheepishly.

"Well that might be so, but you need to be more ladylike at the table. Take smaller mouthfuls and chew gracefully please." She orders whilst eating her dinner in a much more ladylike, gentle fashion, nibbling away at small mouthfuls.

"Leave the girl alone Virginia, she is clearly starving. Poor little thing, she is so skinny she could do with a bit of fattening up." Dad states, whilst winking in my direction.

"For goodness sake George! Don't encourage her to be disgusting at the dinner table. She looks like Bertie gobbling up his dog food! Just like it is going to run off the plate if she doesn't eat it as fast as possible!" Mum shouts back at Dad, as he chuckles quietly to himself. "It's not funny George!" Mum shouts, as I struggle not to laugh.

"Yes sorry dear." Dad says to Mum, just to save an argument.

"I am sorry too Mum. I will try harder to be more ladylike." I say in a pleasing manner. I always try to behave in the way my parents want me to, I hate to disappoint them.

I sit up straight and eat the last of my dinner in a more acceptable way, to please Mother. I chew every mouthful slowly and deliberately despite an overwhelming desire to guzzle up the lovely food in front of me. I drift off into my own world again, imagining Kala eating food in Adia. I am certain nobody tells him to stop guzzling his food. I wonder to myself what they eat in Adia, it probably isn't the same kind of food that we eat. I should ask him next time I speak to him and find out what kind of food they eat.

Once we are finished eating supper, I decide to go back to the library to have a look at the book about magic again. It is still sitting where I left it on the table and I sit down and open it, flicking through the pages looking for some more interesting information. As I look through the book, I drift off again into my own little world imagining life in Adia. I picture what it is like in the beautiful forest, the sky is blue and I am with Kala. I feel so happy, lost in the dream world that I am creating. I know what I have to do now.

I stop flicking through the pages of the book and stare straight ahead of me as I have a revelation. I don't want to be a part of this world for another minute, I am bored, lonely and unhappy. Kala makes me happy and the thought of having a new life in a new place is so exciting. I have to find a way to be there with him, I don't want to be without him. I just hope he feels the same way about me, because if he doesn't then I can't go to his world, I will make a fool of myself.

I start to worry, thinking that perhaps we are too different and things can't work between us. However, I can't shake the feeling that we have something very special and we were brought together for a reason. Suddenly, it dawns on me that being together may not be very easy - if it is even possible. I start looking through the book again frantically trying to find a clue of how I could be with him. My efforts come to nothing as there is no information about other worlds never mind how to travel to other worlds.

I go upstairs to my bedroom to have another look at the notepad, in order to investigate whether there would be a way I could be with Kala. I look through the whole book and when I come to the last few pages, I realise that there is nothing much to advise me any further. The author has noted, in his words, "I long to travel to the other world but it does not seem possible". I feel saddened as I read this but I haven't lost hope that there might be a way to be with Kala.

I scan the notebook again to try and locate even the smallest clue about how to travel to Adia, but I cannot find a thing. I find myself falling asleep trying to read the rest of the notebook. I decide to put my pyjamas on and go to bed. I lie in bed thinking about a way to be with Kala on the other side of the mirror, but the more I think about it the more impossible it seems. However, speaking to a boy on the other side of a mirror in another world didn't seem possible, only days ago.

The only option for me is to speak to Kala when I see him tomorrow. Firstly, I need to find out whether he feels the same, and wants me to go there and be with him. Secondly, if he does feel the same I need to ask him if he is aware of any way I can travel to Adia to be with him. I feel a knotted, sick feeling in the pit of my stomach as I think about the possible outcomes.

I can't stop thinking about being there and getting away from the boring world I am living in at the moment. All the thoughts rush through my mind and I struggle to fall asleep, but I need to if I am going to be up early to meet Kala tomorrow morning. As I finally drift off to sleep, I dream about Adia and Kala. It is not a happy dream. In the darkness of bushes, I hear rustling and when I look, eyes peer out at me from the darkness. The eyes glow with a menacing stare and when I go to Kala, he is gone. It feels so real when I wake up I believe that I have been there and have lost Kala forever.

I try to shake it off and tell myself it was just a stupid nightmare and there was nothing 'real' about it, but I begin to realise just how much Kala means to me and how sad I will be if I lose him. It might have only been a few days but I have become really attached to the idea of his world, and how free I could be if I went there. Perhaps the nightmare is just because I am nervous about everything going wrong. It could also be my fears about losing Kala forever. The situation is so surreal in the first place, I have to pinch myself now and again to make sure this isn't a very realistic fantasy, brought on by the boredom of my mundane life.

Chapter 5

After my late night, I thought I might be sleepy this morning, but I am quite the opposite. I am wide awake and excited to see Kala and hurry around, getting ready to see him. I rush around so much that I forget to dress up and do my hair and make-up. As I speedily munch my breakfast I think about the fact I look rather plain and boring again, but if he likes me as much as I like him I begin to think it shouldn't matter how I look. My mum is always telling me that people should see the beauty on the inside.

Once I am finished my cereal, I move my chair over to the fridge to get the key and hurry downstairs to the basement. I am more excited than I have ever been before to see Kala. I notice the room isn't glowing with the beautiful blue colour that I usually see under the door and I worry that he will not be there. I hold the crystal out in front of me, it does not glow. Suddenly, I feel terribly nervous. *What if this was all just a dream? Did I just imagine all of this? Am I crazy?*

As I sit down on the floor and cross my legs I will the crystal to work, the room is so dark, I feel scared, not being able to see a foot in front of me. I look into the mirror but I cannot see a thing and my hands begin to shake a little.

"Please work, please work, please work." I whisper repeatedly whilst closing my eyes tightly shut, clutching the crystal in both hands.

If it wasn't so dark I could check what time it is, maybe I came down too early or maybe Kala has been distracted. I open one eye and notice the crystal is glowing with a white light, and the room is starting to fill with the beautiful blue glow that I love. I feel the crystal become warmer and it starts changing colour. I feel less worried, my heart races with the excitement of knowing I will be seeing Kala any minute now. A part of me is still nervous that he won't feel the same as me.

I look up and see Kala smiling back at me, and I feel that funny feeling in my stomach like butterflies. I sit quietly for a moment, smile at him and wave, he waves back at me. I know this is real and he can see me and we exist in some sort of parallel universe, it all makes perfect sense, yet, it makes no sense at all.

"Hi Kala. I have been thinking about some things. I have a couple of questions for you but I am a little nervous about asking them." I speak nervously, not making very much eye contact with him.

"Hi Melody. Just go ahead and ask. I have been thinking about a few things as well. Maybe we are thinking the same thing?" He replies warmly and reassuringly, building my confidence.

I feel a little less nervous but I still find myself pausing to think about the precise question before I go ahead and ask it. Part of me wants to change the subject and talk about something else. I could ask him more questions, find out more about Adia or his friends and family, but I know I need to ask him because being there is all I can think about. I open my mouth to speak and nothing comes out. I take a deep breath and try again, but when I open my mouth again my voice appears to have left me. I scratch my head and look away from the mirror thinking again about how I should ask the question when suddenly, Kala's voice breaks the silence.

"Is there something wrong Melody?" He asks sweetly, making me feel more relaxed.

"No there is nothing wrong. If I could find a way to be with you in Adia would you like that? It's just because I really like you and my life is so boring here. I would love to come visit you in Adia and get to know you better. Just if you feel the same though, there is no pressure." I speak more bravely, but in the same instance feel my stomach doing somersaults.

"Oh that's great! I really want you to come and visit me here!" He responds enthusiastically and I am instantly delighted.

"I am so pleased to hear you say that, I was worried you wouldn't want me to. Do you know how I can travel there and be with you?" I ask hopefully.

"I am not sure, but there is somebody that I can ask. There is a lady that stays here, in the forest, she is called Stormie. She can tell people about the future and has an awareness of all things magical. Maybe she will know how you can visit me here." He speaks encouragingly.

I feel a little relieved now that I know there is somebody who might be able to help me travel there, and I am completely overjoyed that Kala wants me to visit him. I don't know if he finds me attractive and part of me wants to ask him. The other part of me is scared to ask, for fear that he doesn't like me as much as I like him. I decide not to ask and wait until I am with him in person and see what happens.

"So, when will you be able to speak to Stormie?" I ask hoping he tells me that it will be soon.

"Hopefully, I will be able to see her today. I could try just now if you like or would you rather talk for a while longer?" I think about this for a moment and decide that the sooner I can visit him in Adia, the happier I will be.

"You should try just now. I am really excited about visiting your world. We can talk more when I get there." I say not being able to contain my excitement. It is only after a few moments that I consider that perhaps this isn't possible, but I don't want to believe it just yet. I have to believe that I can get there and meet Kala in person, not just on the other side of this mirror.

"Okay, I will aim to meet you here in a short while. Then I will be able to tell you if Stormie has any idea of how you can travel here." He explains carefully.

"That's great I will see you later." I reply cheerfully, smiling and waving at him.

I leave the room filled with hope, but whilst I close the door I feel a little sad that I am walking away from him again. I wonder how I will pass the next few hours as I wait to see him again. I make my way upstairs and put the key back, before going to the library. However, when I get to the library I just stare at all the books and can't bring myself to pick one up. I can tell the next few hours are going to feel like an absolute eternity.

I turn to the window and look outside, it is a nice sunny day again so maybe I could take Bertie for a walk. I go to the door and call for him but he doesn't appear, chances are he is probably sleeping. I suppose it would just cause difficulty anyway because he will likely jump in the river and get covered in mud again.

I go upstairs to my room and sit in my window seat, staring out over the beautiful gardens. I imagine playing in the garden with my friends from school, running around and laughing together. It's not exactly much fun, stuck out in the middle of nowhere by myself. I look at the pink clock on my wall and I am upset to notice that it has only been twenty minutes since I left the basement.

Time always passes so slowly when you are waiting for something to happen. I think it is a good deal worse because I want it to happen so much. I decide to go downstairs and watch some television. I grab the remote and turn on the television then, I look through the guide to see if anything good is on. None of the daytime chat shows look particularly interesting. Further down the list, I notice there is a documentary about jungle tribes about to start. This sounds a little more interesting than middle-aged women discussing how dysfunctional their lives are.

I start watching the documentary and find myself engrossed in the tales of life in the jungle, and how different the people are. Even although I share the same world as these people our lives are completely different. I wonder what it would be like to live without electricity, a clean bathroom, computers or mobile phones. Part of me thinks it would be really boring and difficult, but another part thinks I would feel free.

I feel like life in the modern world, compared to that of life in the jungle, is quite restrictive. In the summer, I am on my own time but I still have to do certain things at particular times. During term time I have to meet deadlines for homework, essays and presentations. I have to do assessments on particular days and if I don't do very well, I will feel like a failure. The jungle is totally different, they don't have watches or deadlines and that's why I think they are free, compared to me.

I begin to think about life in Adia and how that might be similar to life in the jungle. When Kala meets with me, he is in a forest, the scenery is definitely similar. He spoke of a tribe that lives in Adia, the *Vultus-Saudades* and how they are protective of their people, and the land they reside on. He made them sound quite threatening and that you are better to stay out of their way.

As the documentary comes to an end, I check the time to see how long I must wait until I meet Kala again. I am pleased to see over an hour has passed. I start looking at the guide again to find something else to watch. I am disappointed to find there is nothing that interests me, and it is mostly the rubbish daytime chat shows.

I think Bertie must have sensed my distress as he suddenly comes trotting in to see me. He looks all refreshed and energised after his nap, which could spell trouble. He clambers up on to my lap with his huge paws weighing heavily down onto my legs. Then he starts to whine a little bit and this means he needs to go outside for the toilet.

"Oh Bertie! Cross your legs. I can't take you out!" I say sternly but he only whines louder and I start to feel guilty. "I'm sorry dog, come with me and we will get your lead because you are not roaming free today. You will get me into all kinds of trouble and today Bertie, I have to be somewhere." I explain to him forcefully.

I walk through to the vestibule and Bertie follows obediently, he always does when he is getting what he wants. His lead has fallen onto the floor so I pick it up and attach it to its collar, tugging it a couple of times just to make sure it it's on nice and securely. I can't have the troublesome hound escaping and getting me in a pickle before my big meeting. I open the front door and Bertie decides to overtake me as soon as it opens and drag me down the steps at high speed.

"Bertie! You behave! I told you not to cause trouble!" I shout at him angrily as he drags me onto the lawn. He isn't taking any notice of anything I am saying as he continues to drag me around the garden. I am determined not to completely lose control because if I mistakenly let go, that will be the end of it, and I might miss meeting Kala.

Bertie drags me to the bottom of the garden and we are near the river like last time. "No don't be a bad dog! We are not getting covered in mud again!" I yell whilst pulling his lead back as hard as I can. He hasn't even had a pee yet which makes me think he might have tricked me into taking him out just to get into trouble or mud-covered. "Do your jobs Bertie and then we are going back to the house. I mean it we are not staying out here all afternoon!"

I realise that I have no idea what the time is or how long we have been out in the garden for. I start dragging Bertie back to the house but he is putting up a fight, he really wants to jump in the river again. Then an idea pops into my head that should definitely get the chubby dog back inside the house. "Bertie, if we go back to the house there is some yummy chewy treats for you. Would you like that? Some nice treats!?" Bertie looks me in the eye, then he looks at the house and looks back at me panting with his tongue hanging out. "Treats Bertie!" I shout again and his ears prick up, I swear that dog has a smile on his face.

He then decides to spring into action and run as fast as he can back to the house and I am sprinting behind to keep up. He suddenly stops at the steps and starts to sniff something, but I am still running and crash into a pillar, bashing my elbow against it and landing on my bottom. "Ouch! Bertie you are going to be the death of me! Oh my funny bone! Ouch, ouch, ouch!" I scream in severe pain and my eyes begin to water. I stand up and dust my bottom down which is feeling a quite sore from landing on the gravel "You silly dog! I am waddling like a duck now!"

Just as I am about to make my way up the steps and into the house Bertie seems to have other ideas. He starts dragging me around the side of the house, sniffing the ground all the way. Something must smell interesting, but I have lost track of time is and I am starting to worry that I won't meet Kala. I just hope he waits for me if I am late, he surely will, I would wait for him. "Bertie, I don't have time for this. Can we just go into the house and get you some of those lovely treats you like?"

Bertie still has other ideas, because he is dragging me around the back of the house now, sniffing at the corner of the shed. He starts to scrape at the door, but I refuse to open it and try to drag him back to the house again when suddenly, I hear a rustling. Perhaps Bertie is actually on the case of an intruder, and I start to feel a little nervous as I look all around us.

All of a sudden, through a small hole in the back left corner of the shed a cat squeezes out and darts across the garden. "Bertie! No!" As he dashes after the little black and white fur-ball, dragging me along with him. The cat disappears through the hedge, seemingly gone forever, whilst Bertie sniffs and digs around in the soil. "Right you bad dog! I am not washing you again, this is ridiculous!"

The cheeky little black and white cat is sitting on top of a wall behind the hedge, looking pleased with himself as a result of making his successful escape and annoying Bertie beyond belief. Bertie starts to bark loudly and repeatedly at the mischievous little black and white cat, but he doesn't seem to care, he disappears over the wall and he's gone for now.

"Bertie, come on lets go back inside." I say to him quietly, I understand by the sad look in his eyes that the cat had fooled him and this had embarrassed him deeply. "It's not so bad Bertie, we still have treats. Not that you should be getting any when you don't listen to a word I say."

Walking back to the house I notice mud all over his front paws and decide that I can't take him inside like this, he will make such a mess. I just hope and pray that Kala waits for me, because I am sure we have been out here for much too long. I lead him over to the hose and rinse off his paws quickly and for once he doesn't struggle, that cat has really knocked his confidence, he's not the same dog anymore.

I lead him up to the house, luckily without much fuss and let him go once we are back in the house. I go into the kitchen to get the key from on top of the fridge and notice that we have been outside for more than two hours when I check the time. Starting to worry, I hurriedly grab the key and rush downstairs to the room, but to my disappointment I can't see the blue light glowing from underneath the door.

"Oh no! He's gone!" I say to myself whilst I walk into the pitch black room. I take the crystal out of my pocket and clasp it tightly. "Please, please, please work. Please be there Kala." Despite all my pleading with the crystal nothing happens, it doesn't light up. I feel like crying, I feel the tears welling up in my eyes because I am so disappointed in myself. *What if he thinks that I have lost interest? What if he thinks I didn't want to go and be there with him?*

I feel like I have ruined everything, I didn't have to take Bertie out and I knew it would lead to trouble, but I did it anyway and now everything is completely ruined. All I have dreamt about lately is meeting Kala in Adia and having a wonderful adventure, now I am stuck here in the most boring place in the whole world. I throw the crystal across the room in frustration and pace back and forth trying to think properly but I am too upset to gather my thoughts.

After a few minutes I feel so frustrated I start pushing my hands against the mirror, banging at the glass wishing I could push through and get to him and tell him I am sorry. But, my energy is wasted, nobody can hear me, the crystal doesn't light up and nothing happens. I slide down to the floor against the mirror and begin to sob, feeling like I should give up because I don't know what else to do.

After a few minutes of sitting with my head in my hands, I look up and notice the room is glowing. I scramble across the floor and pick up the crystal feeling that my prayers have been answered. I turn around to face the mirror, looking for Kala, but I see nothing. The crystal does not change colour, it might just be taking a little longer than usual.

A few more minutes pass and the crystal is glowing, but I can't see Kala and the room does not start to change, nothing is happening. I wonder if it is broken because I threw it or maybe something is wrong on the other side. I am not really sure what I should think anymore. I feel the anger and frustration building up again because I feel helpless. I throw the crystal at the mirror in a dangerous move without even thinking, letting out a scream as I do so. Something isn't quite right.

The mirror should've smashed but it didn't. The mirror appears to be in one piece, well if that's what you could call it. It has taken on a very strange glow, like the blue one, but it looks like water in a fish tank swirling and bubbling. I stare at it for a few moments in shock because I am not really sure what to make of this. I look at the crystal on the floor, still glowing white, so I step towards it and pick it up. It feels warmer than usual, I look at the crystal closely then look at the section of mirror I threw the crystal at, I look back at the crystal again, and then, I look around the room. I feel absolutely puzzled by what I can see in front of me, I can't believe my own eyes.

I edge close to the mirror, I am slightly apprehensive about what could happen if I go near to it, but I feel drawn to it for some reason I am not entirely aware of. Maybe it was good for me to break down and lash out in the way that I did, because feeling hopeless has left me with much less fear than I had before. I raise my hand up to the mirror which feels warm, I do not touch it straight away as the swirls and bubbles make me a little nervous.

I think to myself about what could happen if I touch it, it doesn't feel dangerous, too hot or too cold, it should be fine. I place my right hand on it, expecting it to rest against the glass but my hand slips right through into the swirls. It feels like putting my hand into warm water, but I quickly remove it just to make sure nothing strange has happened. I look at my hand feeling more puzzled than I did before as I notice my hand is all wet. I bring my hand close to my face to smell it but there is no scent but, I am not courageous enough to taste it. *Is there water on the other side of this mirror?*

I prepare and steady myself, rooting both my feet to the ground in front of the mirror and raise my hands in front of me, facing the mirror. I push both my hands into the mirror, which doesn't seem very much like a mirror anymore. I feel the warmth in my hands and the beautiful colours, swirls of blue and turquoise makes me want to immerse myself in its heavenly, bubbly, warmness. I take a step closer and my arms are now in the warmth on the other side and I realise that this is really happening, I am on my way to Adia. My wishes have come true, but I am still a little apprehensive about going through the apparent portal, as I stare with my eyes wide open. *If it's water what if I drown?*

I throw away all fearful thoughts and with great gusto jump up in the air, throwing myself through the mirror and my body is immersed in the lovely warm liquid. Once inside, I look around me but alarmingly I have now become completely disorientated. I look back at where I came from, but all I can see is darkness, and when I look forward I see bright blue water. I am confused but have to try not to panic or else I know I will drown. I start to swim in the direction that I guess is towards the surface of the water and hope that it is not too far because, I don't think I can hold my breath for too long.

Chapter 6

I think I am at the surface of the water, but I am completely disorientated and begin splashing about wildly. I don't even have any time to think about being scared, I am just trying to get my head above the water so I can catch my breath, but I am struggling. Unexpectedly, I feel someone grab hold of me and drag me out of the water. I begin to cough and splutter, then, I finally can catch my breath with huge relief.

I look around me and it is clear that I am in the middle of a forest with a lake in front of me. I sit up and look at the lake, the colour is a beautiful deep blue then I look up at an opening between the trees and notice the sky is a stunning sapphire blue with stars of all different colours twinkling, pinks, reds, greens, yellows, oranges and purples. The colours are enchanting, similar to the crystal when it flashes which reminds me I had it in my hand and now it's gone. *How did I get out of the water alive?*

I pad my hands against the ground and look around me, but I can't see the crystal. I notice I am sitting on sand and I am soaked through, I must look like such a mess. I hoped I would see Kala, but now I am worried that if he sees me looking like this he will find me completely unattractive. I attempt to dust myself down as I let out a big sigh but it seems hopeless, there isn't any chance of me looking even remotely presentable. I hear rustling behind me and I jolt forwards frightened by the sudden noise, scaring me as it broke the silence. I nervously look behind me and there is a young lady peeking at me from behind a tree. She looks as if she might be more nervous than me.

"Hello." I say quietly and smile whilst waving at her trying to look friendly. She doesn't respond and just stares at me silently. I put my hand back down and blush, embarrassed by my failure to communicate with her. I look at her for a moment whilst I decide what to do next, she is young and pretty with long deep-blue hair. She has bright green eyes which are very striking, very similar to Kala. She has delicate facial features with a button nose, her skin is incredibly, and beautifully pale, also similar to Kala, and her clothes are nothing like what we wear at home, more like a golden coloured long dress.

I stand up and dust myself down, looking around me again I still can't see the crystal anywhere much to my disappointment. The girl is staring at me from the tree, I make my way slowly towards her with my arm outstretched, in order to try and shake her hand but she just looks at it blankly as she takes a step back so, I put my hands down by my side because I don't want to scare her.

"I am Mel-o-dee. Me, Mel-o-dee." I say slowly sounding out my name deliberately and quietly, trying not to scare her whilst pointing at myself. Standing close to her now I can she just how beautiful she is, she almost looks like a china doll because her skin is so perfect and pale, not a blemish in sight. She has a cute button nose, green eyes which sparkle and beautiful rosy red lips. Her face has lit up because she has begun smiling back at me. "Not from here." I say pointing around me and shaking my head, hoping she will understand what I mean.

"Well I can tell you are not from here. You look different. Your clothes are strange." The girl speaks suddenly, startling me and I find myself taking a step back from her now. Her accent is pleasant and she talks slowly, soothingly, calmly - she does not sound threatening. However, I feel apprehensive because she is so unsure of me, but I understand why she would be wary.

"Did you pull me out of the lake?" I ask quietly not really making any eye contact because I feel awkward.

"Yes." She responds as she sits down in a bright green bush that strangely appears to mould to her shape as she sinks in comfortably.

"Thank you for helping me. It is quite strange how I came to be here. I was supposed to meet a boy called Kala. Do you know him?" I ask hopefully.

"Kala comes here often. My name is Indiara and Kala is my brother. I have been looking for him because my family are worried. He was expected to come home earlier in the day, but when he did not return my Mother sent me to look for him." She explains carefully, I can sense that she feels concerned about him.

As I process the news that Indiara has just given me I feel slightly disheartened because I didn't expect that I would actually make it here, but in some cruel twist of fate that I would not finally meet Kala in person. Now I feel stupid for being so worried about how I look. I also realise I will have to explain to Indiara exactly what has happened and hope she believes me.

"Can I explain to you about how I met Kala and how I came to be here?" I ask nervously, but looking her right in the eyes now in the hope she can see I am genuine. "I would like to help you find him if that is okay with you."

"Yes, come here, sit with me." Indiara smiles at me, patting the bush beside her, so I go to stand beside her. I look down at the bush before turning around to face away from it, but I am scared that if I sit on it I will fall. I crouch down a little and pat the bush underneath me. "What are you doing!?" Indiara barks and grabs my arm pulling me down beside her. I am frightened I will fall, but in the same way the bush moulded itself around her I sink into it perfectly as it moved to fit my shape. It is more comfortable than any seat I have ever sat in or any bed I have ever slept in and as I look at the scenery around me, which is so stunning, it feels like I am in paradise.

I spend a while explaining to Indiara about how I come from another world, about the crystal, how Kala and I met and that we wanted to meet each other today. I explained that he said he was going to see a lady called Stormie, in the hope she would be able to explain if there is a way to travel to Adia. Lastly, I explain how I was late for meeting Kala and that I lost my temper, throwing the crystal and somehow the mirror transformed into a portal that led me to here.

Indiara was surprisingly understanding despite the very strange situation we had found ourselves in. Something told me that very strange situations might happen quite often in Adia. Indiara was very easy to talk to and I hoped we could be friends, not just because the thought of being alone in a strange place scares me, but she appears to be a genuinely lovely person.

"I know where Stormie lives, we should make our way there right away. Even if he is no longer there, she might know of his whereabouts." She stands up and offers me her hand to help me out of the bush. I feel much better knowing she is not going to leave me alone in the forest. There have been some unidentifiable noises whilst we have been sitting talking, and it occurs to me that in a place like this anything could be lurking behind the bushes or trees. I realise that I am very lucky that Indiara has taken me under her wing. I take her hand and bring myself to my feet, and as I do so the bush transforms back from my shape to looking like it had never been sat upon in the first place. I find this remarkable and wonder to myself if these extremely comfortable bushes are easy to come by in the forest.

I follow Indiara through the trees, making our way to find Stormie, she doesn't speak to me much, but I don't really notice because I am so completely mesmerised by the scenery around us. The trees look tall enough to touch the sky and the leaves range from bright greens to lime greens. I can see the stunning sapphire blue sky between the treetops, not a cloud in sight.

"Do we have far to go?" I ask Indiara curiously as we walk briskly, the grass and twigs crunching underneath our feet.

"No, it's not very far from here." She explains in a flat tone, like she is concentrating on something else. Perhaps feeling concerned for her brother or contemplating my presence. I mean if I feel strange being here, she must feel strange having an alien in her homeland – effectively I am precisely that, an alien. *What a strange situation to be in, fancy me being an alien?*

Walking along through the trees I feel myself getting my hopes up that perhaps Kala will be with Stormie and I will meet him, and we can go for a walk together. I want to get to know him better as I fantasise about seeing him in person, looking into his gorgeous green eyes and he smiles sweetly at me. I am jolted out of my fantasy with a slight shock as Indiara grabs my arm forcefully.

"It is just over there. We shall go inside and speak to Stormie. When you enter the room you must bow before Stormie, then sit on the cushion on the floor." Indiara carefully informs me as she points to a small cottage, covered in greenery, at the bottom of a dirt track, in the middle of the trees. We walk towards the cottage, which looks very small, it could even be described as looking more like a hut. I couldn't imagine living in such a small abode compared to the huge mansion we have at home. There are pretty flowers along the outside of the cottage some big and some small in shades of pinks, purples and blues.

We approach the battered old front door which creaks noisily when Indiara pushes it open. I am surprised at the door being left open like that when I look behind me into the trees I can only imagine this place could be quite lonely at night and anyone could walk in. When we get inside there is a dark hall which seems to disappear into nothingness. Indiara steps in front of a door on the left and knocks three times before entering.

I watch Indiara enter the room and she bows before a little old lady, I presume she must be Stormie. She is sitting on a chair at the back of a relatively dark room. The only light comes from a few candles, there are drapes covering the windows. The room looks somewhat larger than I imagined. On second thoughts the room IS bigger than the outside of the cottage, this cannot be possible but it would appear that in Adia things don't always seem to make sense.

I bow before the little old lady and I sit down on a purple velvet cushion on the floor beside her. The little old lady is sitting quietly, with her eyes closed and her hands pressed hard against the arms of her wooden chair. She is wearing a long purple dress with sparkling stones twinkling in the candlelight. Her grey hair is tied in a tight bun at the back of her head with a purple flower holding it in place.

"*Shamala*, my friend, what brings you here?" The old lady speaks softly using some form of greeting, I presume.

"*Shamala*, I have lost my brother and my friend from another world is looking for him also. Her name is Mel-o-dee." I want to correct Indiara, but decide not to in the current situation out of respect and besides, I feel honoured that she referred to me as her friend. I look up at the old lady and her eyes are wide open now. She is staring right at me and it's making me feel terribly nervous. I smile at her hoping she realises I am a nice person. Thinking about it, she is a psychic, she should already know that I am a nice person. I look at Indiara out the corner of my eye and she looks at me. I wonder if I should say something and my jaw drops slightly as if to speak, but no sound leaves my lips.

"You are not from here my child that, I am certain of. It must be a very faraway place, a very strange place because I cannot see it in my mind's eye and you different from anyone I have ever seen before." The old lady spoke slowly and gently, it was almost hypnotic. I am not sure whether I should speak so I just nod and smile. She continues to stare at me and I begin to feel incredibly uncomfortable, looking at Indiara pleadingly for assistance.

"Stormie, perhaps may I explain about how my friend came to be here?" Indiara asks politely whilst looking almost as nervous as I do. Stormie glances painfully slowly over at Indiara, looking right at her, then she nods for her to continue before closing her eyes again. "She comes from a place called the United Kingdom, it is a faraway land. She came to the lake because she wanted to meet my brother, his name is Kala. She had been speaking to him through a mirror in her home and found a way to come here using a special crystal. Kala was also in possession of his own special crystal. When she came from her world into ours, he was not there to meet her and if I hadn't heard her struggling in the water, she may have drowned. Before Mel-o-dee came here she had been speaking to Kala and he said that he would be visiting you. Is there anything you can tell us which can help? Please Stormie."

I could see from Indiara's expression and hear from the tone in her voice, she is deeply concerned for her brother. I want to do anything I can to help and not just because I feel I have fallen for him, but now that I see she is very worried I begin to feel it too. Stormie has sat in silence for what seems like an eternity when suddenly, she lets out a humming noise and opens her eyes.

"You will have a long journey to find Kala. He came to see me in order to ask me some questions about Mel-o-dee. He told me that he was desperate to see her as he had fallen in love with her but could not see any way to be with her." Stormie's words made my heart skip a beat. For just one second I had forgotten the fact that he had gone missing and I felt elated by this news. "I could not help him because I had not heard of such stories about another world. My psychic visions do not extend to this other world. It appears that other world does not exist, but clearly it must because you are here with us dear Mel-o-dee. I told Kala about Tikto the Dopostetis, and that he may be able to help. Do you know where he lives?"

"He lives across the valley. It will take more than a day to get there on foot." Indiara gasps. "What if he isn't there when we get there? Have u not one vision Stormie? Not a clue of where he might be?" Indiara asks desperately, as I ponder what a Dopostetis could be.

"I have told you all I can." Stormie responds bluntly, with a blank expression before hanging her head. I can see the disappointment in Indiara's eyes as she stands up and turns to me. I stand up and follow her out of the house wondering where our journey might take us now. There are so many questions I want to ask her, but I am unsure whether it is appropriate because Indiara seems so concerned and in a hurry. I follow along behind her, waiting for her to speak as we make our way back through the forest along the same path.

"How can she call herself a psychic? She must know where my brother is. Why won't she tell me? There are many strange things happening. I have to find him as soon as possible." Indiara rants as I respond with sounds of agreement, concerned that I may say something to upset her or that she may blame me for all of this.

"What are we going to do now?" I ask gently as we walk further through the forest. I notice the sky that was so blue above has changed to a dark purplish-blue and the stars in the sky are twinkling more brightly now with all the colours of the rainbow. I would love to be wandering through the beautiful forest, hand-in-hand with Kala as dusk approaches. My mind is lost for a moment in a romantic fantasy that I hope could soon become a reality.

"We must go back to my village and tell Mother that we need to look for Kala. She will be worrying about me as well as Kala. I have been gone for a very long time." Indiara explains seemingly troubled by the thought of worrying her Mother.

I realise that I have no concept of time and I wonder if my parents have noticed that I have gone. I am concerned they will be worried about me and begin to search for me, or that they would have to call the police to help find me. The problem is, they won't be able to find me, there isn't a hope of them finding me now and I am not even sure if there is any hope of me ever returning home. The thought of going back into the water frightens me after I nearly drowned, I am sure that is the only possible way for me to travel home. Then I remember the blackness of the lake and consider that perhaps there is no way back. The prospect is now quite scary but I must focus on finding Kala.

There are a variety of strange melodic sounds, some are lovely and some make me feel extremely nervous as we walk between the trees with very little light shining down from the sky to help us see where we are going. Indiara seems to know the route very well as she marches ahead of me. She doesn't appear to be even so much as slightly afraid of the howls and growls coming from deep within the darkness of the trees. I have the distinct impression I am being watched as I look all around me, I cannot see anything but I feel like there could be eyes peering at me, drilling their way into my soul. At least the fast speed we are walking at gives me little time to worry about any creatures living in the forest. I just hope we can find Kala sooner rather than later, and finally everyone can relax.

Chapter 7

After walking for a short while, we come to a clearing in the woods with a number of small houses. I can hear the sounds of what I assume to be birds tweeting and I smell a fire burning nearby. There is a glow coming from a number of small houses in the area. Behind the small houses there is one larger house, which looks grand compared to the rest, but still basic compared to the mansion I live in back home. There are a number of people wandering about, socialising near a large bonfire. I notice that many of the young women have varying shades of blue hair and the men striking flame red hair. The village looks partly tribal whilst appearing somewhat modern.

"This is my home village, we are a small community and there are many of these throughout the forest. We choose to live a more quiet life, away from the modern advances of the city. Some of the outsiders think we are strange, but we are happy living out here in the peace and beauty of our natural surroundings." Indiara informs me in a way that suggests she wants me to understand her culture. However, the world she lives in is completely strange to me; wonderful but strange.

"Where do you live?" I ask curiously looking at the houses trying to guess which one might belong to Indiara and Kala.

"I live in the large building at the back." She points to the big house that I was quickly drawn to when we first came to the clearing. "We must find Mother and tell her we need to make our way to visit Tikto."

I follow Indiara along a dirt path, between grassy plains which leads through the village, between other houses, right up to her front door. I become aware of people turning to look at me as we walk towards her house, their eyes stare at me, piercing through me and I truly feel like an outsider, an alien to these people. I hear gasps coming from the villagers as we pass them, Indiara hushes them, making me feel more protected than I would if I was alone here. I am truly thankful for her friendship because I have no comprehension of what would happen to me if I was alone in this place. People might see me as some kind of threat and leave me to fend for myself, or worse, try to attack me and cut me open like one of those alien autopsy stories!

As we approach the door I notice Indiara raising her hands to a panel, which has a large green button directly next to it. There are two high pitched bleeps before a number of clicks, then the door opens. I am quite surprised by the futuristic method of unlocking the door and realise the people adopt some modern technological advances, whilst living in a traditional setting. It occurs to me that living in the city might be extremely advanced compared to back home and now I am curious to visit.

We enter the house which is quite plain, with white walls and wooden floors, a number of pictures are mounted on the wall. I notice a photo of Kala wearing some golden coloured robes and he looks so very handsome. I walk over to the picture and stare at it intently touching the frame, looking at every detail of the picture, the beautiful purple and yellow flowers in the background, the bright green trees towering above him. Indiara has walked ahead, she turns back to look at me.

"Come Mel-o-dee! We need to speak to Mother." Indiara breaks my trance with her firmly enforced instructions as she grabs my arm. I am taken by surprise at the harsh nature of her words and actions. I feel aggravated, I want to correct her because she keeps saying my name wrong, but I realise she is the only friend I have and I feel the need to keep quiet for just now and perhaps raise the matter politely at another time.

She leads me into a room which I assume is the kitchen, there seems to be a number of appliances and pots in there. Indiara looks around into the back of the room, apparently looking for her Mother. There is a small silver box on the wall with a screen and she presses a button which flashes red whilst making a bleeping noise. Eventually, the screen lights up blue and a messages appears 'scanning in progress' then almost immediately a robotic voice comes from the box, "Good evening Indiara. Ready for your command."

"Find Mother." Indiara speaks to the box and it registers her command before coming up with a flashing message 'Searching'. Then an image appears on the screen which looks like an older lady. "*Shalama* Mother, where are you?"

"*Shalama*, I am visiting your Grandfather, Indiara I have been worried about you. Did you find your brother?" Indiara's Mother asks concernedly.

"It is a very long story. We have to make our way to visit with Tikto, I believe he went to see him." She explains hurriedly.

"But that is very far away! I don't want you walking there alone." Indiara sighs at her Mother's concern, the same way as I do when my Mum worries about me.

"I won't be alone and even if I was I would be alright, I can defend myself you know!" Indiara shouts angrily at the screen, in a way that I would never speak to my Mum and this takes me by surprise. It was so forceful and I could hear her Mother making grumbling sounds as she processes what Indiara had said to her.

"That's fine! But I want you to wear the band and keep in touch with me so I can send help if you are in trouble." Her Mother instructs powerfully.

"Okay I will do that for you." Indiara responds showing more respect and understanding.

"Who are you going with?" Her Mother asks directly. Indiara rolls her eyes at the constant questioning.

"My friend, Mel-o-dee." Indiara responds to the question with less confidence.

"Who is Mel-o-dee? I have never met this person! What a strange name!" Her Mother barks.

"Mother! She is helping us find Kala! You are wasting time asking so many questions." Indiara reacts more aggressively again, angrily thumping the button and ending their conversation. "I must get changed before we go on our search for Kala."

Indiara marches off into another room, apparently irritated by the whole situation and by how her Mother spoke. I feel guilty for causing all this trouble, if it hadn't been for me Kala wouldn't be missing and everybody is terribly worried about him. It must be unusual for him to be gone for so long and I can only be to blame for him attempting to find me. I look around the kitchen, the walls are plain white and the floor is some kind of white stone. Some of the appliances look interesting, I don't want to touch them for fear I could break something and I certainly don't want to annoy Indiara anymore than she already has been.

I walk through to the back of the room and stand at a large window which looks out onto the trees. It is very dark and I feel slightly nervous about our imminent trek into the forest, but Indiara seems confident that she can handle herself so I hope we will be fine. Indiara reappears wearing some trousers which I can only described as the kind of pants a genie would wear, they are black with a shiny gold thread weaving through that sparkle underneath the kitchen light. She has a cosy looking black jumper with flat black boots, which look ideal for walking long distances. She makes her way over to a cupboard and takes out two silver bands. She puts one on her wrist and presses a small button which is on the side, then, she comes over to me with the second band.

"Hold out your arm Mel-o-dee. This band is to help protect you, when I push the button it tracks your whereabouts and we can contact each other at all times." A small heart shaped light on the band illuminates as Indiara is speaking. "The device is known as the 'heart on your sleeve' band. The heart changes colour depending on your mood. Yours is black at the moment which means you are anxious and stressed. Do not worry Mel-o-dee, soon we will find Kala and everything will be fine. Tikto is a nice man and he will be able to help us find Kala." Indiara tells me reassuringly, this may be a little presumptuous but she now appears to be enjoying the control of having such a huge task to undertake.

"If you want to call me, you press the button three times quickly and it will ask for your command. Say the code number 3201, then my name and it will begin bleeping and then, when I press the button on my band we can speak to each other."

"Ok, I understand, thank you." I say smiling at Indiara, appreciating her helpfulness and as she smiles back at me, I realise I am safe with her and the anxiety about the trek has all but left.

"Your heart is turning blue. That means your becoming calm!" Indiara exclaims happily. "Come, we must leave immediately." She directs me towards the door.

As we leave the house there is a village gathering outside, no doubt the local people are waiting to catch a glimpse of the outsider. They all stare at me silently which makes me feel anxious, and when I look down at my heart it has turned black again. I look to Indiara, she is looking at each of the villagers from left to right with an angered expression on her face.

"Why are you all just standing there!? Mind your own business!" Indiara shouts at them crossly. The village people begin walking away, some look back at me clearly curious about who I am, but continue to move along. However, one man stays standing there, just staring at me. "Do you want something?" Indiara focuses right into his eyes, with a burning vicious stare, he nervously starts muttering.

"Em, it's, it's, j..j..j, just strange!" The man stutters, he's an older man with a pained facial expression, he isn't making any sense. I feel a bit sorry for him, he is stood in white robes and doesn't appear to be a confrontational character.

"What is strange!?" Indiara is becoming more frustrated with the man as she makes her way down the three steps from her front porch. I follow behind her obligingly, but I am careful not to move too closely because I feel worried that I am scaring the man. I feel my eyes starting to well up with tears and I take a deep breath because I don't want to cry in front of them, partly because I am scared I wouldn't stop.

"The, the, the girl! Where did she come from? Is she? Is she!?" He stutters loudly still making little sense to us both.

"Is she what!? Spit it out!" Indiara barks impatiently with her hands on her hips.

"Is she an alien? Where did she come from?" The man asks fearfully looking at me then, looking back at Indiara. It's like he wants to look at me, but he is too scared because to him I am some sort of creepy alien from outer space.

"You don't need to be scared of me. My name is Melody and I suppose I am an alien. Don't be afraid, I come in peace." I say holding out my two fingers like they do in the sci-fi films, but he starts stepping backwards, now looking more frightened than he did previously.

"What are you doing!?" Indiara turns to me seemingly irritated by my feeble attempt to befriend the man.

"Sorry I just wanted him to realise I am nice, not scary and I want to be friends." I whisper to Indiara hoping she will understand the reasoning behind my actions. Indiara stares at me for a moment but my eyes drift over her shoulder and Indiara turns to look.

"He's gone. We must go, we have wasted enough time. Follow me!" Indiara tells me before walking ahead of me.

Indiara walks around to the back of her house and then follows a dirt path between the trees as I follow quickly, striving to keep up with her. It is very dark and I feel more scared than ever now, the twinkling light from the stars no longer can light our way because the trees are so thick at this part of the forest. Every noise, tweet, howl, crunch and bang seems to be amplified in the darkness of the forest.

"What are those noises?" I ask feeling ever so slightly fearful of anything that could be lurking behind the trees.

"It's animals that live in the forest and noises of the trees moving. You must not feel scared. Animals can smell things that people cannot, they can smell the fear and that will make them want to hunt you down!" Indiara speaks forcefully.

"Why would they want to hunt me down?" I ask quietly.

"Because you would make a nice dinner for them, they like to eat people. Maybe because you are a strange person they would leave you alone." Indiara chuckles as she tells me this. I would find this funny, if it wasn't that now I am really scared and if some animal smells me right now it will want to eat me and I DO NOT want to be eaten! I look down at the wrist band to see what colour the heart is, but it must be black again because I can't see anything.

"How am I supposed to cover up my fear now? I am frightened! I don't want to be food." I say feeling panicked whilst looking for reassurance, rather than to be the butt of any more of her jokes.

"You will be fine, I won't let anything eat you, I promise." Indiara replies chuckling again.

"Thanks, I feel so much better." I say sarcastically. I am not best pleased about how she thinks my fear is a funny joke. I am not from this strange place and I can't defend myself. I only have Indiara to help me and I need her reassurance, not to be made a fool of. I am trying to think of calm thoughts, to rid myself of the fear of being attacked by some giant monster or being eaten alive. I imagine arriving at Tikto's house and finding Kala, and the joy I feel that we are finally together for the first time. I dream of lying in the field with him outside under the stars, mesmerised by the twinkle of all the different colours and talking to him about everything and nothing. I look at the band on my wrist and the heart is glowing purple.

"What does the purple heart mean?" I ask curiously.

"It means you are happy. How can you be happy just now?" Indiara snipes at me.

"I was thinking of Kala." I reply honestly and Indiara stops for a second and turns to look me directly in the eyes, she looks like she is going to speak but she simply says nothing and nods. I am not sure what she is thinking at this precise moment, but I hope she knows that I really care about him. There are so many things I want to ask her, but it seems she snaps at most questions and I don't want to offend her. Maybe people in Adia are very shy and prefer not to share too much information. I don't want to appear to be rude by being overly curious, but I can't shift the desire to learn about this place, it is truly fascinating to me.

It feels like we have walked for miles and my feet are sore, my eyes are struggling to stay open, my back is aching and I just want to sit down. Indiara marches up ahead like a bold soldier, she is taller than me and more muscular, she appears to be well accomplished at venturing through treacherous conditions. My petite frame is weakening and not used to all of this exercise, I don't feel like I can travel much further tonight. My stomach embarrasses me by letting out a thunderous rumble, drawing attention from Indiara.

"Was that you?" She asks raising one eyebrow at me, looking me up and down in a seemingly critical manner.

"Yes, I must be hungry." I apprehensively reply, feeling as though I will be holding her back because I am weaker than she is.

"We must rest. Sometimes I do not know when to stop. We must settle in a place, have something to eat and sleep for a while. If we keep going when we are tired we might become sick." I am grateful to hear Indiara speak these words so that I can take a break from the trekking. I want to get to Kala as quickly as possible, but I will never make it if we don't at least stop to refuel.

Indiara nimbly climbs a tree nearby, so high that I can no longer see her. I am scared of being left alone in the darkness of the forest. I don't want to shout out to her in case I disturb any creatures lurking in the trees. I feel a presence from above although I cannot see her, then without warning something touches my shoulder, I jump a foot off the ground and spin right around at the same time letting out a pained squeal as I go.

"Shut up Mel-o-dee!" Indiara is facing me upsides-down with an angry expression. Her legs wrapped gymnastically around one of the trees branches, I am amazed by her strength.

"Sorry, but you frightened me! Don't go off and leave me like that again, and my name is Melody not Mel-o-dee,

Melody!" I say sternly showing a side to myself she had not seen before.

"Can't you climb trees, little *parci*?" Indiara uses a word I am not familiar with, she appears to be making fun of me again.

"Not really. Why did you just call me that? What is a little *parci*?" I ask becoming increasingly frustrated as she grins at me cheekily.

"You don't know what a *parci* is? You don't know anything!" Indiara shouts at me. I am finding it hard to tell whether she is joking with me or being serious. I just wanted to know what it was, it isn't really fair to make fun of somebody when you don't know what something means and it's not like there is anybody else around to laugh at her "hilarious" joke. She is swinging about shaking the branches of the tree, part of me wishes it would snap - she wouldn't be so smart then. I imagine her falling to the ground and being ashamed of herself, but in reality I very much doubt that would happen.

"A *parci* is a little bird that cannot fly, it is stuck to the ground. That makes you a little *parci*. You need to be stronger like a *madocio* if you are going to survive." Indiara informs me, whilst insulting my placid nature.

"So, what is a *madocio*?" I ask curiously.

"It is a large fire breathing lizard, with many stripes of bright colours on its scales. They live up in the mountains and it is safer to stay away from there, most explorers who venture there never return. The ones that do return tell terrifying tales that I do not want to repeat to you. You must be tough like a *madocio.*" Indiara tells me seriously, looking me in the eye still upsides-down. I imagine this strong, majestic, fire breathing lizard with its coloured skin.

"Indiara, there are bushes, trees and twigs everywhere. Where are we going to lie down to sleep?" I ask feeling concerned that I am in for a rubbish sleep tonight.

"We were going to sleep in the tree! But you, like a little *parci,* you are just standing there staring at the tree instead of climbing it! You won't get any food for your noisy, empty belly if you do not climb. Now come!" Indiara orders me, but I am frightened I fall because I am not used to climbing like she is. I very rarely climb anything at home and when I do it is no more than a couple of feet off the ground, not high up like this tree is. She smiles at me and holds out her hand to pull me up onto the branch she is on. "We must go higher, it is safer and the fruit grows further up." She tells me as she points to the sky. Indiara climbs more slowly now so I can see her as I follow behind. I precariously climb upon every branch wobbling and shaking, eventually we find a large part with leaves and come to a stop. Indiara sits down and pats the ground as a signal for me to join her and I do. As we lay looking at the stars, the leaves feel warm underneath me and surprisingly comfortable. I forget all about being hungry and drift away into a much needed deep sleep after the long journey so far.

Chapter 8

My nose is itchy. I roll over and scratch it feeling irritated, I can hear the gentle twittering of birds and I feel the comfort of my bed. Something nudges me in the back, it must be Bertie, I move over still enjoying my sleep in the hope he will leave me alone, but I get another heavier shove this time. "Go away Bertie! I want more sleep." I mutter incomprehensibly.

Suddenly I am jolted out of my sleep by a sharp kick on my back side, I open my eyes and I am reminded that this isn't my bedroom. I am right at the edge of the large leaf we went to sleep on last night. I am about thirty feet off the ground and I feel like screaming as I look down at the forest below. Indiara grabs my arm and rolls me over which is easy for her because I am as light as a feather and she is incredibly strong. She is standing above me with a handful of red ball shaped objects and then she shoves one at my face.

"You must eat before we start walking again." She tells me whilst shaking the red object about a centimetre from my chin.

"What is it?" I ask unsure about whether the object is safe for me to eat, trying to focus on it with Indiara holding the thing so close to my face.

"It's a fruit that grows from the trees, very good for you. You need to eat it because there are no other foods in this part of the forest." She informs me as she sits beside me and I take it from her hand. She can tell I am still confused by the fruit because of the way I am looking at it. "It's called a *boon*. You just bite into it, it tastes sweet."

I open my mouth and apprehensively bring the strange red fruit to my mouth, as I take a bite my teeth sink into the fruit easily. It tastes delicious and sweet on my taste buds before travelling down to my stomach, making me feel absolutely ravenous. I rapidly scoff the rest of the fruit and hope there is more to eat, I turn to Indiara showing her my palms, smiling cheekily.

"Oh so you want more, do you?" She asks me with a wink before throwing another *boon* in my direction. As I wolf the second one down I hope she has another, I am absolutely starving. I look up at her and she knows instantly, kindly throwing me the last one which I gobble up, letting out a huge burp.

"That's disgusting Melody! I will leave you in this tree if you do that again!" Indiara shouts at me jokingly.

"Pardon me. I ate them a little bit too fast." I respond bashfully as she bursts into fits of laughter. I stand up on the branch whilst she continues to giggle, I look down but can't see the ground below, just green leaves and trees. I look up at the sapphire blue sky and notice it never really gets bright and sunny here. Perhaps that's why the people are so pale-skinned here, unlike me, I must look rather strange. The sky is beautiful and clear, the deep sapphire blue is striking and mesmerising. I stand and stare for just a moment; Indiara has stopped laughing and is standing right next to me looking up at the sky too.

"What are you looking at? There is just sky, nothing to see. We must go." Indiara tells me harshly. Sometimes I think she forgets that I am not from here and the surroundings are fascinating to me.

"How am I going to get back down?" I am concerned because in the dark last night I didn't realise just how high up we had climbed.

"That's easy little *parci*." She responds cheekily before disappearing up even higher through the trees. Her fearlessness is wonderful and I wish it would rub off on me so that maybe I can stop being called a little *parci*. After a minute or so Indiara speedily drops down the trunk of the tree apparently abseiling using a large vine, she stops at the branch where I am stood and wraps a second vine she had dragged with her around my waist before tugging it to ensure I am secure however, I am definitely not convinced how safe it is.

"I am going to lower you down slowly. Shout when you get to the bottom." Indiara instructs me before grabbing the vine tightly in both her hands. I position myself against the trunk and lean back with my feet against it, I look nervously at her and then close my eyes because I am frightened if I look down I will panic. "Are you ready?"

"No!" I yell frightened that something terrible could happen, the vine might snap or it might not be long enough or I could get stuck.

"You have to get down from this branch so let go of your fear! I will start lowering you down now." She shouts at me to jolt me out of my 'frozen to the spot' state. I feel the vine slacken and naturally start to push my legs against the trunk to help lower myself down. The vine feels sturdy so I begin to relax and enjoy the abseil.

"I'm at the bottom!" I yell loudly to make sure Indiara can hear me, I hear my voice echo through the trees. I feel like I want to climb back up the tree so I can abseil down it again for fun, but we need to focus on finding Kala. I stand looking up to the top of the tree but I can't see Indiara anywhere, I'm not sure if she heard me so I shout again, "Indiara! I'm at the bottom!". The echo of my voice through the trees again is so loud, she must have heard me. It feels like she is taking ages to come down, I stay firmly stood where I am at the bottom of the tree.

As I wait for Indiara to climb down the tree I become aware of a rustling in the bushes and I look around anxiously to see if I can spy anything or anyone nearby. "Oh hurry up." I mutter to myself out of frustration at being alone in the forest again. The rustling gets louder and I feel increasingly afraid as I back against the tree, but I can't see anything nearby at all. The shrubbery is so thick here I can't see anything apart from green leaves, perhaps if I just stay quiet whatever it is will go away.

The rustling does not stop and I suddenly become aware of a large animal in the bushes, I can see a dark furry animal pacing around. I am so frightened I start to shake uncontrollably, I look around but I can't see anywhere to go, I look up but I can't see Indiara. *I don't know what to do!*

My hands are sweating as well as my forehead, I feel a drip down the side of my face. All of a sudden a huge cat-like animal jumps out from the bushes and is standing about two feet away from me. There is nowhere for me to go, I look up desperately again, but still I can't see Indiara anywhere. I can't believe she hasn't made her way down the tree yet, it shouldn't be taking so long. The huge cat is snarling at me and growling, it starts circling me. I close my eyes and hope that it can't see me anymore, because my eyes are closed which of course is ludicrous!

As the huge animal continues circling me, I can't understand why it hasn't eaten me already. Perhaps it is the unusual look about me, it isn't sure whether or not I am safe to eat, just like Inidara joked about before. This thought came too soon as he stands directly in front of me lowers himself close to the ground before pouncing on me, pushing me against the tree. I don't care anymore, I start screaming like a banshee, I think I'm done for, a goner, I am about to die a painful, horrible death. The huge cat pinning me against the tree is so heavy I feel crushed under the weight, I continue screaming even as it shows a huge set of sabre teeth it is ready to eat me with. It looks like something out of the books I read at school about prehistoric animals, apart from its coat which at first looked silky and black, but close up it is more of a deep purple shade.

I close my eyes tightly and I am filled with fear as the massive beast snarls at me, enthusiastically preparing to murder me. I have stopped screaming now because I have no fight left in me. I have accepted the inevitable. Suddenly, I hear a strange noise in the background of all the snarling. It sounds like rustling and a loud screaming noise, but I am too scared to open my eyes. I hear a huge thud and I have somehow become free, I open one eye nervously to see what is going on and there is Indiara riding around on the huge cat that only seconds before was going to make a meal out of me.

I now begin to realise just how strong Indiara is as she takes control of this massive beast, which is at least twice the size of her. She has a firm hold of the skin on the back of his neck which aggravates him a great deal as he tries to shake her off but she hangs on tightly. I watch as she skilfully manages to pull something from her pocket which is cylindrical in shape. She pushes the tip of the object into the neck of the large cat-like animal for a few seconds and with that it stops fighting back. Indiara hops off the back and walks towards me putting her hand on my shoulder.

"Are you ok?" She asks between breaths, clearly exhausted from her scuffle with the enormous beast.

"I think so. How come you took so long to come down? What is that thing?" I ask breathlessly

"I'm sorry Melody. The vine became tangled around the tree so it took me a few minutes to straighten it out." Her apology was genuine, she kept turning back to check the large cat wasn't about to attack again, luckily it was slumped on the ground. "He is a *joomokie*, I gave him an injection to calm him.

He will be friendly now, but it wears off eventually so we should move quickly."

Indiara makes her way over to the *joomokie* and signals for me to join her, she begins stroking his head and scratching his chin like he was a pet cat. "Stroke him because you won't get a chance to come this close to one again." I am not really sure whether I should accept her command because he tried to eat me only moments ago. I don't feel very friendly towards something that was so intent on finishing me off for good. I reach out my hand slowly, and reluctantly pat him on his head.

"You seem nervous Melody. Here in Adia we love all animals, he didn't mean to scare you. His instinct is to find something for dinner, but I don't think he would eat you anyway. You look a bit funny to him, he was probably just teasing." Melody informs me whilst grinning but I don't see the funny side. "Come now, we must visit Tikto today."

We begin our trek again through the forest but I have become more aware of everything around me now. I notice the heart on my wristband is black so I must be anxious and stressed. I doubt I will be able to calm down now I am so filled with fear after the *joomokie* attacked me. I was like fresh meat for him and that was a big cat, there could be other huge beasts living in the forest, but I don't want to know about them. I am sure I could ask Indiara, but I think that it would just increase my anxiety. I just hope that after what happened she will try not to leave me on my own again. I am thankful she saved me, controlling that huge beast with all her strength, she is quite possibly the most amazingly strong girl I have ever met.

We walk for about another hour and come to a river running through the forest, I am extremely thirsty and feel the urge to jump right in and enjoy immersing myself in the lovely cool water. Indiara makes her way to the edge of the river bank, kneels down, scoops up some water in her hands and drinks it. I kneel down beside Indiara and copy her scooping up the water, it is so fresh and thirst quenching I quickly scoop up more and slurp it joyously. The water is like nothing I have seen before, it sparkles so beautifully blue and it is crystal clear. I would never drink river water back at home, it never looks clean enough, but here it looks too good not to drink it.

"Does that feel better? You must have been very thirsty." Indiara asks caringly as she continues drinking.

"Yes I was, this water is lovely and fresh. I could dive right in!" I reply enthusiastically.

"We don't have time, we have to go now." Indiara states while she stands up and signals to a bridge, a little way downstream. We begin to head to the bridge but as we get closer I realise it looks old and unsafe. I start fiddling with the band on my wrist because I feel nervous, something I usually do with my watch at home.

"Indiara, are you sure that bridge is safe?" I ask tentatively and as we approach nearer a screeching alarm starts going off. "What is that!?" I scream over the high pitched din. Indiara looks shocked and grabs my wrist, at this point I realise the alarm is coming from me. She holds both my hands in hers and appears to be saying something, but I can't make it out. Within a short space of time the alarm stops and the heart on my wrist which was flashing red has turned back to black. "What happened?"

"You must have pressed the panic button. I am sorry I forgot to tell you about that." I am immediately angered by this information and simply must say something to Indiara.

"There is a panic button and you forgot to tell me? You forgot to tell me about a panic button? Is that what you are telling me? You forgot to tell me there was a panic button and if I knew that, I could have pressed it when that *joomokie* tried to eat me for his dinner, but I didn't know about it so I couldn't!" I shout angrily at Indiara completely losing my patience because I am absolutely stunned at the fact she didn't inform me of this indispensable function that could save my life.

"I'm sorry Melody." Indiara looks genuine as she apologises to me and I am not the sort of person to hold grudges. Not only that, I am very much on my own here and I actually have become very fond of her and don't want to argue, she is like a sister to me.

"Apology accepted." I reply and reach out to give her a hug, but she just stares at the ground. I decide to walk over to her and give her a great big cuddle. She stands there solid as a rock whilst I squeeze the life out of her. "What's wrong? Do people not cuddle here?"

"Yes they do, but I'm just not that kind of person and I don't know you very well." For the first time Indiara looks very embarrassed as she stamps her left boot into the ground, I feel sad for her because she doesn't like hugs, everybody should like a good cuddle. I decide not to go on about it because I don't want her to feel more embarrassed than she already does.

"It's ok, just where I come from you can say sorry with a hug when you care about someone." I explain to her softly because I want her to know how much I care about her. "Let's cross this bridge then, but I am scared. Can you help me?" I ask partly because I am genuinely afraid and the other part of me wants her to feel useful and back in control again. As I expected, she stands up straight and stops stamping her feet into the ground and walks up ahead to the start of the bridge.

The bridge is held together by ropes that are attached to logs and looks fairly dangerous, I do not want to fall in the water again after nearly drowning when I arrived here. Indiara is ahead of me and stands up on a large log that lies in the middle, pushing it with her foot a couple of times to check it is sturdy and then she climbs on fearlessly.

"I will go across first and wait for you at the other side. It seems strong enough for one person to cross at a time." Indiara calls to me as she starts making her away across the bridge, putting one foot in front of the other. Watching her balancing precariously on the log I'm not sure whether I am going to be able to manage to cross it as skilfully as she is able to. The problem with me is, unlike Indiara, I am filled with fear.

She approaches the other side and I know I will have to make my way across the rickety old looking bridge. She waves to me from the other side, signalling for me that I should start crossing. I place my foot up onto the log and as I put one foot in front of the other I decide that it is not so bad. After a few more steps, I realise that I spoke too soon. As I get nearer to the middle of the bridge, the log is thinner and my balance becomes unsteady. I wobble from side-to-side extremely ungracefully, nothing like Indiara when she nimbly hopped across the bridge only moments earlier. Now I have one leg dangling in the river and one leg trying to stay desperately on the log, which actually feels more like a twig at present.

"Come on Melody! Stop dancing around and get to the other side! I want to find my brother now!" Indiara boldly yells at me as I flap about like a demented chicken. Somehow, I manage to grab hold of the ropes at either side of the log and straighten myself up. I concentrate hard on being brave and try to forget my fear of falling into the turquoise fast-flowing river.

I move quicker than before whilst imagining I am a superhero and that nothing can stop me from doing anything I want to do. My plan works and I arrogantly step off the other side of the bridge looking Indiara right in the eye. She smirks at me and pats me on the shoulder as she senses my new found inner strength. I just hope that I can be this brave no matter what stands in our way. I can't be sure and I doubt she would ever want to say anything, but I am almost certain she looks impressed with me and I am impressed with myself.

Chapter 9

It feels like we have been walking forever, my legs are heavy and my feet ache from the lengthy journey that we have embarked on. It feels like days have passed, whereas in actual fact I have only been here for two days. I can barely remember what it is like to be back at home with Mum, Dad and Bertie. I would spend days trying to fill my time by finding tasks to do and still be so bored. Yet, I still don't know whether this is the kind of fun that I planned on having. Anytime I feel like laughing just now it is hampered by the feeling that I have somehow let Kala down. I am afraid that Indiara resents me for her brother going missing, despite her keen effort to look after me. The way she barks at me every now and again makes me think that she is angry with me, if it hadn't been for me Kala wouldn't be missing.

Indiara and I reach the top of a large hill and we can see for miles across Adia, it is starting to get dark and I wonder if perhaps it is time for a rest. The beautiful twinkling stars look close enough to touch now that we are so high up on this hill. I wonder how much further we will have to go and I am not even sure that I can manage much further. Indiara is looking around at the scenery as if she is trying to see something in particular, perhaps she is hoping to see her brother, but we are too high up to identify anybody across the valley.

"See over there." Indiara points to an area of bright lights and tall buildings in the distance. "That's Cordovan.

Some people call it; 'The Big City'." She has a certain excitement in her eyes as she states this.

"What's it like there?" I ask curiously.

"I have only been there a few times, it is wonderful Melody. When we find Kala we should visit there, you will like it." Indiara need not convince me, I am already completely intrigued. I can only imagine that 'The Big City' is incredibly exciting and I have built up an image in my head already of fancy lights, big buildings and flashy cars. I remember Indiara telling me that her standard of living was quite basic, so I assume that the city would be some thrilling futuristic kind of place. I feel energised from the knowledge that I could be visiting Cordovan. I want to find Kala as quickly as possible so we can go there.

"Do we have far to go now?" I ask Indiara which prompts her to look around at the ground below.

"Hmmm. Do you see that small house just down there?" I see she points over to a small building near the bottom of the hill and I nod in acknowledgement. "That is where Tikto lives, once we are at the bottom of the hill it is only a short walk."

With my new found energy I go marching off ahead of Indiara, making my way down the hill and she has to catch up with me for a change. The grass on the hill crunches under my feet as I march quickly in front, trying deliberately not to allow Indiara to catch up with me. I hear her feet crunching more quickly behind me as she begins to catch up which makes me speed up even more until I am eventually running down the hill.

"Hey! You can't outrun me!" Indiara shouts as she catches up with me. I feel her hand on my shoulder and try to run even faster but instead trip over my own feet. As I tumble to the ground I catch Indiara with my foot and she lets out a scream before falling on top of me. We roll down the hill for a minute or so scrambling, trying to grab hold of each other before finally coming to a stop. Indiara is lying on her back with her head pointing down the slope and I am sitting up alongside her facing the opposite direction. We are both covered in grass and twigs, Indiara starts to giggle, her laugh is infectious, I start to chuckle along with her. Indiara lifts herself up off the ground and squats down as she dusts the twigs off her clothes, she looks at me with a cheeky glint in her eyes. She catches me off guard by pouncing on top of me and we wrestle and start to roll down the hill again laughing all the way.

A little way further down the hill we come to a stop again giggling and laughing, then we stop breathlessly and we look at each other smiling. She is sat right in front of me but I look slightly to the right of her shoulder, trying to decipher how much further we have to go. She turns her head to try and see what I'm looking at and then looks back at me smiling again.

"I have something to tell you Melody." She states smiling with her eyes wide and sparkling.

"What's that then?" I ask happily.

"You're okay." She smiles sweetly at me and finally the fear that I felt about her resenting me has lifted. I feel accepted by her and have realised perhaps she is enjoying the adventure of trying to find her brother. Perhaps Indiara felt the same way as I did before I came here, maybe her life was boring too. If she can look after herself and fight huge sabre tooth cats, I would imagine Kala can look after himself in much the same way as she can.

"You're okay too." I reply winking at her. She slaps me hard on the shoulder and I let out a yelp before standing up and dusting myself down. Indiara brushes the grass of my back and turns at me signalling to do the same for her. I finally feel like we are friends and I can't stop smiling. I'm reminded of my best friend back home and I miss her very much. She is called Bryony, and she has the most beautiful golden long blonde curly hair, with a smile that can light up the whole room. We talk as often as we can on the phone, but I next to never see her since we moved out to the countryside. She would love to hear all about what I am getting up to just now, but I don't suppose there is any way I could speak to her. It's as if I am in some kind of parallel universe and for the first time home seems like farther away than ever before.

At least for now I have Indiara as a friend, she seems like a true friend now and I am sure I will be able to tell Bryony all about my adventures when I return home. As we walk further down the hill I am suddenly hit with a reality that stops me in my tracks. *What if I can't go home?*

"What's wrong Melody?" Indiara realises something is bothering me as I stand, staring at the bottom of the hill which is not very far away now.

"I'm worried about something." I say rather blankly as I am deep in thought.

"What is worrying you? You're heart is black again, are you afraid of something?" She asks genuinely concerned by my apparent unease.

"What if I can't go home? I love it here but I need to go home at some point. My parents will be worried sick about me and I have to speak to my friends." I say with a shaky voice and feeling that I am on the verge of tears.

"If you could come here, there will be a way to go back again. You have nothing to fear,I will help you. We will find Kala like you wanted to so much, and then you will be happy."

She tells me so sweetly and calmly. There is something hypnotic about Indiara, when she softly speaks with her gentle intonation. It could make any fear or worry float away in the breeze.

I say nothing and start to walk down the hill once more and she accepts that for now I do not want to speak about my fears any further. I feel content in the knowledge we are closer to finding Kala once we visit Tikto, because that's where Stormie said he would be. The fear that came on all of a sudden has disappeared just as quickly, mostly thanks to Indiara and her reassurance in her soothing manner that is so completely different to the snappy side of her when she is losing her patience.

We make it to the edge of the valley which, looks bigger than it did before at the top of the hill. I can see the house nearby where Tikto lives and feel relieved to finally have arrived here after the long and dangerous trek. I feel a little anxious about meeting Tikto, I can only hope that he will be able to tell us where Kala is. Part of me is worried we have travelled all this way for nothing.

Indiara walks ahead of me and approaches the small house which is very plain, it looks like it is made out of some sort of reddish-brown concrete with a small chimney on top, puffing out smoke repeatedly up to the deep purple, early evening sky. There is a button and a screen on the wall beside the door. She pushes the button and it makes a bleeping noise, a white flash lights up the screen.

"*Shalama,* Can I help you?" An elderly looking man appears on the screen smiling, I assume he must be Tikto.

"*Shalama,* I wonder if you can help me. I am looking for my brother and I was informed that he had come to visit you. His name is Kala." Indiara states in a way that is rather matter of fact.

"Ah yes! You must come in." The old man sounds friendly and helpful as he opens the door.

A blue light flashes above the door and there is a buzzing sound as it begins to unlock, clicking and clunking as the cogs twist to open the door. I notice the door is heavily reinforced and would be impossible to break through, much more secure than the other houses we have visited whilst I have been here. When the door finally opens the old man is standing there smiling. He is quite tall and wearing some white robes, he has a bald head and big bright amber eyes.

"Come in!" He says cheerfully signalling for us to enter the house. "You are the girl he told me about! You don't look like one of us do you? I am sure you have wondrous tales to tell me. My name is Tikto and your name is?" He asks, but before I get a chance to open my mouth. "You're Melody aren't you? What a beautiful name, I haven't heard that name before."

We enter the house and Tikto ushers us into a room, through a door to the right, it is dimly lit. There is a large rug on the floor and Indiara instantly sits down and crosses her legs, so I decide to do the same. I find it a bit strange that he knew my name before I even told him and I begin to wonder if he is psychic, like Stormie but I dare not ask. I have started to notice in the houses we have been in there hasn't been any furniture to sit on. I wonder if I could invent the sofa here and make a fortune! But, on second thoughts, I have never heard anybody mention currency of any description, maybe there is no such thing as rich, maybe I could be famous though, seeing people already seem to know my name when I have never met them!

"Would you like a cup of tea?" Tikto asks thoughtfully after our long journey.

"Yes please!" I reply excitedly, simply over the moon that Tikto has offered us a cup of tea, just like home. I am incredibly thirsty and thrilled at the thought of a nice cup of tea, which is something I never thought would be particularly exciting before, but then I have never been this thirsty before.

"Yes that would be nice, thank you." Indiara responds less thrilled than I.

Tikto leaves the room to make tea and we sit in silence on the floor of. The room is very interesting as I look around at all the ornaments, pictures and trinkets. There appears to be some kind of symbol represented by some wooden ornaments sat on the floor beside a fireplace which is in the middle of the room. The objects are made into the shape of a man, a woman and a child. Another object appears to be in the shape of a duck-billed animal, which looks rather odd. It appears to be large and plump with a textured coat. I want to ask what it represents, but I am not sure whether it is polite to speak seeing Indiara hasn't said a word since he left the room.

On a shelf up to the left of the room, there are what appears to be hundreds of bottles filled with potions against the cream walls. I am itching with curiosity to know what these potions are for, they come in a range of colours; blue, red, yellow, green, orange, purple, pink, black, gold, silver. They also come in a variety of shapes and sizes, some bottles are cylindrical, some are square and others are unusual shapes. I can see the bottles are labelled and I would love to have a look at them, but I don't want to do anything that might upset Indiara or Tikto.

The pictures on the wall appear to be paintings of the valley, some on bright days with blue skies, others at night under the beautiful sapphire sky and twinkling multi-coloured stars, some under the purple early evening sky which makes the land glow in a stunningly soft light, absolutely entrancing. One picture, however strikes me more than any of the others. It appears to be a kind of thunder and lightning storm, the sky is a blood red colour with the blackest of black clouds above, flashes of white light strike the ground in the valley. That picture looks extremely menacing and is very hard to imagine after the gorgeous landscapes I have witnessed since I have been here.

Tikto appears back in the room with a wooden tray, carrying a matching orange coloured tea set. He pours the tea before sitting down and I am instantly struck by the smell, I am instantly aware this wasn't the kind of tea I had expected. It must be some kind of herbal tea, like my Mother drinks back at home. It looks too hot to drink, but I am desperate to take a sip despite it not being the kind of tea I was hoping for, my mouth is as dry as can be from the long journey. My legs and feet are relieved to be resting on the floor after such a long hike as they ache from exhaustion.

"Do you know where Kala is?" Indiara is as straight to the point as ever.

"I can't say for sure. He came to visit me yesterday because Stormie had sent him to ask for help. He was looking for you, my dear Melody, but he did not know how to find you. I had heard of the other world, many years ago. I thought it was perhaps some sort of mythical tale at the time. But, when Kala came to me ask for my help I realised this world must exist and now after meeting you, Melody, I know that it does! Unfortunately, I could not help him with his request to meet you in person, because I was not even sure whether this world truly existed before now. I gave him the address of a woman who came to me many years ago. She told me of a similar situation where she had met someone in the other world and could not meet with them in person. Her name is Mahari and after a while she gave up trying to meet the man and moved to the city of Cordovan, I believe she lives on Ellico Square in the north part of the city.

Indiara sits quietly for a minute processing the information. I don't know what to say, I sit quietly waiting for her to speak. My tea finally looks cool enough to drink, so I decide to take a sip. When I taste the tea it is not unpleasant but I can't pinpoint the flavour to anything I have ever tasted before. It has a sweet taste with a hint of an earthy flavour which is quite different to anything I have experienced at home. I drink the rest very quickly and still find I am thirsty for more. Tikto, being an attentive host instantly fills up my little orange cup with more thirst quenching delicious tea.

"I can't believe he would go so far without telling us where he was going, especially when he is not wearing a band." Indiara finally speaks.

"He is a strong, energetic, young man. You have nothing to fear and he will be home very soon. Perhaps you should go home to your family and wait for him to return. You should stay here tonight, it is not safe to travel through the night and you will both need to get some rest, you must be tired with it being so late." Tikto said in a very caring, fatherly manner.

"Yes we are tired, thank you Tikto." Indiara responds graciously.

"You are very quiet Melody. I would be very interested to hear all about where you come from." I am grateful to Tikto for being so kind to me and will happily tell him all about my life back home.

"Do you have a piece of paper and a pencil? It might be easier for me to explain if I can draw you some things from where I live." I ask hopefully, I love drawing pictures.

"I am sure I will have a piece of paper and a pencil for you to draw with." Tikto replies as he gets up and leaves the room. I wait for a few minutes and find my eyes are drawn to the potions on the shelf again and feel that perhaps I will be able to ask Tikto if I can have a look at them after I explain to him about my world.

After a few minutes, Tikto returns with a couple of sheets of paper and a brown pencil that appears to have been sharpened using a knife. I sketch the outside of our home and the gardens around it, I sketch dads expensive car parked in the driveway and Bertie sitting waiting for us at the door. We talk for hours and I sketch all sorts of objects; our phones and how we use them, our computers and how we search the internet, our televisions and the informative programmes I like to watch and the trashy soaps my parents tend to follow in the evenings, the sports we play and the friends and family I have. I sketch the royal family and the parliament, I even attempt an atlas to show him what the world looks like.

After what may have been hours of talking and sketching, we become aware of it being very late in the night, although there has been no mention of time since I have arrived here. Tikto seemed to enjoy the stories about my life back at home, and I was happy to tell him. He shows us to our room, which to my happiness has two comfortable looking beds, I feared with all the sitting on the floor that we may have to sleep on the floor.

Indiara and I climb sleepily into bed without saying a word to each other and as soon as I lay down and my head touches the pillow, I am fast asleep. I dream of the big city of Cordovan and my imagination runs wild with the thought of tall buildings, bright lights, exciting people with blue and red hair, wearing fashionable clothes, some driving fancy cars, some travelling by a monorail in the sky. As the images swirl and blend in my mind, I have a wonderful sleep and feel completely rested when I awake. I am not sure what the next day will bring, but one thing I am sure of is that I am eager to discover where our journey will take us next.

Chapter 10

I wake up after a peaceful sleep and almost forget where I am again, although when I open my eyes and look around the room, I remember we are staying with Tikto. There is a shutter covering the window and the room is quite dark, I look over at Indiara, she is lying with her arm and leg flopped over the side of the bed and she's snoring. I let out a little chuckle at her snorting like a pig in her sleep.

I am wide awake now and want to get up, but I want to let Indiara sleep for a little longer. I quietly get up and out of the bed, then grab my shoes before slipping out through the door as silently as possible. I sit at the top of the stairs and slip my shoes on before gently tip toeing down to find Tikto. I hear a rustling noise coming from a room towards the back of the house and notice the door is slightly ajar. I make my way through the hall and push the door gently open into the kitchen where I find Tikto busy making some tea.

"Would you like a cup of tea?" Tikto asks me politely as he notices me entering the room.

"Yes please." I reply cheerfully and I watch him as he promptly takes another cup out of his cupboard.

"I enjoyed your tales about this United Kingdom place you speak of." Tikto tells me pleasantly, passing a full cup in my direction. "It seems a shame you will be leaving here today. I would very much like to spend more time with you and find out more about your world. Promise me you will visit again very soon, perhaps once you have found Kala. Will you come back?"

"Of course I will Tikto!" I really mean it too, I would love to come back and visit with Tikto again. I take a sip of my tea as I wonder whether I could ask him about the potions in the front room. "I will definitely be back to visit you, even if it's just to have more of this delicious tea."

Tikto smiles and signals for me to follow him through to his front room and we both sit on the floor. I look up at the shelf with the various multi-coloured potions and feel an overwhelming desire just to come out and ask what they are for. I sip my tea quietly but I find myself drawn to the potions and staring at them.

"You seem to be very interested in my medicines and concoctions Melody. Would you like to have a look?" It was only a matter of time before he noticed my intense glaring at the colours and interesting liquid filled bottles.

"Yes please! I'm not sure why, but I have just been drawn to them. What are they for?" I ask very curiously.

"They do many things my dear. Some of them are for healing and others can do magic." His words send a shiver down my spine. He looks excited by the potions and I am more intrigued by the knowledge that they can do some kind of magic. A couple of days ago I would never have believed that magic could happen, but now I truly believe that anything could happen, much further than my imagination could ever travel. "Go on my dear, you're very welcome to take a look." Tikto speaks encouragingly, much to my delight.

I make my way over to the shelf, filled with numerous bottles of colourful liquids. I pick up a star shaped bottle, which I am particular drawn to because the contents sparkles dazzlingly with all the colours of the rainbow. I turn the bottle, shaking it gently to make the colours sparkle even more. I want to open the bottle to look at the fluid inside but the lids are sealed tightly on all of the potions. There is a label attached to the lid which has the word "Tavi" written on it.

"What is this one for?" I quietly ask whilst still staring at the sparkly mixture and spinning the bottle around, utterly intrigued by its sheer beauty.

"Oh my dear that is a very special potion. It is very difficult to make and I only have two bottles left at the moment.

When you drink the contents of that bottle you become one of the Tavia." Tikto explains quietly.

"What are the Tavia?" I ask becoming even more intrigued.

"The Tavia are small creatures that live in parts of the Sigsana wood and some even live as far as Yuli beach. There are different kinds of Tavia with different abilities that we Adians do not have. All kinds of Tavia have wings and can fly, they can be quite mischievous beings, but they do not do any harm." He explains cheerfully and I listen joyfully.

"Are they fairies?" I ask perhaps naively, but that is what he appears to be describing.

"What is a fairy?" Tikto responds, obviously puzzled by my question.

"Oh it doesn't matter. It just sounds like a fairy, they aren't real and you said they were called Tavia, so it can't be the same thing." I realise I have no clue what I am trying to explain and Tikto nods, but does still appears to be a little confused by my ramblings.

"Here this will help you understand." Tikto tells me, at the same time he hands me a book. I open it up and realise the potions are listed under their names and colours. I immediately begin reading through them to find out what each and every potion can do.

<u>*List of Concoctions*</u>

1. Blue - Instant Calm, Sleep
2. Red - Courage
3. Orange - Strength
4. Purple - Heals Wounds
5. Rainbow - Become Tavia
6. Gold - Grants one wish
7. Pink - Attractiveness
8. Green - Cures Tiredness
9. Brown - Cures Illness
10. Grey - Protective Shield
11. Black - Invisibility
12. White - Vivid Dreams
13. Yellow - Weather Changer

The list goes on much further and I want to try all of the potions to see what would happen. I am not sure if he would require some kind of payment for the potions. I am sure he doesn't just give them away for free.

"How do you make them?" I ask inquisitively. My question causes Tikto to chuckle.

"Now if I told you that my dear, everyone would be able to make my concoctions and I would no longer be able to work. Although I am sure you have noticed that I am an old man and one day I won't be able to work anymore. Not all the potions function in the same way you see, some of them I need to perform certain rituals in order to help people when they come to me. It is a very complicated process, which takes many years of studying and practising in order to understand how these mixtures work. My father taught me and his father taught him, and I have been teaching my son and daughter how to heal, and they will also be handed the recipes for the variety of concoctions that you see before you." Tikto explains sincerely.

"I see, sorry I didn't mean to pry. I am just fascinated because I have never seen anything like this before." I utter apologetically.

"Oh my dear, you have nothing to be sorry for. You are very welcome to ask me anything, however some things have to be kept a secret for the sake of my family." He explains and I give an understanding nod, I appreciate that he must protect the secrets of his potions.

"I would really like to try one of these concoctions." I say as my curiosity to experience one of these fascinating potions is overwhelming. I am still looking through the different bottles on the shelf trying to match the colour to its description in the notebook.

"Some pay me in Barra which is the currency used here in Adia, others pay me with a service. I suppose you provided me with a service by telling me all about your homeland, a lesson you could say. Perhaps, I could let you try one of these concoctions, but because you have never tried one before I don't want there to be any ill-effects, so is it permissible for me to choose which one you should drink?" With these words I believe I should listen to Tikto, because I don't want to risk anything bad happening to me. I nod and sit back where I was before and sip the rest of my tea whilst Tikto looks through the bottles on the shelf, choosing a potion for me.

I notice him selecting a black potion in one of the square bottles and he inspects it before opening the lid. He then measures out a particular amount, in a small cup and brings it over to me. I look at it nervously before looking up at his eyes, he is smiling so there can't be anything to be worried about.

"I have just measured out enough for this concoction to last for a brief period. This one will make you invisible, nobody will be able to see you." Tikto tells me informatively. I nod and take the cup from his hand and drink the whole lot with one big gulp. It didn't taste of anything much really, just like water and I don't feel anything strange. I look down and I can still see myself, so I don't believe it is working. Tikto is standing there in front of me with a huge smile right across his wrinkled face.

"Has it worked?" I ask suspiciously.

"Yes I can no longer see you." He responds enthusiastically.

"But you can hear me?" I ask still unconvinced.

"Yes I can only hear your voice." Tikto says before laughing quietly.

"I can still see myself." I explain confusedly whilst looking at my arms and legs.

"Yes of course you can. It's just everybody else who will be unable to see you. Why don't you have some fun with your sleepy friend?" Tikto says cheekily, chuckling to himself. I decide to take his advice, this could be a lot of fun after all the mischievous comments and jokes that I have had to put up with from Indiara, I could get my own back, now, the joke will be on her.

Tikto picks up his cup of tea and leaves the room to go back through to the hall and then, into the kitchen. I decide to sneak through quietly and make my way upstairs to the bedroom where Indiara is sleeping. The door is still slightly ajar, just the way I left it which gives me enough room to slip through and indicates that Indiara is still asleep. Indiara appears to have just woken up as her eyes open and she lets out a long, loud sigh. I tip-toe over to the bed and realise she really can't see me because she hasn't reacted at all to my presence.

Indiara rolls on to her side and she is now facing me, she definitely can't see me, this is going to be fun. I sneakily creep over to her bedside, and once I am stood right there I quickly grab the top of her cover with both hands and rip it off. The shocked look on her face makes me want to burst out laughing, but I have to hold it in which is a huge struggle.

"That was strange." She whispers under her breath before getting up and sitting on the edge of the bed. She pulls on her boots and ties the lace on her left boot before lacing up the other boot. As she laces up her right boot I sneak over and begin to untie her laces on the left one. She begins to stand up, so I jump out of the way, as she begins to walk her boot slips off, again I want to burst with laughter, but I have to keep it in but it's getting harder and harder not to explode. "Hey! How did that happen!?" Indiara shouts, clearly irritated by what I am doing, making my invisibility even more fun.

She bends down in order to tie up her boot obviously not realising there has been some trickery afoot. I sneak carefully up behind her and tap her on the right shoulder and she swiftly spins round, looking all around the room. "Who is that? Who is there?" She spits aggressively. I sneak around to her other side and tap her on the left shoulder which causes her to swivel round to where she was facing before. "I warn you, I will attack!" she bellows which causes my laughter to burst out uncontrollably, I just can't hold it in anymore.

"Melody? Where are you?" She asks confused because she can hear my laughter, but can't see me anywhere. She looks all around the room, looking under the bed and inside the wardrobe, on the other side of the door before turning back as she can still hear me laughing. "Where are you?" She asks again sounding a little irritated.

"I am invisible." I say trying to contain my laughter.

"What? How did you do that?" She asks clearly puzzled, but realising my voice is right beside her, despite her facing the wrong way and talking to the wall, making me giggle and laugh again.

"Tikto gave me a potion to make me invisible." I explain more calmly letting out a giggly sigh.

"Are you standing in front of me?" She asks insistently.

"I am standing beside you. You are talking to the wall." I say beginning to laugh again.

"Oh, it's so very funny! Stand in front of me!" Indiara demands pointing aggressively and deliberately to the floor, I dare not argue, that girl could eat me alive. I move round to where she is pointing to the floor the expression on her face is not a happy one, she looks serious, frowning slightly.

"I am standing in front of you now." I tell her sharply.

"Right, can you feel me doing that?" She asks as she prods me right in my stomach.

"Ouch! Yes that was right in my tummy." I moan upset by her vicious prodding.

"Haha!" She sniggers and continues to prod at me.

"Ouch! Ouch! Ow! Stop it!" I yell before jumping just out of her reach.

"You're not so funny now, are you?" She asks audaciously.

"It was funny seeing your face when you didn't know what was going on, that made it all worthwhile." I tell her as I begin laughing hysterically.

"Aaaaah! That's really weird!" Indiara shrieks, pointing to my left arm.

"What is?" I ask because I can't understand what is scaring her.

"It's your arm! It's just appeared there and I can't see the rest of you." Indiara stands in front of me still pointing to my arm with a surprised expression on her face. I find this quite funny and start waving my left arm at her, which causes her to screw up her face like she is disgruntled by something. Then I start making spooky, ghostly noises and walking up to her shaking my left hand near her and then prod at her playfully. "Stop that now! I don't like it." She barks at me.

"Who is laughing now?" I ask cheekily through another burst of laughter.

"You're not funny and besides the rest of you is starting to appear, the potion must be wearing off." She informs me indignantly, with folded arms and a rather smug expression.

"Oh well, never mind, do you want to get some breakfast?" I ask, consciously changing the subject.

Indiara nods and we both make our way back downstairs to the kitchen where Tikto is cooking breakfast and the aroma travelling towards us both is absolutely delicious. Indiara makes her way into the kitchen first and I follow behind, we sit next to each other at the table as we watch Tikto serve some food onto a plate.

"I hope you like this Melody, I am not sure what you eat so I prepared a breakfast that we usually eat here in Adia." Tikto tells me considerately as he puts a plate of food in front of me and another in front of Indiara.

"Thank you very much." I say graciously.

"Thank you for everything, we are very grateful." Indiara speaks thankfully before tucking into her meal.

I look at the food on the plate which is hot, like a cooked breakfast, but I don't have any idea what it is or whether I will like it. It certainly does smell good and I remember being unsure about the fruit when we were in the forest and it turned out to be delicious so I decide to tuck in all the same. I want to ask Tikto what it is but I don't want to sound offensive when he had taken the time to prepare food for us. It appears to be some kind of green mush on one side of the plate and some small round things that look like pancakes. There is a clear brown sauce drizzled atop four spherical objects that are a darker brown colour.

"Did Melody give you a fright there? I gave her one of my potions and we thought it would be fun to play a little trick on you." Tikto spoke to Indiara cheerfully as he eats his breakfast. I bravely take a mouthful, I am aware that I am in need of some sustenance if I want to survive the next leg of our journey. Yet again, I am pleasantly surprised by how delicious this food is, the tastes are more what I would expect for dinner back at home, similar to vegetables and potatoes but lovely all the same, especially when you are starving.

"Yes, you both got me there! But, I got her back so now we are even. Perhaps would we be able to purchase a concoction from you, or two? It might be helpful to us, for this journey to have them in the event of any unexpected situations." Indiara asks confidently.

"I would happily come to an arrangement with you Indiara. The cost of each concoction varies in relation to the ingredients that I use, some are more expensive than others." Tikto explains, Indiara seems to squirm slightly in her seat with her head down.

"I don't have very much Barra and I would prefer not to spend what I do have because there might be an emergency where I need it. I could contact my Mother and she could pay the bill, if you don't mind that is." Indiara seems slightly nervous at this request, I would imagine she doesn't want to make promises she can't keep.

"Certainly, if you want to call your Mother I can speak to her for you." Tikto offers politely.

"Thank you." Indiara smiles and continues eating her breakfast, I have shovelled mine down already. I wait patiently for them both to finish their breakfasts whilst I contemplate which concoctions we are going to choose. I still feel intrigued by the one that sparkled and I wonder what becoming a Tavia would be like, I would love to be able to fly, even if it was just for a few minutes, like when he let me try the invisibility potion.

"I will call my Mother just now and ask her if we can have some of your concoctions." Indiara explains before leaving the room to make the call. I can hear mumblings coming from the hall, but I can't make out precisely what she is saying and feel I shouldn't be listening to her conversation anyway. After a few minutes she comes back into the room smiling, she looks at me and then looks at Tikto. "Let's choose our concoctions! Mother said she would rather I used any means necessary to be safe and to send her the bill!" Indiara explains excitedly.

I am completely thrilled by the news and I can tell by the way Indiara's eyes have lit up, she is just as excited as I am. Tikto stands up and waves his hand as a signal for us to follow him, he opens a door to the right of the kitchen where there is another room. We follow him into the room which is dimly lit. I feel slightly apprehensive at the sight of what seems to be lots of dust and cobwebs hanging from the ceiling. I wonder what the insects are like here, I don't like spiders very much. I try to put it out of my head, as so not to creep myself out. There are a number of shelves on one wall, filled with empty bottles of all different shapes and sizes. In the middle of room there is a huge table with tubes connecting to bottles and more tubes leading to dishes and pots bubbling, appearing to be in no particular order, but they surely must be for the sole purpose of making the highly interesting concoctions that I studied so carefully in the front room.

"This is my laboratory where I carry out all my work. I also try to invent new types of concoctions, so that even more options are available to people. There is one in particular that I am working on that is very exciting, but I would prefer to keep it a secret for now, if word gets out I fear that I would be continuously monitored and harassed by the city guards, possibly even the Emperor!" We listen intently to Tikto's words, he has perhaps gone a little off topic and I am keen to select our potions and continue with the journey, which is turning into a real adventure.

"Do you have the list so we can choose which potions we would like?" I ask eagerly, Tikto points back to the door before walking back through to the front room and again we follow him enthusiastically. He picks up the book from the shelf where I had left it, hands it Indiara to have a look at and I peer over her shoulder to be reminded of what each concoction can do.

"Can we have two purple, two rainbow, one grey, one brown, one blue, one orange and one green please?" Indiara decides very quickly the precise potions we require and I am so glad she asked for two of the rainbow, that means one each so maybe my dream will come true and I will get to fly. I am glad that my input didn't even seem necessary because the Tavia was the main potion I wanted to try, although I begin to wonder if I could be granted one wish.

"Indiara, can't we just get the gold potion and make one wish for Kala to come back?" I ask hopefully.

"Can you afford the gold one? The ingredients for this one are extremely rare, I can sell for no less than five million Barra." Tikto interjects with a most surprising answer to my question, five million sounds like a huge amount.

"We certainly cannot afford that one, can anyone?" Indiara sounds shocked by the price of the gold potion.

"I have sold one before yes, to the Emperor himself." His eyes light up as he shares this information.

"What did he wish for?" I ask intrigued by how a man, so rich, could need one wish.

"That, I cannot tell you but I will say one thing, making wishes is something that must be given a great deal of thought. We need to be very careful what we wish for because when the wish becomes a reality it might not make us as happy as we initially thought." Tikto advises proverbially.

The three of us pause in thought for a moment, processing what was said, I imagine what I would wish for in the whole world, it would be Kala but I know in my heart we will find him soon and that we don't need a wish to make it come true, just our willpower. Tikto nods and smiles before heading back to the laboratory, again we follow behind him patiently, this time standing just inside the door so as not to get in his way. He opens a cupboard in the far corner of the room, there are shelves filled with bottles of his precious concoctions.

He pulls a bag out from the bottom of the cupboard and begins to fill it up with the potions Indiara requested. Two of the sparkling rainbow Tavia potions in star shaped bottles, two of of the purple potions for healing wounds in round bottles, two of the black invisibility potions in square bottles, one orange to provide strength in a cube shaped bottle, one grey that provides a protective shield in an oval shaped bottle and one green to cure tiredness in a long cylindrical shaped bottle.

"Won't they break all clanging together in the bag like that?" I ask nervously aware of how precious his concoctions are. I definitely do not want to break them when they are important for our trip.

"They are made of a special material that is virtually unbreakable. Do not worry Melody they will not break and this bag is very secure. That will cost three hundred Barra." Tikto said as he handed the bag to Indiara.

"Three hundred!? Mother did say to get whatever I needed for this trip but at that price I think she might be annoyed. I think it is important to have them so I just hope she will understand when you send her the bill." Indiara states, alarmed by the seemingly huge cost.

"I have enclosed a list of instructions that you should read before taking any of the concoctions. Make sure you read them thoroughly." Tikto instructs importantly with a serious expression on his face.

We both nod at Tikto in acknowledgement, then he leaves the room and we move back to the front room as he shuts the door to his laboratory. He enters the front room with some form of chunky looking gadget in his hand. He seems to be typing some form of information onto the device, he then presses a number of buttons quite speedily.

"What is your house code?" Tikto asks softly.

"It is: 1722TAPK." Indiara informs him of the code as Tikto appears to tap this in the hand held device.

"Thank you, I have forwarded the bill to your Mother." He advises happily.

"Ok thanks, I suppose it is time we should be on our way. Thank you for everything, we are truly grateful." Indiara speaks kindly and genuinely flashing Tikto a rare smile.

"You are very welcome, come back and visit me any time." He responds earnestly.

"Thank you, it was a pleasure to meet you." I say feeling honoured to have met such an interesting, kind and helpful person. Tikto shows us to the door, I feel excited that we are making our way to find Kala again. I just hope that I don't have to wait much longer, and that we find him as quickly as possible. He opens the door to the valley and its spectacular views, the emerald green grass in the daylight is truly inviting.

Chapter 11

As Tikto closes the door behind us we look out into the valley ahead of us and I realise we have another long trek ahead. Indiara pauses for a moment and then looks over to a very dark cloud that is floating, at what seems to be an unusually low level, it looks very odd.

"If we make our way toward that cloud, it takes us near the outskirts of Cordovan." Indiara explains pointing to the low cloud in the distance.

"It looks a little strange." I say curiously.

"I suppose it does, but it will make more sense when we get there. It rains there quite often." Indiara explains, seemingly unphased by the bizarre looking cloud.

Since I have arrived, here there has been a great deal of extraordinary things happening and I am sure there will be many more. Indiara has begun marching ahead as usual and I run behind her, eventually catching up. Again she seems completely focused on the task ahead, quiet, not wishing to discuss anything and we walk in silence. It dawns on me perhaps this is her way of helping to conserve energy, so that we can travel further and hopefully find Kala more quickly.

Despite the silence between us, my head buzzes with internal conversation. I wonder if my family are worrying about me, if they have called the police, whether or not they are out looking for me. My parents can be annoying sometimes, but I love them very much and the last thing I want is them worrying about me. Then again, they should be worried considering a giant *joomokie* tried to eat me.

As we walk further into the valley I realise that there are no other houses in view, Tikto really doesn't seem to have any neighbours. It reminds me of home, but it is definitely more exciting here in comparison to where I live. I look at my feet crunching through the grass and notice how green it is, a much deeper emerald green to match the stunning sapphire sky.

After walking for about an hour I notice several large furry animals grouped together and I start to feel my heart race, frightened they may attack. Indiara marches ahead seemingly not noticing my pace has slowed considerably. She doesn't seem to be concerned by the animals. I assume she must have seen them because they are directly ahead of us. I am now rooted to the ground, too fearful to walk any further, I am clueless as to what I should do.

"Why are you just standing there?" Indiara finally notices as she turns round looking at me with concern.

"What are those big furry things?" I ask pointing at the group of large furry animals.

"They are called *fuzzles*. Don't be afraid, these animals are intelligent, they can talk and also they are very gentle. They only eat plants and vegetables so they will not attack you." Feeling reassured by Indiara's explanation I begin walking again.

"They can really talk?" I ask feeling surprised by this revelation, I have always wished Bertie could talk to me.

"Yes. Just like you and me. We can go and talk to them, they might have seen Kala."

Indiara walks ahead more speedily this time, swinging her arms seemingly keen to speak to the group of *fuzzles*. I follow obediently behind feeling considerably less afraid, now that I know the *fuzzles* are harmless. As we get closer to the group of animals I can see there is a pond with a small stream running through it where they are surely gathering to drink water.

Some of the *fuzzles* are dark brown, some are orange and there are small *fuzzles* that look like babies that have white fluff, instead of the dark fur on the larger animals. We begin to get much closer to them and now that we are up close beside them, I realise they are actually very cute despite being massive. They have big fuzzy round heads with large orange beaks, like that of a duck, which looks very unusual. The older *fuzzles* appear to have bristly, thicker coats and the smaller animals look soft and fluffy. Now that we are stood beside the animals, I realise the smaller ones aren't so small after all, about the size of a big dog, like Bertie. The fully grown *fuzzles* would be similar to the size of a cow, maybe a little bigger and, if it wasn't for Indiara telling me they are friendly animals, I would feel very intimidated by their size.

"Hey! Would you be able to help us? I have lost my brother and we believe he might have walked through this valley." Indiara speaks loudly and informally to the group of *fuzzles*, perhaps animals don't require the same kind of greeting as the Adian people do. The *fuzzles* turn to look at her, the white fluffy babies run awkwardly behind the larger animals before stopping to peak round from behind their chubby round fuzzy figures of what I suspect must be their Mothers, and I could see the bright orange beaks of the young animals sticking out quite clearly. A large brown fuzzle comes closer to us, with a smiling happy face and I can see that these animals are friendly.

"I haven't seen a single soul. We are normally resting in the forest at this time of year but we were driven out by the *Vultus-Saudades*. We are trying to decide where to move to next but it can't be too far for the little ones to walk." The *fuzzle* speaks in a low manly sounding voice which takes me by surprise.

"Why did the *Vultus-Saudades* drive you out?" Indiara asks inquisitively.

"We don't know why because we cannot understand their language. They chased us away, out of the trees screaming and shouting at us. Even though we didn't understand their words we knew after that we could never return, it's not safe with the little ones, they had a terrible scare." He explains in a distressing tone.

"I am very sorry to hear that, I hope you find somewhere else to set up home very soon." Indiara speaks gently before she hangs her head in genuine sadness for the group of animals. The large brown *fuzzle* turns to face the other animals with his big fuzzy bottom facing us and his tiny tail wagging fiercely.

"A boy is missing!" He announces loudly to the group of *fuzzles* listening intently, there are perhaps around thirty of these friendly animals standing in the group. "Did any of you see a boy walking through this valley?"

Some of the *fuzzles* shake their heads, others let out a resounding 'no', I can see the disappointment written all over Indiara's beautiful face and it makes me feel saddened. Suddenly, there is a shuffling noise and the *fuzzles* start to look all around them, they are quite clumsy looking objects and probably can't see past their big round behinds in order to discover where the noise is coming from. Indiara is hanging her head clearly concerned for the welfare of her brother, now that he has been gone for two days and she is so deep in thought she hasn't noticed all the commotion coming from the *fuzzles*.

I can see a cute, fluffy, chubby, white baby appear from behind the big male *fuzzle* that we initially spoke to. I imagine this big male is the leader of the group and the little baby feels safe beside him. The fluffy baby moves so slowly and clumsily, which I find even more cute and adorable. I feel like chuckling as I realise the leader hasn't worked out where the tiny movements are coming from and is still looking around him confusedly as the little baby moves towards us. The baby gets closer to his front legs and pokes him hard in his side with its bright orange beak.

"Oh! So it was you making all that noise little one!" The leader said cheekily as he turns his big fuzzy body to face the little baby.

"Yes, it was me! I have something to tell you" A squeaky little voice shouts up to him.

"What is it?" He asks gently.

"I saw a boy walking through the valley when I got lost yesterday. I was at the edge of the forest, but I didn't want to tell anyone because they might be angry at me. I am really sorry." The baby *fuzzle* looks at the leader with big appealing eyes, hoping for some forgiveness.

"You didn't mean to get lost, don't worry little one. It is honourable of you to come forward and share this information. Can you describe the boy?" The big male speaks reassuringly, I feel they must be a very kindly group.

"His fur was bright red, spiky too, stuck right up in the air. He had big black feet and a white coat." The little baby states clearly. I look towards Indiara, the disappointment seems to have left her and she looks more hopeful.

"That sounds like him, that sounds like his hair and he was wearing his big black boots, black trousers and a white jumper the last time he was seen." Indiara explains to the *fuzzles* before she bends down and strokes the fluffy baby on its back. "Thank you little one."

The little *fuzzle* looks happy that he was able to help and seems to enjoy Indiara stroking him as he giggles and wriggles cutely. I step towards him to join in and as I lay my hand onto his fluffy head I feel how lovely and soft he is. His fluffy coat is nothing like any other animal I have ever petted before, it must be softer than cotton wool, I lean down to rub my face against his back and feel his silky coat against my cheek whilst wrapping my arms round him to give him a cuddle. I feel his warmth as he snuggles back into my side and I am overjoyed to have made a new friend.

"Bye bye, little ball of fluff." I whisper gently to the cute little fuzzle before looking to Indiara, she stands firmly staring into the distance and I know we have to go.

"Did he go this way?" Indiara asks pointing towards some tall buildings in the distance. The little fuzzle shuffles along beside her, rubbing against her leg and looking up at her sweetly with his glittering eyes. Indiara looks down at the cute fuzzle and smiles, he nods and points in the direction of the tall buildings with his beak, stretching his neck in the direction as much as he can in order to show us the way. Indiara crouches down and puts her arm round the fuzzle, giving him a gentle squeeze. "Thank you very much, you have been very helpful. I hope to see you again one day."

Indiara stands up and begins walking in the direction of the tall buildings, which look to be miles away. I quickly skip along to catch up with her briefly turning back to the group of fuzzles and waving to them as they watch us leave.

As we make our way across the lush green valley again I realise that we are nearing the large city, I don't know whether to feel nervous or excited. I can see the tall skyscrapers in the distance and the bright lights glistening in the sapphire blue sky, which is gradually becoming darker. I walk faster, jogging for short distances and walking again when I get tired because, I want to reach the city before night. I do not want to be stuck out in the middle of the valley with the *Vultus-Saudades* wandering about bullying and intimidating people. If they are willing to frighten poor defenceless animals, goodness knows what they could do to us.

I am now jogging so quickly that I have overtaken Indiara and she has started to jog to keep up with me. We don't talk but I sense she is just as eager to get there as I am. I don't know if it is wrong to feel like I do but I am not just excited to see Kala, I am also really thrilled to be heading to the big city. I can't even imagine what it is going to be like and I realise that nothing here is what it seems or what you would expect it to be, so I have no expectations, just a feeling of wonder and excitement rushing through me. At the same time I feel guilty because everybody is so worried about Kala. I am less worried now that I know he has been seen travelling across the valley, I have a strong feeling that he is safe.

As we near the outskirts of the city I can see bright lights clearly against the dark-blue sky as the evening begins to set in. There appears to be bright lights moving across the sky that are similar to aeroplanes, but they can't be because they seem to be flying very low. I can feel questions running through my mind and I want to ask Indiara yet, we still don't speak to each other as we hurry to the city. We are both conscious of the sky becoming darker and we want to get to the city before night falls to ensure out safety. I certainly don't want to sleep outside again after what happen in the forest.

All of a sudden the valley becomes very dark and we are still quite far away from the city. Indiara stops and looks up towards the sky, I immediately stop behind her feeling very anxious about the unexpected darkness that has engulfed the valley. I stand next to her and look up towards the sky, I notice that it appears to be a very black cloud that is directly above us. I look towards Indiara with my mouth agape, not sure what to say or do, hoping for some suggestion.

"It's a storm cloud, run!" Indiara yells and sprints away, I follow her by running as fast as I possibly can. As we hurry further across the valley, we come to a huge dip and have no choice but to run down the slope. I can see a large house in the middle and Indiara seems to be heading for it although we still have some distance to go just as a huge thunderous rumble shakes the world around us. I flinch momentarily but somehow I manage to keep running for fear of being caught up in the storm. I see huge purple and blue streaks of light shooting out of the sky.

"Is that lightning?" I manage to shout although breathless from sprinting.

"Yes. We need to get to safety." Indiara screams back at me and I realise for the first time she is genuinely afraid. The lightning although frightening is incredibly striking, with the purple and blue shafts of light zapping into the ground around us, far too close for comfort. The sky lights up, like some sort of aggressive mammoth outdoor disco with lights flashing wildly in gorgeous colours and deep rumbles thumping through the sky.

Half way down the hill, the storm seems to have passed over us and we are able to slow down, both of us exhausted from running so fast. Indiara reaches into the bag of potions and pulls out the green one and passes it to me.

"Just take a small sip Melody, it will help us continue for longer and we will still have some left." Indiara advises and I feel so physically drained I decide it's the right thing to do. As I take a small sip from the bottle I feel a warm trickle run slowly down my throat that is extremely comforting. I pass the bottle back to Indiara and she puts it back in her pouch.

"Shouldn't you take a drink?" I ask between pants, still feeling the after effect of what we had just been through.

"No, we must save it in case we need it. I will be fine." Indiara replies without a pant, she has totally recovered from the sprint, she must be a great deal fitter than I am. She does have a very athletic build, far more muscular than myself with my skinny arms and legs. Suddenly I feel a massive drop of water land right in the middle of my head. I notice Indiara has held her hands out in front of her and again is looking at the sky.

"It's about to rain!" Indiara shouts to me. "We need to run!"

Indiara begins to jog ahead as the rain comes down speedily and heavily with giant droplets pummelling into the ground and onto our skin. The rain water is warmer than at home which isn't quite as bad, at least we are not freezing cold whilst trekking through the valley. The potion begins to kick in and I feel wide awake and ready to jog as I dash ahead to catch up with Indiara.

The huge drops are coming down thick and fast causing the ground to become extremely slippery, slowing both of us down as we try to get safely down the hill. Before we know it there is a river running down the hill and we are directly in the middle of it. I fall over into the stream and it drags me down the hill on my bottom and I let out a scream. Indiara loses her footing shortly after me, I turn back to look and she is coming down speedily behind me, she is lying down with her arms and legs crossed like she is on a water slide at a swimming pool. She doesn't make a sound as she slides down the hill, whereas I continue screaming petrified about where we will end up.

I seem to be sliding rapidly towards the house in the middle which is surrounded by a huge pool of water. I take in a huge breath fearful that the water I am about to plunge into is deep, and for the first time since I tumbled into the fast flowing stream I am silent. After a few minutes I plunge into the black water which has surrounded the house at the bottom of the hill. Back under water like I was before, I feel terribly frightened and I start to panic whilst scrambling under the water, not being able to decipher which way is up.

In an instant I feel a presence alongside me and a force pulls me out of the water. I am still splashing about frantically and gasping for air when I realise I am right in front of Indiara who is standing calmly attempting to stabilise me. As I come to my senses and stand up beside Indiara, the water is only just above my waist so not as deep as I believed it to be and now I feel extremely embarrassed. Indiara laughs at me but pats me on the back reassuringly.

"Stop laughing! It's really not funny. I thought I was going to drown." I whine pathetically feeling helpless and sensitive.

"It's a little bit funny." Indiara states as she chuckles to herself.

I shrug off her teasing and start to wade through the waist deep water trying to take in our surroundings. Indiara also inspects the house in the middle of the huge pool of water, which suggests to me that she has never come across this place before. The house looks abandoned in the dark, filled with water there is an eerie atmosphere as the rain eases off. As we wade through the water all you can hear is the trickling and pouring sounds of the water as it moves through the building and around the bottom of the hill. If anything it just looks like a house dumped in a pond but I get the feeling there is something more sinister about this place. The black cloud seems to be hovering above us filling the sky. I begin to realise this was the odd looking cloud we could see in the distance when we were leaving Tikto's house.

"Have you still got the bag of potions?" I ask Indiara wondering if any could help.

"There is no need to use any of them. Look at the sign up there, somebody must live here." Indiara replies bluntly.

I look up at the sign which states, in what can only be described as quite quirky flashing red lettering, "The Flooded House" and underneath in smaller letters "Mr. Fishman". I ponder the possibilities of whom this Mr. Fishman could be before relaying them to Indiara.

"Maybe the man is some kind of fisherman and he spent time catching fish in his sort of, combination house-pond set up, that he seems to have here or maybe the house got so flooded he has had to flee." As the words roll off my tongue I realise that any ideas I may have are nothing more than a waste of my time, you would think I would have learned by now that in Adia things are not what they seem. I could never have imagined all the things that have happened up until this point, never mind speculating about Mr. Fishman and how his house came to be so filled with water.

"Why don't we just go in?" Indiara asks but rather than waiting for my reply which would have been a firm "NO" she grabs a hold of the window ledge with water pouring towards her and drags herself in against the flow using all her strength.

"Great" I whisper under my breath sarcastically.

"I heard that, come in - you are being a little *parci* again." She shouts from inside the house.

"Yeah, yeah I know, try to be more like *madocio*." I grumble quietly and sarcastically as I make my way to the window.

"I heard that as well." Indiara barks and then starts to giggle and I can hear splashes so she must be having fun in there. *How scary can it be?*

I wade over to the window and start to pull myself in but struggle against the weight of the water, I am completely soaked which is adding to the difficulty of getting through because I feel heavier than usual. Indiara appears at the window smiling and reaches through to me, I grab both her arms and she pulls me through. Once inside there is some nice music playing and there is beautiful turquoise glow, it feels like we are inside an aquarium. The ground feels soft on my feet and there doesn't seem to be anything scary at all, quite relaxing despite the outside being so dark and creepy. There is the noise that sounds like a waterfall pouring through in another room. Indiara swims her way over to the door to find out where the noise is coming from. I follow more cautiously than her, aware that we could be inside a house that belongs to someone and we have no idea what this someone will be like.

As Indiara grabs onto the door and peers round into what appears to be a hallway, I look over her shoulder the water is much louder now. I look up towards the ceiling and see the water pouring down from what appears to be a second floor and the water is cascading down what I imagine to be a staircase. There is an intense purplish-blue light glowing in the hallway that is quite mesmerising as it twinkles and flickers in the water. I hear a splashing behind me and I spin round quickly to see if somebody is there. Indiara swivels around to look and we both notice bubbling under the surface, we turn to look at each other wide-eyed. I for one do not have a clue what is about to happen and going by the expression on her face, neither does she.

The bubbles become bigger and wider as the noise builds up into a crescendo, then all of a sudden there is a huge splash that hits both of us, now we can see a huge figure in front of us and I am terrified of what could happen. I try to figure out how to escape the flooded house, but we are trapped because the mammoth figure is blocking the window that we originally had dragged ourselves through. Frantically searching my memory, I recall there being quite a few windows but without knowing our way around the house I imagine we might struggle to get out. Indiara grabs my arm as she tries to swim against the flow of the water, the huge build of the creature has made the house seem very dark from his shadow and he laughs in a deep booming voice at our pathetic attempts to get out of the room. *Why is this happening to us!?*

"There is no point in trying to get out that way. Neither of you are strong enough to get through my flooded house!" The creature bellows loudly to us both as we scramble desperately at the door, trying to push our way through. "You are wasting your time, what made you think you could just come into my house? Haven't you heard of knocking!? This is trespassing!"

We are still trying desperately to escape the house ignoring the loud, angry howls from the giant creature. I am not even sure if it some kind of monster or if it is another type of Adian but whatever it is, I am scared of it and we need to get out immediately. Eventually, Indiara manages to get through the door but she is then pushed along the hallway with the apparent great force from the downwards flow of the water. I am left stranded alone and struggling to fight my way through the doorway, despite my desperate attempts to get away.

"I have had enough of this utter nonsense!" The creature roars angrily and with that I start to feel myself being dragged backwards. I try to swim but there is no hope of me fighting against the massive force that is pulling me backwards. In a desperate attempt to save myself I spin myself around only to be face-to-face with the gigantic creature and despite all the fear, I am faced with a most unimportant but puzzling question. *How does a huge thing like that live inside such a normal sized house?*

I look up at the enormous creature pleadingly with wide eyes, hoping he will take pity on me. He is a rather odd looking creature, like nothing I have ever witnessed before, not even in cartoons or story books. The expression on its face is of plain disgruntlement and that wouldn't be unfair considering we did just invite ourselves into the house. Its skin is all scaly, like a huge fish but it talks like a person and seems to be quite human-like. It has huge eyes and gigantic lips, with a fin on its back, it has arms and hands, its large tail sticking out from behind, just visible above the water. It looks like a cross between a man and a fish so I am certain this must be Mr. Fishman himself.

"Please don't hurt me." I whimper quietly not really knowing what else I can do. The huge creature grins back at me, letting out a chuckle whilst staring right at me with his huge dark eyes.

"It would be cruel of me to hurt such a small, strange little object like you." He states rather insultingly. I find it hard to believe he is calling me strange when he looks like a cross between a man and a fish but never mind. I decide to try and use my charm on him to perhaps, win him around as it doesn't look like I am going to be able to get out of this situation very easily and now I have no idea where Indiara is now.

"I am sorry we came into your house without permission, but we thought with all the water pouring in that perhaps you were in trouble and we wanted to help. We fell down the hill in the storm and we were both terribly scared." I lie hopefully in a convincing manner.

"I see. Well it wouldn't be the first time this has happened, usually nobody comes down here because it is always flooded. Most days there is a storm outside and the rain pours down the hill and all through my house. It suits me because I prefer to be in the water but as you can see I have arms and legs so I don't have to live underwater." He says, kicking out a creepy leg from underneath the water. "My name is Mr. Fishman and who might you be?" He explains more calmly.

"Well my name is Melody. I am not from Adia, I came from another world but I am here looking for a friend Kala. We think he might have gone to Cordovan, he has been missing for days and that's where we were heading when we accidentally stumbled upon your house. Is it possible you might have seen him?" I ask him optimistically.

"No as I say you and your friend are the first people to have been in my house for a very long time. I have not seen your friend so I think it is time you should leave and don't go trespassing again! I don't know how you do things where you come from but here you must knock first." He tells me this information like it is some sort of foreign concept, but I nod and accept that I am in the wrong and it is probably better he thinks that knocking is unusual where I come from because he seems to have taken a little pity on me because I am not from this world.

"Sorry I will leave immediately, can you please get Indiara for me? You know the girl that was here a moment ago?" He starts to look angry at this request and the last thing I want to do is make this enormous creature annoyed. "Oh well, I will just go and find her myself if that is alright with you?" I decide to follow up what I said in an obliging tone.

He does not reply apart from letting out a single snort, I turn around quickly and make my way to the door hoping that he will allow me to get Indiara and leave the flooded house in one piece. I am aware that I might struggle to get through the door because I couldn't make it through before, but as I approach the door suddenly there is a huge force behind me and it pushes me through to the hallway. Mr. Fishman must have decided to help me after all, despite me annoying him. I don't want to spend too much time thinking about it as I keep my eyes peeled so I can find Indiara.

I swim through the hallway past the water pouring down the staircase and along to a door on the right, I peer inside a room that has red-orange lighting which hurts my eyes but I hope that Indiara might be there. I can't see any sign of her so I swim further up the corridor to another room that is quite dimly lit, I call her name hoping she might shout back in order to tell me where she is, but nothing. I feel exhausted and cold in the water, not knowing which way to turn, I certainly don't want to go bothering Mr. Fishman again in case he gets more annoyed with me. As I pause to catch my breath I hear a slight splashing sound at the window of the dimly lit room. I look over to see Indiara waving at me from outside of the window, I speedily swim over to her and she drags me through to the outside of the house.

"I was just about to make my way to the other side of the house to rescue you. How did you escape?" She asks with an expression of sheer amazement.

"Well, I spoke to Mr. Fishman, just used a bit of charm." I say winking at Indiara.

"You are becoming strong Melody, no more little *parci* anymore! Now we nee to get back up the hill." Indiara gives me a rare compliment which fills me with joy and I smile at her, letting her know I appreciate her consideration.

"Perhaps one of the potions could help now." I suggest in the hope a potion might bring us to safety as we both begin to get colder and start shivering from being in the water for so long. Indiara rummages in her pouch out and after looking through it for a few moments she pulls out the little cube shaped bottle which I recall being useful for strength.

"I will drink this orange potion and it should give me the power to carry you up the hill without slipping and sliding down again." Indiara explains as she pulls the stopper out the top of the bottle. She drinks the potion down quickly and as she does her skin seems to glow, within a few seconds she looks more wide eyed, strong and alive. "Come here." She demands.

I make my way over to her and she lifts me up over her shoulder without any difficulty at all. The results of drinking the whole potion have given Indiara much more strength than ever before. As she climbed up the slippery hill without difficulty, marching up to the top much like a superhero with special powers. I look down at her feet and they are pushing deep into the soaking ground leaving a huge track of footprints in a perfect straight line all the way from the bottom. Indiara puts me back down at the top of the hill and looking over to the distance Cordovan is not very far away now.

"Do you wish for me to carry you the rest of the way? You must be exhausted, the heart is grey on your wrist and since drinking that potion I feel stronger than I ever have in my entire existence." Indiara offers kindly.

"Okay, I feel like I am going to fall asleep any minute. Does grey mean tired?" I ask curiously.

"Yes. I will throw you over my shoulder again, we are nearly there now. Just go to sleep on the way if you want to." Indiara speaks nicely and opens her arms directing me to come over to her. I walk sluggishly over to her and she lifts me up over her shoulder again.

Indiara starts walking but eventually builds up to a sprint, then she begins leaping across the ground like an athlete executing perfect long jumps, over and over again. She is crossing the countryside quickly and powerfully, yet so smoothly that I fall asleep on her shoulder without much difficulty at all. I can't fight the tiredness anymore and I need rest before we arrive at Cordovan in order to be in the best state of mind to find Kala.

Chapter 12

I hear a strange buzzing sound as I wake out of a dreamy haze, rubbing my eyes I sit up and begin to take in my surroundings. We must be in the city because there are huge buildings nearby and the noise of vehicles passing. The place I am sitting in is dark, and full of shrubbery. I look around and spy Indiara, fast asleep on the ground. I suppose the potion had to wear off eventually, she must have been very tired. I can hear voices passing and footsteps, curious to see our exact location I peer out through the shrubs, but I am wary of being spotted by the locals.

I stay crouched and move towards Indiara tapping her gently on the shoulder to see if she will wake up. She shuffles slightly and opens her eyes, looking at me and then looking around the space we have slept in. She has her head rested on a large grey bag that we did not have before I went to sleep.

"What's in the bag?" I ask inquisitively.

"We need to wear special outfits so that we don't stand out in the city. I have some special serum to make you look more like one of us and some blue dye for your hair. If you stand out too much, questions will be asked and we don't need that. I visited a special shop last night whilst you were asleep to obtain the necessary materials. There is a back entrance to this building, we should be able to sneak inside. It is a hotel, but I am unable to pay for a room, so I will go in first to make sure the coast is clear and then I will call you."

Indiara gets up off the ground and dusts herself down, I am quite glad we have new clothes, because we are both covered in dirt now. I hope we can get a shower in this hotel and freshen up. Indiara picks up the grey bag and signals me to follow her through a gap within the shrubs. She stays close to the side of the building with her back against the wall, she looks all around, I guess that she is making sure the coast is clear, nobody seems to be around. She quickly opens the door and enters the building, I stay behind the shrubs awaiting the call. She seems to take ages, but it may have only been a few minutes, it feels like I have been waiting forever.

I notice that the heart on my wrist has turned black and suppose I do feel extremely anxious again. I am concerned that somebody might spy me in the shrubs and be frightened by me, then who knows what could happen. Maybe I would be arrested, or taking away as some kind of science experiment. I notice I can still here the strange buzzing and wonder what on earth the noise is, perhaps it is some kind of generator. Finally, the band begins to make a bleeping sound and I feel a little relief as I press the button to answer.

"Come in through the door quietly. I am stood just inside the first door on your left." Indiara instructs me before cutting off. I take a deep breath and stand against the wall looking for anyone passing by. Luckily, there doesn't seem to be anyone around, I speedily run to the door and open it as gently as possibly. There is a slight squeak that makes me cringe, but I manage to close it quietly. I am stood in a corridor that is very dark, with a dim light in the distance. I see the door on the left and tip-toe my way towards it, it is slightly ajar and I am skinny enough to slip through without making a sound.

Indiara is stood there waiting for me in the dark. She raises her hand to her mouth, signalling not to talk to each other and grabs my hand. She opens a door to the left corner of the room, inside there is a brightly lit stairwell and we start climbing. We reach the eight floor and pause for a moment to catch our breath before Indiara opens the door extremely gently.

We are now on a corridor, with a few doors at the top of the building. It is well lit and the floor is a beautiful shiny white stone with a silver sparkle, the walls are bright white. We have to step lightly to avoid making a sound with our shoes against the stone floor. Indiara stops at a door marked with a blue star, she removes a key from her pocket and opens the door to the room. When we get inside, the room is simply marvellous, it must be some kind of penthouse suite as my jaw just about hits the floor in sheer amazement. We walk along a small cream carpeted area and down a few steps into the main part of the room, it has a huge square seat in the middle, the size of a double bed and covered in fluffy cushions. There is a glass table in the middle, which has a square area glowing green.

At the other side of the room there are huge windows going from the floor to ceiling and just as I am about to run towards them, Indiara pulls me back shaking her head. I suppose we can't take the risk of being seen at the window. Indiara takes me to the bathroom and pushes a button on the wall. The water starts to flow and she signals at me to get in.

"Excuse me Indiara, but I am a little nervous about getting undressed in front of you." I explain sheepishly.

"Ok, I will turn around, but I need to help you with your hair." She explains as she hands me what appears to be shower gel. I take off my clothes and climb into the shower, the water is lovely and warm, with jets shooting water from every angle. For the first time in days I feel relaxed and I enjoy every moment of being in the shower, rubbing the luxurious soap into my skin, it smells heavenly and lathers up instantly. I step out of the shower and wrap myself in a huge towel.

"Are you ready for your hair?" Indiara asks in a very enthusiastically.

"Yes, although I am a little nervous, I have never had it coloured before." I say as I sit down on a stool, in front of a sink that is in the middle of a long unit, with a shiny cream stone effect and a large mirror. Indiara opens a cupboard underneath and rummages around, she removes a glass and presses the button on the sink, a tiny jet shoots out blue liquid and she fills the glass.

"Here, you should have a drink." She says as she hands me the glass filled with bright blue fluid.

"Is that water?" I ask puzzled by the colour.

"Yes it is, don't you have water back where you come from?" She asks confused by my reaction. "We drank some from the river of course that water is less blue because it hasn't been filtered. It won't hurt you."

"Oh yes sorry, just that the water back at home is clear." I explain before taking a sip, it tastes lovely and fresh. I begin to wonder if my mum is looking for me, or my dad is panicking and calling the police. I hope they are not afraid, or even better that they haven't noticed that I have gone. Indiara opens a tube and shoots out blue paste into a bowl she found in the cupboard. She mixes it up with her hand and then starts massaging it into my hair, starting at the roots and working her way down to the ends. My hair is no longer straight and has gone back to its usual curliness.

"You must sit for a while to let the colour soak in. I will have a wash, while you wait and then you can go in to rinse the colour out." Indiara explains helpfully, I turn to face the other way and close my eyes so she can get undressed and jump in the shower.

I notice some of the blue dye has dropped down so I wipe it with a bit of tissue. I wonder how I will look with blue hair and even paler skin than I already have, I also wonder whether I can pass myself off as an Adian. I feel quite excited that soon I will be looking at a new version of me and the prospect of fitting in is a rather good one, I will have much less to fear when we are out in public now.

I hear Indiara switch the shower off, she comes over to the mirror and she is wearing a fluffy white robe. She inspects my hair closely and gets a bit of the blue dye on her hands which she washes off immediately in the sink.

"It is ready to wash out, make sure the colour is completely washed out" She informs me whilst drying her hands. She leaves the room and I get back into the shower to rinse my hair. I stand in the lovely warm water jets again, rinsing my hair and I notice the dark blue dye running in the bottom of the shower, down several holes at the bottom, it disappears. Once the water begins to run clearer, I guess that it must be washed out so I hop out of the shower, wrap myself in the towel and look in the mirror and see that my hair is now completely blue.

I walk out of the bathroom and through to the living area where I see Indiara looking in a fridge. She hands me a can of juice which I immediately open and start drinking, it tastes awful and I want to spit it out but I continue to drink seeing it is better than nothing at all.

"What is that stuff? It's really bitter." I ask between coughs.

"It is an energy drink, good for keeping your strength up." I understand what she explains I need to do, I drink it as fast as possible, trying not to taste it. Just as I finish forcing down the last of the horrible tasting drink, she launches a packet at me from across the room. "Eat that, I don't know when we will get to eat again."

I open the packet, inside there are little round gold shiny snacks, I put one in my mouth worried it will taste disgusting, but I am pleasantly surprised that they taste quite sweet and delicious. I gobble them up sitting on the floor beside the table, I notice the green glowing square looks like some kind of screen built into the unit, perhaps it is a television or a computer. Meanwhile, Indiara has gone back into the bathroom.

The door opens and Indiara appears looking completely different to how she did only an hour ago, it's as if she stepped into a time machine and went hundreds of years into the future. She did explain before that they live a more simple life compared to that of the people in the city, however I didn't expect their existences to be at such polar opposites with one another. She is wearing an all-in-one white suit with a silver wavy line that starts at the top of the right side of suit and stops at the top of her leg. She also is wearing silver long boots, that look really trendy and on the other side of her suit there are several tiny lights that are glowing red, blue and green. Her long blue hair flows down over her left shoulder and looks absolutely perfect, not one single hair out of place, she is the most beautiful girl I have ever seen.

"Indiara! You look amazing!" I shout excitedly.

"Shhh. We must stay as quiet as possible. You should dry yourself off in the pod." Indiara advises me quietly.

"What is the pod?" I ask keeping my voice as quiet as I possibly can, whilst still being audible.

"You go inside and push the button. The door closes and it dries you and your hair, it also puts you into your outfit. I have loaded your new clothes into the machine and keyed in the code. You just need to stand in the pod and press the blue button."

I go back into the bathroom and turn to the left where there is a door that was closed before, I assumed it was a cupboard but now that it is open I can see the pod inside. I drop the towel and climb inside, I look inside for the blue button but I can't see it so I turn around to face the door, where I see a bright blue button and a keypad underneath. I press the blue button and with that the doors close quietly and there is a slight clicking noise as the pod begins to start up.

The pod becomes warm and there is an orange glow from a lamp above, it feels a little bit strange. There is a slight whirring noise and warm air blows out all around me, within seconds I am completely dry, when I look down at my hair it has gone into tights curl. I notice two bright blue spots light up underneath my feet and above my head there are white lights beside two handles.

"Stand facing the front of the pod, place your left foot within the blue light on your left and the right foot within the blue light on your right. Hold the handles above your head." A soothing, computerised lady's voice delivers the instructions from a speaker next to the keypad.

I immediately place my feet on the spots and grab hold of the handles, I feel slightly apprehensive, not sure what is about to happen. Suddenly, there is a louder whirring sound and within an instant I am fully dressed in a suit much the same as Indiara's but in pale pink with a silver swirl down the right side and small lights on the left hand side that light up purple, blue and white. I am also wearing a pair of silver boots, they have a small heel on them, I hope I can manage to walk in them. Mum and Dad never allowed me to wear heels at all at home, I feel like I am breaking the rules.

"Keep looking straight ahead." The computerised voice instructs again.

As the pod begins making a clicking noise, I can feel something on my head sucking my hair inside. After less than a minute, it moves away with a final whoosh the door slides open and I am free to step out of the pod. I walk towards the mirror to have a look at the new Adian version of me and I am completely shocked by my different appearance. I barely recognise the girl staring back at me, my dark blue hair is long and wavy, it looks thick and perfectly styled with huge curls. I look at the all-in-one suit with the twinkling lights, much better than the boring clothes I was wearing before. I love my new look, it's hard to imagine ever living in the United Kingdom or even to remember anything about my boring life that I had before I came here, I almost don't want to go home ever again but, perhaps I never will be able to go home again, and that in actual fact scares me a great deal no matter how much I like Adia. I don't even think my parents would recognise me with my new look and they certainly wouldn't appreciate the blue hair.

I walk out of the bathroom and into the main sitting-room where Indiara is clipping a tool belt around her waist, she places the potions into pouches along the belt amongst other useful items, including her knife, snacks and juice. Indiara looks up at me and smiles.

"Come here, I need to put the serum on your face. You almost look like a true Adian but your skin is too pink, you must be white in order to deceive people into believing you are from here. We can't get caught in the city, because if they think you are an alien, the guard might take you away for experimentations." Indiara explains what could happen and I am not surprised, I am truly relieved that she is helping me blend in.

I walk over to where Indiara is sitting on the floor and lower myself down, crossing my legs directly in front of her. She removes the tube of serum from a pouch on her belt, as I close my eyes she begins massaging it onto my face gently. It feels a little tickly as she spreads the serum across my face and neck, covering every single part slowly and carefully. I then feel her take my left hand and I open my eyes to see her begin applying more serum onto my arm and hand, she then moves over to do the right arm and hand, taking special care to get in between every finger.

"Will this stuff stay on?" I ask, worried that it may wipe off and revealing my real appearance to the locals.

"Yes, it should stay stuck to your skin for a few days." Indiara explains as she finishes off applying the white serum. "You should have a look in the mirror Melody, you look like a real Adian and nobody will ever be able to tell the difference."

I get up and walk through to the bathroom, then I stand in front of the mirror and look at my reflection, the transformation is complete. Looking in the mirror I feel like I have left my old self behind and changed into a real Adian. My skin paler, my long perfectly placed dark-blue hair, I look taller because of boots and the suit makes me look like I have some curves, all grown up like a woman. I turn to the left side and then spin on my heels to the right. I pose a little, smiling, swishing my hair, then pouting like a model, I have never thought of myself as being an attractive young woman before but it feels really good, although it does cross my mind that perhaps Kala won't recognise me now.

I hear the door open and I turn around to see Indiara standing there, signalling to me with her hand to come out of the bathroom. I wonder why she isn't talking and I suspect something might be wrong. I walk towards her and she puts her finger up to her mouth to tell me to be quiet, so I tip-toe over to her. She takes my hand and leads me through the room and back to the front door. She gently opens the door, trying to be as quiet as possible. There is a slight creaking sound.

"Is somebody there?" A voice calls out from the bedroom.

"Run." Indiara whispers loudly and with that, we sprint down the hallway and back towards the stairs. We don't even look back to see if we are being chased, we just run as fast as possible, down the stairs, back along the other corridor to the back door. We both pause for a moment, our breathing rapid and heavy, Indiara is bent over with her hands on her knees. She looks all around her, taking in her surroundings before signalling with her hand, for me to follow her.

We walk up a street which is quite different to the streets back at home, there doesn't seem to be any cars from what I can see as we walk along. The buildings are really tall and striking with silver walls, the windows appear to be black or tinted in some way because you can't see through them. There are bright lights and signs in all different colours, some are flashing, advertising products or marking entrances to buildings. I hear a whirring noise above my head and a huge shadow comes over me that causes me to flinch and gasp with fear. I look up and see what I can only describe as an unidentified flying object passing by. A round shaped flying spaceship of sorts, floating along the street with blue flashing lights all around the circumference of the spherical shaped vehicle. I stop walking and gasp at the extraordinary sight before me.

"Haven't you seen one of those before?" Indiara stops and turns towards me, having noticed my mesmerisation at the flashy, flying saucer passing, up above our heads.

"No. It is truly spectacular." I whisper, still fixated on the flying dish which is gradually moving into the distance now.

"That's a *hilo,* it is how the wealthiest Cordovans travel in the city. The one with the blue lights is a standard model that seats four, there is one with green lights that seats six and the white light model seats eight." Indiara describes fascinatingly.

"That is extremely cool." I say, eyes wide and feeling full of joy at my new discovery.

"Cool?" Indiara asks confused by the expression.

"Oh. Where I come from, it means something is good." I explain to her and she nods in understanding. "So how do people travel around if they don't have a *hilo*?"

"Well they can walk, or they can go to the *'Travel Cube'* stations located all across the city." Indiara explains another object I have never heard of.

"What is a *'Travel Cube'* station?" I ask curiously.

"You go into the station, a kind of giant glass cube and type in the coordinates of where you wish to go and it teleports you to your destination." As she explains further I feel thrilled at the idea teleportation.

"Can we try it?" I ask, keen to experience what it is like to travel in this way.

"I suppose we could. You should see one, they are very big." Indiara advises.

As we walk further along the road I keep looking out for one of the *'Travel Cube'* stations, even although I don't really know what I am looking for. Indiara seemingly is keeping a look out for one as well, I assume because of the way she is looking all around her. We walk for another few minutes, not very far as we have slowed down now when suddenly, Indiara grabs my shoulder, I see she is pointing to a big glass cube that is brightly lit on a different street to our left.

"That is a *'Travel Cube'*." She states. "Do you want to try it?"

"Yes I do, but may I ask what happens when you teleport?" I ask nervously.

"You have nothing to worry about Melody, it happens so fast you don't even know how you got from one place, to the other. You will see." Indiara advises reassuringly.

We walk down the street closer to the huge glass cube on the street corner. Indiara skips ahead of me and presses a blue button on the cube which begins to flash on and off. As the button flashes, the door to the cube speedily slides upwards so we can step inside, there is room for about fifteen people in the glass space, once inside the outside has become blurry and unrecognisable, the door slides back to a closed position.

There is a keypad on the inside of the cube where Indiara has already begun to type in some details. A map appears on the screen in order to show you where you are going, Indiara pushes a button which appears to go to a live picture of Ellico Square, which is much larger than I imagined. The screen flashes up with a question, 'how many travellers will there be today?' Indiara types the number two into the keypad and there is a beep once this information is entered. Now, there is a whirring noise and two squares on the floor begin to flash blue.

"Please stand on the marker." A digitalised feminine voice delivers instructions within the cube. Indiara steps onto one of the flashing squares and points to the other one, signalling for me to step on it, after less than a minute the whirring gradually becomes louder. I feel slightly more nervous because I am not sure what is about to happen, it crosses my mind that because I am not from this world perhaps something could go wrong. I look over to Indiara who is standing rather casually with her hand on her hip, if she isn't worried I suppose there is no need for me to be. Just over the loudness of the whirring, I can here several beeps followed by a blue flash.

Chapter 13

I have no idea what happened and I do not know how I appeared inside this glass cube, but here we are. Indiara and I are stood together in a different street. The last thing I remember was the loudness of the whirring, the beeping I could hear and then a bright blue flash, then nothing, quite possibly the weirdest experience of my whole entire life.

Indiara pushes a button and casually strolls out of the glass cube we have arrived in. I follow along behind puzzled by this new and strange trip as a novice teleportation traveller. I am not sure what to make of the whole experience, it's obvious Indiara has done this before as she acts so casual.

"What did you think of the trip?" She asks grinning slightly.

"Weird." I say, lost for any other way to describe it.

"Weird? Yes I suppose I thought it was strange the first time." Indiara states agreeably.

"Yes strange, I mean I just don't understand how I got from there to here and have no memory of it." I try to explain.

"It is because you are transported at such a high speed there is nothing to remember, you can't possibly see or do anything and you're quite literally gone in a flash. A blue flash to be precise." Indiara explains before laughing.

"So where do we go now?" I ask unsure of our surroundings, I look around at the buildings visibly built in a square shape. Ellico Square is similar to the last place we were, tall tower blocks that stretch into the sky but with a little more character than the last place. These buildings have balconies and big windows that are lit up in the dark blue sky. The materials that the buildings are made from seem to have a kind of blue sheen to them.

"This is Ellico Square where Mahari lives, the lady that had a similar experience to you. This should be a very interesting meeting." Indiara speaks very sure of the situation, I don't have the same level of confidence.

"Where does she live?" I ask, looking around the square, overwhelmed by the large size of the buildings.

"This might be a problem Melody. Tikto said she lived in Ellico Square, but he didn't say which building. We will need to ask around to try and find out where she lives, this could take some time." Indiara explains and with that we embark on the mammoth task of trying to find out exactly where Mahari could be.

We walk around the street, asking a variety of people if they know Mahari, if they have any clue where she might live in one of these large buildings but nobody has heard of her. I notice that people are dressed in similar all-in-one suits, the men wear bulkier black boots. They have lots of different coloured hair, some dark, some light, flame red, emerald green, sapphire blue, neon pink to name a just a few, I have never seen so many amazing colours of hair. Some Adians have asked us whether or not we know her family number. We stop for a moment to sit on a bench outside one of the buildings in the square, I read a sign with shiny silver lettering: "Ellico Square Towers", I wonder if we are sat right outside the building where Mahari lives.

"What is a family number Indiara?" I ask curiously.

"Every family in Adia has a number, the emperor and his wife are family number one. My family is number three hundred and forty five. If you know the family number it makes it easier to find somebody." Indiara explains carefully.

"I understand, back where I am from we have last names." I say, trying to make a comparison.

"You have more than one name?" Indiara asks curiously.

"Yes, it is Melody Elizabeth Virginia Berrisford." I respond proudly.

"That is a wonderful name." Indiara speaks warmly.

"What do we do now? How are we going to find Mahari?" I ask getting back onto the task at hand.

"I do not know what to do Melody, without a family number or even a building name it is very difficult to find her." Indiara looks me in the eyes, very seriously. "We may never find her." She says desperately as she puts her head in her hands, clearly upset that we have come this far and now we have nowhere to turn. I look around the area where we are sitting, I try to imagine what Mahari would look like, I focus on every individual that walks past trying to decipher if it could be her. The truth is I really do not have any idea who Mahari could be, I guess she would be an older woman but it could be anyone.

Indiara still sits with her head in her hands, she appears to have given up, but I know that she is just strained and tired. If there is one thing I have learnt about Indiara, it is that she is one of the strongest people I have ever met. I start to feel guilty again, I believe that I need to do something that could really help instead of following her around hoping she knows what to do next. I have to take charge of the situation because this is my fault, we are in this position because of me, Kala is missing because he wanted to meet me.

"Indiara, it is going to be ok, I promise." I speak softly as I place my hand on her shoulder, hoping to bring her some comfort. Indiara lifts her head out of her hands and pats my hand gently.

We sit for a few minutes staring when out of the blue, a lady walks past and she looks at us both, particularly staring at me like she knows something is strange about me. I turn my body away to avoid her gaze whilst nervously peering at her from the corner of my eye. The woman has long faded blue hair tied up in a pleated bun. She appears to be older as she has lines on her forehead, around her eyes and mouth, but not as old as I would imagine Mahari to be. Having said that nobody has looked particularly old apart from Tikto, maybe Adians don't age as quickly as we do back at home.

As the lady walks further down the street, I turn to look at her more directly, she is walking quite slowly, weighed down by heavy bags she is carrying. She turns to look back at me again, I bashfully look away not wishing to make eye contact with her, but at the same time feeling the overwhelming urge to go over to her. I wonder why she keeps looking at us, perhaps it is because it is unusual to see two young girls sitting in the street or perhaps she knows something about us, it does seem quite peculiar.

The lady walks around a corner, disappearing from sight. I pause for a moment and take in a deep breath, looking back to where the woman went. Then I realise, this could be an opportunity wasted and I had just finished making a pact with myself to do something to actually make a difference to this situation. *I have to do something.*

"Come on Indiara." I say loudly as I grab her arm.

"What are we doing?" She asks, slightly puzzled by my sudden animation.

"We need to find out where that lady is going!" I shout back to her as I run ahead, conscious that she may be gone already and we will never find her. Indiara follows me without asking questions, she doesn't take long to catch up with me as we rush around the corner to track down the mysterious lady.

"She was wearing a long grey dress and she can't be walking very fast, her bags were weighing her down." I explain to Indiara as we run down a narrow lane, which passes through an archway, opening up into a beautiful secluded garden filled with blue, purple and yellow flowers. To my surprise, the lady has sat down on a bench to take a rest and instantly spots the pair of us as we come bounding into the garden noisily and coming to an abrupt halt. I put my arm out to stop Indiara running any further. The woman stares at us with one eyebrow raised, probably puzzled by our behaviour. I want to say something, but I am unsure how to explain our reasons for bursting into the garden the way we did.

"Are you following me?" The lady asks, rather unexpectedly.

"Well, um, yes we are." I say through deep breaths, exhausted from running.

"Why!?" The lady asks bluntly, eyeballing us both critically, seemingly aggravated by our behaviour.

"We do not mean any harm. We are looking for a local in this area, her name is Mahari. Would you know where she lives?" Indiara takes over, far more equipped for handling these situations than I.

"What do you want to speak to her for?" The lady asks curiously.

"It is about my missing brother, Kala, we have been searching for him for days now. If you could help us we would be very grateful." Indiara pleads.

"You tell me the truth right now child." The lady states abruptly.

"The truth?" Indiara says, puzzled by the harsh tone of the lady. "I am telling you the truth."

"That girl, she isn't from around here, her accent is strange. I have heard it before, she is not from here." As the lady speaks, it becomes clear she is in fact the exact person we have been looking for.

"Yes Mahari, she is from another world. Can we please discuss this somewhere in private?" Indiara asks very calmly, but forcefully, as she steps closer to the lady, confidently making the assumption that she is in fact, Mahari.

"Okay, you may come inside, but how did you know it was me?" Mahari asks looking particularly intrigued by Indiara.

"I think my friend here must be psychic." Indiara directs her words at me and smiles. I feel quietly proud of myself, I finally managed to do something to help find Kala. However, I am very concerned that my transformation did not fool Mahari. *What if somebody realises I am an alien and the guard takes me away?*

Mahari leads us to a door at the side of the huge tower block, along the lane we had just passed on our way to the garden. She stands in front of a door before raising her hand to a pad on the wall, there are a few bleeping sounds which come from the pad, before it lights up blue and starts flashing. After a number of clicking sounds the door slides open in a vertical direction and we are now stood at the entrance to a large corridor. The first thing that strikes me is how clean and shiny the building is, I notice the floor is some kind of dark metallic grey material which looks similar to marble. The walls are also a shiny material, a bright pearly white shade and the sparkle from the soft lighting is quite mesmerising.

As we follow Mahari through the corridor, we pass a number of doors and I am curious to see what is behind them. We come to the end of the corridor and I notice a large glass tube that disappears up into the ceiling. Mahari raises her hand to a pad on the wall, beside the tube and the door slides to the left. She signals for us to enter the tube. She presses three buttons on the inside of the tube, a bleeping begins and the door slides back into place. There is a flash of white light and a whirring sound.

Less than a minute has passed and we are still in the tube, but it becomes clear we are in a different place, the door slides open and we begin walking through another corridor that seems to go on forever, we pass a number of doors before coming to a stop outside one in particular. Mahari raises her hand to a pad to the right of her door which begins to fade, seemingly dissolving into thin air and we are now able to walk through.

As we enter her home, I look behind me to see that the door has come back into place, feeling slightly bewildered by the complexity of this. I look around the room, noticing the modern furniture and style combined with some objects that look more traditional. I take particular note of a vase that looks rather sinister, the detail painted on the vase depicts a forest in dark green, the top of the vase is blue which I guess would be the sky, at different points in the forest there are red piercing eyes. I walk away from the vase, I find it slightly disturbing and sit alongside Indiara on a sofa.

"Would you girls like something to drink!?" Mahari shouts from the kitchen.

"Yes please!" Indiara calls back to Mahari.

After a few minutes Mahari appears with a tray of glasses, filled with green liquid and what appears to be a plate of biscuits. Mahari lays the tray down on the table in front of us, she passes a glass of the green drink to Indiara and then one to me. I inspect it suspiciously, meanwhile, Indiara is guzzling the stuff as fast as she possibly can.

"I don't mean to sound rude, but what is in this?" I ask shyly as Indiara begins tucking into the biscuits on the plate.

"You do not sound rude at all child. This drink is called *Lazooki*, it is full of vitamins and minerals, it will keep you strong and healthy. You should eat a little something, try the snacks, they are good for you." Mahari offers, she seems more caring than before.

I taste the juice which is sweet and fruity, then, I try a snack that tastes strangely like a ready salted crisp but thicker and wider in size. Happily, I finish off the juice and have a few snacks, I am very hungry and thirsty.

"Thank you so much for your generosity Mahari, the juice tastes wonderful and the snacks are great. Perhaps we should talk about why I am here?" I speak nervously.

"You are very welcome. I am interested to discover how you came to be here, I must say if you hadn't spoke to me I doubt I would have realised you were from the other world. However, I did have a strange feeling there was something unusual about you when I walked past you both in the street. How on earth did you manage to come here? I spent a number of years trying to find a way to meet a wonderful man from the other world but, I never succeeded. Eventually, I had to stop going to see him because the pain inside me became so great. All because I could not meet with him and it was too much for me to cope with. That is when I decided to move to Cordovan, so that I could try and move on, forget the past although I suppose I never really can, no matter how hard I try" Mahari explains openly to us both and we listen intently, embroiled in her words, a sad tale of love and loss. Everyone is quiet, deep in thought, I decide this is the right time to explain about how I came to be here.

"Well, I suppose I came here because I was angry. I met Kala a few times and it sort of all happened by accident. I was becoming frustrated with a magical crystal that I found and I threw it at the mirror, smashing it and opening up some kind of portal. The next thing I knew, I had walked through the mirror and on the other side I was under water. I began to drown, that is when Indiara rescued me and she has been looking after me ever since." I say winking at Indiara and she gives me a lovely smile, I see her blushing with embarrassment.

"You are so young. I am very happy for you, because you will not have to suffer the pain I did. It was very difficult not being able to meet with Stanley. It was hard to leave, but it was even harder to stay knowing I could never meet with him. I was very much in love." Mahari speaks solemnly.

"I read his notes Mahari, one day I will show you them or maybe I could find him and bring him to you. You could finally be together!" I say enthusiastically, but I see Mahari's face does not show any sign of joy.

"I never found anyone that meant as much to me as Stanley. I dated a few different men but they didn't have his charm or his sweet voice. I gave up on finding a life partner and I never had children. I am sure with all his wonderful qualities he found a delightful partner to spend the rest of his life with, once I had left and stopped holding him back." Mahari says with great sadness.

"He must have meant a lot to you." I respond sorrowfully.

"Yes. I am sure as much as Kala means to you dear child." Mahari smiles sweetly at me. "You must find him! I couldn't imagine finally arriving in the other world and not being able to find Stanley. I will do anything I can to help." I am now delighted that Mahari is so keen to help us and truly understands how much this means to me.

"Have you seen him? Did he come here? I was told he may have been looking for you Mahari." Indiara asks beginning to sound agitated, I imagine this is because she doesn't want to waste any time.

"Yes he came to visit me, he asked me to help him. I told him that I couldn't help and I apologised." As Mahari spoke, Indiara's face filled with disappointment. "I didn't know what to do, I told him he may never be able to meet you. I told him that Stanley and I could never meet. I told him the same story that I have just told you. After we spoke, he explained to me he did not want to give up but he had to go home. Perhaps if you contact your Mother he will be safe at home with her by now."

Indiara nods before standing up and looking round the room, she lifts up her wrist and speaks clearly into it. After so many days she is calling home. Mahari points her in the direction of a room across the lounge so she can have some privacy. I have never felt so hopeful and excited, yet so full of sadness and homesick at the same time. I desperately want to speak to my own Mum and Dad, I want to give Bertie huge hugs, I long to have girly chats with Bryony over the telephone, telling her all about my exciting travels. I am so very far away from home and I have no idea if I can ever go back.

I can hear the mumbles of Indiara speaking in the other room, I hope for some good news and that we have found Kala. Anything that could lift the feeling of hopelessness would be wonderful, it would make all the pain and effort worthwhile. I feel a great pain in my stomach, a nauseous feeling, fearful and lonely. My mind fills with thoughts, like a mental fog, words, faces, images, memories spinning through my mind. My boring old life is now flashing through my mind, like my very own home movie being fast-forwarded before me. I begin to sob.

Mahari instantly notices the distress I am engulfed in, an emotional whirlwind culminating into a flood of helpless tears. Mahari takes me in her arms and holds me gently as I cry into the softness of her jumper. Somehow, despite all the upset I notice how sweet she smells and how warm she is, I feel a great sense of comfort. I wish I could reunite her with her beloved Stanley, she deserves to be with him.

"What is wrong Melody!?" Indiara shouts across the room, running towards me.

"I..I..I." I can't speak, I want to, but I can't. "I miss home." I utter painfully to Indiara. "I really wanted to see Kala, but I didn't want all of this to happen." Indiara grabs me and I sob against her shoulder as she holds me tight.

"Hush, Melody." She speaks so softly. "We will find him and everything will get back to normal. He hasn't returned home as yet, but he will, you must have faith."

Indiara continues to hold me as Mahari leaves the room, I hear some noises coming from the kitchen, clicks and clacks then the sound of running water. Mahari returns and passes me water to drink, lifting my head I grasp the glass and take a tentative sip, my hand still trembling. I notice that the heart on my wrist has turned blue so, I guess it must be the colour for when you are feeling sad.

"I think you girls could do with a rest, you are welcome to stay here tonight." Mahari very kindly offers.

"Thank you for the generous offer Mahari, but we have already troubled you enough and I feel we should be making our way home." Indiara explains softly and I nod in agreement, despite feeling exhausted. I see no need to rush either, Kala is more than likely heading home so I don't feel we should rush off to try and find him, we know he is well because of all the people who have seen him.

"Girls! Don't be silly, you need to rest, you have been no trouble to me at all. If anything it helped me to talk about Stanley, I have never been able to tell a soul since leaving the village for fear they would think I was some sort of crazy lady." Mahari reveals as she crosses her eyes together, and shakes her head about making us begin to laugh and soon enough we are all smiling.

"Ok, we shall take you up on your kind offer." Indiara accepts the offer and Mahari gives her a gentle pat on the shoulder before leaving the room. Indiara continues to sit holding me, we can both hear Mahari in the other room, she returns after a few moments with blankets and cushions which she lays down on a seat beside us. She proceeds over to the large window at the front of the sitting room and pushes a button on the wall, screens slide down making the room go very dark. I hear the flick of a switch and two lights at the side of the windows provide a warm glow. Mahari then pushes another button, suddenly the floor slides open and two beds rise up fitting into the space where the floor had previously been. Mahari proceeds to make the beds up for us to sleep in, and lays down pyjamas for us to wear.

"Would you girls like a hot drink before bed?" Mahari asks softly.

"Yes please." Indiara replies and then looks at me.

"Yes that would be lovely." I reply through snivels, Mahari smiles sweetly at me. She leaves the room so we can get changed and get comfortable in our beds for the evening. The pyjamas are an all-in-one purple suit, which are soft and comfortable. I snuggle down and Mahari reappears with a nice hot drink for us both. I leave it to cool for a moment before taking a sip, it is lovely, warm, creamy and sweet, similar to milk.

After I finish my drink I try to settle down for the night, but I find it an enormous struggle. I toss and turn in the bed but can't get to sleep at all, I should be very tired after recent events and the bed is the most comfortable one that I have ever been in. The trouble is I couldn't stop thinking, the thoughts kept running through my head on a loop, relentlessly looking for peace and not being able to find any way of resolving the conflict in my mind and at least getting some sleep. I felt confused and alone, my head started to ache, I want to get up but don't feel I can in a strange place. I don't want to be seen to be acting strangely or disturb anyone by getting up and wandering about. The noise in my head is unsettling, aggressive and tiresome, I feel like screaming but I remain silent on the outside. I have never experienced anything quite like this before, the hullabaloo in my head, the internal monologue like a vicious argument that I am having only with myself and there can be no resolution, no apology, no end and no peace.

The more I worry about not getting to sleep, the more I focus on it and the greater the tension builds. Images flash through my mind, I see every scenario of what could happen, what could go wrong, what could go right and what I imagine happening at home, one after the other but in no particular order. I see my parents talking to a police officer before going out to search for me, worried sick about me, fearing the worst. I see Kala lost and confused, looking for answers but not being able to find them, I see him giving up on me and going home. I drift into sleep only to start having nightmares where I can see Indiara and I, losing each other in the wilderness and being scared, it is dark and I don't know where to go in the strange environment I find myself in. Suddenly, I find myself to be surrounded by the *Vultus-Saudades*, staring at me with their bright red eyes, burning like angry flames into my terrified soul. The wicked tribesmen terrorising me, pulling at my hair and wiping off my make-up revealing the frightened foreigner underneath.

I wake up with a shock, struggling to catch my breath and pouring with sweat. I feel like crying, Indiara notices my distress and gets out of her bed and lies down beside me on top of the sheets. I instantly feel calmer knowing she is beside me, when Indiara is around you don't need to be afraid, she is the most brave person I have ever met.

"Why are you so upset Melody?" She asks quietly.

"I had a bad dream." I whisper sadly.

"It's just a dream Melody. You must never be scared of a dream, because you created the dream. If you can control your thoughts, then you can control your dreams and you never have to be scared again." Indiara speaks in a courageous way.

"I don't know what you mean." I say, baffled by how this could be possible.

"Think positively Melody." She says soothingly whilst resting her head on my shoulder. "Find a way to overcome your fear in the dream and triumph. Or, you can imagine things happening that will make you feel happy."

"Do you mean like finding Kala?" I ask intrigued by what she is explaining.

"Exactly like that Melody, now try and get some sleep, we won't get very far if you haven't rested well enough. You need all your energy and strength to find Kala, otherwise you won't be able to keep up." She strongly advises me and I already know I need to rest. I try not to get frustrated by what she is saying.

"I will keep up, don't you worry." I say feeling a little more competitive.

"Then get some sleep." She instructs me firmly.

"Ok, good night Indiara." I say softly and with that she gets back into her own bed and settles down to go back to sleep.

I lie there for a few minutes thinking more positively now, I think about meeting Kala for the first time. Because of the struggle we have been through, the lengthiness of the journey, the fear and struggles we have faced so far, it has begun to seem like meeting Kala is completely out of reach. However, now I am beginning to feel more positive, I know this is not impossible, meeting Kala seemed impossible but it isn't. I got angry before and when that happened I found courage and abandoned any fear that I've ever had. The thing that strikes me the most, is that my feelings for Kala must be so strong that I am capable of things that I never thought I would be able to do before. I fall asleep thinking about how possible finding Kala actually is, it's more than possible, it is going to happen and it will be the best moment of my life.

Chapter 14

I wake up feeling rested and hop out of bed, Indiara must already be awake because her bed is made. I energetically skip through to the kitchen expecting Indiara to be there, but she isn't. I look around the kitchen unsure of whether I can help myself or not, I decide I should probably wait for Mahari so I go back through and start making my bed.

Suddenly, Mahari rushes through to the kitchen and begins clattering around in the cupboards. I immediately dash towards her concerned by her franticness, feeling that something appears to be wrong. When I get to the kitchen she doesn't even notice me standing there, she is kneeling on the floor looking through a cupboard agitatedly and I realise that something is wrong.

"Mahari, can I help? What's wrong?" I ask concerned as to why she is so anxious.

"Oh, Melody, Indiara is sick." She informs me in a clearly upset tone.

"What!?" I respond shocked by the statement.

"She has been sick through the night, she is very poorly, I have been trying to make her comfortable but she can't stop vomiting." Mahari tells me with huge concern in her voice and a desperately worried expression. I immediately rush through to see Indiara, her skin is grey, her eyes are red and she has a bowl in front of her.

"Indiara! Is there anything I can do?" I wail, worried by her condition.

"Yes, remember the brown potion, it is on my belt. On the table beside the bed, you must bring me it so I can drink it. Conceal it from Mahari." Indiara speaks as loudly as possible between gritting her teeth, clearly in pain and distress. I dash through to the other room and straight to the table, but when I get there I can't see the belt and I begin to feel anxious. I look on the floor, all around the bed. I lift up the pillow on her bed and underneath I find the belt and start to feel a little calmer, letting out a big breath as I open the pouch to remove the bottle of the brown potion. As I clasp it in my hand I remember Indiara telling me to conceal it from Mahari. I can't understand why she doesn't want her to know that we have these potions.

I put the belt back under her pillow and rush back through to Indiara, she is leaning into the bowl vomiting, coughing and spluttering. I wince, covering my mouth and nose with my arm. I step towards her looking over my shoulder to make sure Mahari isn't there. I slip the bottle of potion into Indiara's hand and she raises her head to look at the bottle. I look around again to make sure Mahari isn't in the room, she is nowhere to be seen. I remove the lid from the bottle and help her get the potion in her mouth. She gasps and pants after swallowing the potion, I watch her nervously as she becomes silent and closes her eyes.

"What did you just give her?" I turn my head to see Mahari standing at the door looking at me suspiciously. I know I will need to think fast to come up with a reason for the potion, I can't believe she saw me give it to her but there is no point concerning myself with that now, I need to explain myself and quickly.

"Indiara has a medical condition and sometimes she can become very sick, she has special medicine that she carries with her to make her better." I lie hoping that Mahari believes my story.

"What condition is this?" Mahari asks, still suspicious of my actions.

"I don't know the name of it but she needs to rest, maybe we should leave her alone." I say before standing up and walking towards the door which prompts Mahari to go back through to the kitchen. Before following Mahari, I look back at Indiara, she is still lying very still with her eyes closed, I hope with all my heart that the potion work.

"I will make you some breakfast, maybe you should go and get ready, I have left a robe on your bed. The bathroom is the third door on the left, press the button twice to open the door and when inside hold the button down to lock the door. To unlock the door press the button twice." I nod as Mahari gives me the instructions although thinking to myself it sounds rather complicated.

The bathroom is very similar to the one we used inside the hotel and I remember how to use the shower. Once I am clean and dry, I put on my robe before checking myself in the mirror, then I press the button twice to exit the bathroom. I walk through to the room Indiara was resting in, but she isn't there. I go back to the bed to get my clothes and start dressing myself. Once I am dressed I realise that my make-up has faded and I need Indiara to put more on, but I don't even know where she is.

I hear a faint swishing noise of a door sliding up and then footsteps coming down the corridor. When I look up Indiara is washed and dressed, looking far healthier than she did only less than an hour earlier. My mouth is now agape, flabbergasted at the transformation in such a short space of time.

"Close your mouth Melody, why do you look so surprised?" Indiara asks loudly.

"Of course I did, I just didn't expect it to work so quickly." I reply and Indiara responds with a wink, grinning slightly at me. Mahari comes into the room with food for us both to have our breakfast, although it feels like there is an atmosphere now. She doesn't seem to have lost the suspicion that arose after the potion situation.

"It is remarkable how quickly you became better Indiara, your medicine must work very fast." Mahari states as she hands Indiara a bowl.

"Yes it is fast acting. I have these stomach problems and sometimes I get very sick, it is a very rare condition." Indiara responds, her explanation doesn't come over as very believable and I begin to worry about what will happen next. Mahari hands me a bowl and doesn't say anything, I look to Indiara to try and establish how she is feeling, but I can't see her face to even begin to gauge the situation. She nibbles slowly at her bowl of fruit and I begin to slowly eat mine also, as Mahari exits the room.

I keep looking over to Indiara but she is concentrating heavily on eating her fruit and doesn't notice me staring at all. I try to concentrate on eating my fruit as I know we will have a long way to go from here and we will need all our strength. I wonder what Indiara is thinking, perhaps she is nervous because of Mahari's suspicion after the potion incident.

"Is everything ok?" I ask between chews.

"Yes, just need to stay quiet and leave quietly." Indiara whispers without looking at me. I am desperate to know what all this fuss is about. I don't understand why Mahari can't know about the potion. I still don't even understand what happened to Indiara or the reason she got so sick. I wonder if I could become sick like that and now we have ran out of the potion which cures illness. *What if one of us becomes ill?*

As soon as Indiara finishes her fruit she signals to me to hurry up so I quickly finish what I am eating. Indiara comes over to me with the white make-up and starts to apply it carefully but quickly. She rushes over to the bed and pulls her belt out from under the pillow and clips it round her waist before signalling for me to follow. I get up from the seat and stand near to her, watching every move, trying to make sure I don't do anything wrong. Mahari enters the room again and looks right at us, she smiles. It is such a relief.

"We must go now Mahari, we are very grateful for your hospitality." Indiara gushes gratefully. "We must get to my brother as quickly as possible, enough time has passed."

"I understand, it has been a pleasure to have you both here, it really has." Mahari speaks fondly.

"Thank you Mahari and one day I hope to reunite you with Stanley." I say wishfully.

"I really do hope so Melody, you have given me hope and that means the world to me." Mahari responds with tears in her eyes and the moment becomes incredibly emotional, I go to her and give her a warm cuddle, the warmest cuddle that ever there was.

We make our way towards the door, Mahari follows behind and pushes the button to open it for us, blowing us kisses and we leave quietly. We walk a little way down the corridor before stepping into the glass box. Mahari waves to us from the door and we wave back, Indiara presses the exit button and suddenly we are transported speedily to the main corridor, near the front door. Indiara walks towards the front door and presses the button to exit and I follow quietly behind, my mind is noisy with questions however, on the outside I am silent. We walk a little way down the street before the noise in my head is too loud and I have to ask Indiara what had just happened in the apartment. I cannot walk any further and I stop, Indiara turns to me with a confused look on her face and opens her mouth as if about to say something.

"What just happened back there?" I ask before she gets a chance to speak.

"You know what happened, I got sick and the potion made me better." She states bluntly.

"There are some things I need to know." I say firmly.

"Like what?" Indiara asks abruptly.

"What was wrong with you back there?" I ask persistently.

"I do not know. Perhaps some illness or possibly I had eaten something that was not good for me. The potion worked and that was why we got it, to cure illness. You knew that." She explains briefly.

"Yes, I did know that but I just didn't consider becoming ill out here. Can I get ill?" I ask with genuine concern.

"I don't know, maybe you could. I am sure Tikto's potion will work for you also, I only drank half." Indiara advises, I feel little reassurance.

"And... if it doesn't?" I ask again not giving up on this matter and feeling frustrated.

"You would need to go to hospital." Indiara replies, clearly not interested in how frustrated I am becoming and walking away from me in an impudent manner.

"That can't happen! They would find out I am not from this world, an alien! Then surely terrible things would happen to me." I start to shake as I realise the danger of my situation and feeling simultaneously angry that she doesn't appear to be taking me seriously.

"Would you just calm down and stop shouting! What if somebody hears us?" Indiara whispers aggressively. "You are panicking about nothing. We will have to cope with that if it happens, but right now you are healthy, it is Kala you should be worried about!"

"I'm not finished." I say stubbornly, Indiara stares at me wide-eyed. "Why did we have to keep the potion such a big secret? What have we got to hide?"

"I just didn't want her knowing about the potions. Some people get greedy and take things that don't belong to them." Indiara explains her reasoning and her apparent distrust for others.

"I know that! I'm not stupid but Mahari was nice, she wouldn't do that. I trusted her and you acted in that way so now she does not trust either of us. She thinks we are both liars!" I snap furiously.

"Why do you even care!? You should never trust strangers." Indiara barks at me, now turning to face me with an aggressive frown on her face.

"That's not a good way to live your life! Sometimes you have to trust a stranger. I trusted you!" I say increasingly furious by Indiara's current disregard for others.

"You had no choice but to trust, you came here and you were completely alone. You're lucky that I decided to take care of you. You need to listen to me and if I say something you should just do as you're told." Indiara orders me like a child, heightening my rage, I clench my fists but I would never attack.

"I can't believe you are saying this, you aren't in control of me. I am my own person and I don't need you. I got myself here and I can find Kala without your help." I shout before walking away.

"Don't be stupid! You will get lost or hurt!" Indiara pleads but I ignore her and continue walking away. What she doesn't realise is that I am not scared to go away on my own because I took some of the potions to keep with me when she wasn't looking and I am so angry with her I simply don't care. As I march off into the distance I am not even slightly concerned about the situation I have found myself in, I assure myself that I am more than capable of finding Kala and that I don't really need Indiara.

I walk through the futuristic streets with the hover, bubble car thingamajigs flying overhead. The flashing lights from the buildings, past some shops selling all sorts of exotic delicacies, some sell clothes and others sell jewellery. Looking around I realise it is not all that different from what I am used to at home, just more modern.

I turn a corner and see a huge space-age looking object, spherical, white and shiny with the city lights reflecting on the underneath, as it floats high above the streets. I find myself slowing down to stare and have to catch myself, remembering I can't look like I am not from around these parts, the Adians may realise and get suspicious, I need to act cool and concentrate on finding my way back. I see the booths on most street corners that are used for transportation. I am not sure about how to use them so I continue to walk along briskly. The further I walk the less tall the buildings become and I head in the direction of a high mountain that I can see in the distance, I decide that surely if I keep walking that way I will leave the city and be able to work out, from there, how to make my way back to the village.

As I reach the outskirts of the city I can here loud music coming from somewhere, I get distracted and begin to follow the sound of the booming beat. As I get closer I can see flashing lights and a huge tower that scrapes the sky, behind a high fence. I walk round towards the entrance where I can see a sign for Barra and I don't have any. Now that I am at the front, I can hear the music clearly which is a fast tempo, electronic and I want to dance but I would feel silly by myself, so I tap my foot along to the beat. The sound is like nothing I have ever heard before, it just adds to the desire to get inside to see what is behind the fence.

I walk around the outskirts looking for a hole in the fence, desperately trying to see what is inside. I wonder if Kala has been distracted by the same hypnotic beat and wandered inside. I continue to walk round the outer edge and eventually spy a hole in the fence. A teeny, tiny opening that is about a foot off the ground and that only my littlest finger can fit through. I lower myself in order to peak through the small hole, but can't see very much. What I can see, are blurry flashes of colours and lights moving speedily also, I can hear laughing. Mostly, I can hear the rhythmic electronic music which makes me feel like dancing.

I continue watching whilst contemplating how I will get inside, so I can discover what all the excitement is about. I start moving again, hopeful to find a bigger a hole, much larger, one that I can fit myself through. Suddenly, there is a loud screeching noise which forces me to cover my ears, for fear that my eardrums might burst. I jump back from the fence and look up at the sky. The huge tower has lit up with flashing white and blue twinkling lights. I can see a spherical shaped object moving vertically up the tower, gathering pace, I am captured by the sight. I keep thinking it is going to stop, but it continues to hurtle towards the sky. I expect that when it comes to the end of the tower it will stop but it doesn't. It careers onwards into the sky, with a swish and a bang, followed by loud cheering coming from inside the compound. It was a spectacular sight, perhaps this is some sort of space station carrying out intergalactic missions and they are having a great celebration about the latest flight.

I begin walking again around the edge looking for a way inside. All of a sudden I feel a force grabbing my arm, I struggle against it, not fully realising what is happening. The force is too strong and I become increasingly confused by what is happening, struggling to get away but eventually I am hauled back and I am now faced with a tall, burly man standing over me. It is now dark, I can't see his face properly which is scary, his eyes are covered by a dark visor and his clothes are also dark in colour.

"What are you doing?" He asks firmly with a deep voice.

"Sorry, I hope I am not in any trouble. I was just curious because I have never been here before." I speak trying to talk with the same accent as Indiara, hoping he can't tell that I am different.

"Are you trying to get inside?" He asks seriously.

"I just wanted to have a look." I respond quietly, looking at the ground.

"Hmmm. Everyone wants to go in here, do you have enough Barra?" He asks with a more friendly tone.

"No." I say still looking at the ground, wishing he would let go of my arm.

"Can you work?" He asks hopefully, whilst loosening his grip. I am suspicious of this and taken by surprised.

"What do you mean?" I ask puzzled by what he is asking, I have never worked before.

"I need somebody to give maps to visitors on entering the park. If you can work while it's busy I will let you stay in the park once it begins to get quieter, for free." He advises in a pleasant tone.

"I can do that. But, why would you do that for me?" I ask surprised by his generosity.

"You will be helping me and I can see you would like to have a look, it is exciting in there. I wouldn't want you to miss out on that because you don't have enough Barra. I might look scary but, that is because I need to work here keeping others safe. I have a good heart underneath all this." He says genuinely and lets go of my arm altogether. "Follow me."

He leads me back to the entrance of the park and as we go inside my eyes widen, the lights are bright, the people laughing and hurrying about, jumping, running, excited to be here. I want to join in the excitement, but I know I am expected to work first, so I do my best to concentrate on the task I have been set. He leads me to a small hut just a few feet from the entrance and points to a high seat, so I smile sheepishly and sit down. There is a stand behind me with a large pile of leaflets on top. He lifts some from the top of the pile and hands them to me.

"These are maps of the park, you hand them to people when they come to the hut. You should study the map so you know where everything is, you may be asked for directions. If there are any problems, pull the cord to your left and I will know you need me to come back." He points to an orange cord hanging from the roof of the hut and I nod in acknowledgement. There is a window at the front of the hut and I lean against it holding the leaflets as the guard leaves.

I open one of the leaflets and begin to study the map which spreads out onto three pages, the park appears to be quite large. There are pictures of the different rides on the map and I want to go on all of them, I can't wait to finish working so I can explore. There are some families that come up to the hut and I hand each of them a map, thankfully nobody asks for directions, this is turning out to be much easier than I first thought. I hope Kala comes up to the hut and finds me here, but I worry he will not recognise me because of how I look now. A lot of people are wearing similar suits to mine, they come in all different colours. Some of the older people are wearing robes in bright wonderful colours.

An elderly man approaches the window and I go to hand him a map, but he raises his hand to say he doesn't want one and I start to worry that he might want directions from me. I smile at him, he smiles back and his green eyes light up, he doesn't have much hair left apart from a few white wisps.

"Can you tell me where I can get something to eat?" He asks loudly to be heard over the music. I decide to open up one of the leaflets and try to point him in the right direction using the map.

"If you continue right to the end of the track in front of you and go to your left, past the souvenir stores you will find the food hall, left again after you come to the souvenir store." I say whilst gesturing in the general direction.

"Thank you sweet child, you don't sound like you're from around here." He looks me in the eyes, making me feel nervous.

"No, I am new to the area." I smile trying to hide the nervousness I feel inside, I can't be found out. The elderly man nods and turns, slowly walking ahead onto the path I directed him towards.

I am distracted by some small children that come up to the box making lots of noise, not really talking specifically to me. After a few minutes they go running off towards the rides. I look up to see the man still struggling along the path I directed him on. I watch him, urging him to get to his destination as he slowly lurches on. Suddenly, out of nowhere, a beam of white light surges down towards the elderly man. I imagine it must be something to do with the park as the light seems to coat the old man, illuminating him. The light begins to grow brighter until he is no longer visible, then the light fades and he is gone. What is left behind is a floating glass sphere and it is sparkling, like a small golden sun.

I scratch my head, curious about what has just occurred, I continue watching to see if anything else happens. Some people walk past and nod, most people don't even seem to notice anything there. The sphere appears to get a little bigger and brighter before disappearing completely, fizzling out. There is a small thud as the small glass sphere drops to the ground, it lights up again only slightly, changing from blue to green, then to purple and back to blue again, it looks beautiful.

Soon there are more people coming up to the booth, I hand them maps, point them in what I think is roughly in the right direction and keep hoping I don't confuse anyone. There is another break in the number of people coming up to the booth and I look over to see the sphere again, still glowing but now in the hands of an elderly lady. She raises them above her head and appears to be speaking although I can't make out what she is saying. After a few minutes she stops speaking and releases the sphere into the sky, it floats up and away. She is clapping as she watches the sphere float away and smiling happily. I wonder what is going on and wish I could ask somebody. There is a knock at the door and my attention is drawn to who is entering the booth. The guard enters the hut, looking serious with his dark glasses on his face, despite it being quite dark inside the booth.

"Another good soul has passed today, in the park as well." As he speaks, I realise what is going on, however, I have no clue what to say because I am scared it will be obvious I don't come from here at all so, I simply nod in response.

"Did you see? Right in the middle of the park, just all of a sudden! Boom! He just changes form." I thought he was speaking about death but now I think perhaps I witness something else happening and I am very confused, so again, I nod.

"You are very quiet. Is everything ok? I am sorry I couldn't check up on you sooner, I am very grateful for your help." He speaks genuinely, smiling at me behind his dark visor.

"Yes I have very much enjoyed working here." I reply positively.

"Would you like a job here?" He offers enthusiastically. "We could do with some hard working people like you around."

"That is wonderful offer but I have to go home and I don't live close enough to work here regularly." I try to explain politely, smiling back at the pleasant guard.

"It has been a pleasure meeting you, miss… um. I don't even know your name." He says looking puzzled and I realise I don't know his either. I can't say my own name and can't pause any longer,

"It's Indiara." I say quietly, feeling uneasy about the lie.

"Pretty name. You have done enough for one night, time for you to go and have fun." He says enthusiastically with arms outstretched towards the door, signalling that it is okay for me to go and enjoy myself.

"Thank you." I say as I hop out of my seat and through the door, I wave goodbye to the guard and make my way along the pathway into the park, partly looking for Kala, partly to see all the exciting things that are going on.

I make my way along the path to the left, many tubular white and blue lights which appear to burst out of the ground, light the way as I make my way along. There are signposts however, I am not really sure where I want to go, I don't follow them or the map, I just want to see where I might end up. I notice the heart band on my wrist sparkling white, I don't know what this means. I feel saddened that I don't have Indiara beside me, only for a moment, then I remember how much she offended me and try to put it to the back of my mind. I pass shops and stalls along the way, selling all kinds of souvenirs but without any Barra I can't buy anything.

As I turn a corner I see a group of people looking up, staring at the sky and I stand beside them and look up. I realise I am at the huge tower, that I could see on the outside of the park, the electronic music is even louder inside and really funky, I want to dance, it is so uplifting. I see groups of people dancing together, making moves and shapes I have never seen before. I don't want to draw attention to myself, so I opt for tapping my foot subtly enjoying the beat instead.

Cables loudly begin to move upwards and a slight whirring comes from the station at the bottom of the tower. A large spherical object slides out from underground and spins into position at the bottom of the tower. A huge cheer erupts from the crowd accompanied by enthusiastic clapping, I join in feeling the buzz and excitement in the atmosphere. The big sphere has long rectangular lights around it that glow blue and a loud swish is heard over the noise of clapping and cheers, a large door slides open and a white interior with white seats can be seen on the inside. The music continues to play loudly and a man appears dressed in a white suit with a similar blue glow, wearing a headset, with wild blue spiky hair and eyes glowing bright, almost fluorescent green.

"Who wants to fly up to the sky tonight!?" His loud voice booms over the noise of the cheer. "I said! Who wants to fly up to the sky tonight!? Who is brave enough to go beyond the stars!?" He shouts emphatically to the bellowing crowd, people holding their hands up, signalling to pick them. I am terrified looking at the huge object and at the prospect of flying beyond the stars, but, I raise my hands above my head and start waving.

The music changes to a slower, repetitive beat and the man makes his way into the crowd. He chooses a girl who looks a little younger than me and her even younger looking brother, they both have really light purple hair and big blue eyes. He leads them up into the tower and into the sphere which encourages the crowd to produce a rapturous cheer.

"Another eight people can board the sphere! Who will it be!? Will it be you!?" He shouts excitedly, enjoying teasing the crowd standing, eagerly waiting in hope to board the sphere. "Did you know this is the only ride of its kind in the land? The speeds and sophistication of the Skyship have been developed by top scientists and universal travellers to develop an out of this world experience for people just like you. Isn't that simply fantastic!?"

The man makes his way through the crowd for another five minutes, choosing people to go, all ages, shapes and sizes can experience the wonder of the Skyship. I don't think he will pick me and I have given up jumping around and trying to get noticed. I stand, watching in wonder at the event unfolding. I watch the excitement on the faces of the people in the crowd when suddenly, I see the man, in his white suit, with the crazy blue hair staring right at me, the crowd parts as he makes his way towards me.

"You!" He shouts pointing at me with a large grin on his face, revealing pearly white teeth. "You will be the last person selected to fly tonight! How do you feel!?"

"Great!" I say smiling nervously, not at all expecting to get selected, he grabs my hand and leads me through the crowd to tower. The roar from the cheers is intense, it doesn't feel at all real. He helps me into the sphere, where I take a seat and an attendant dressed in a white suit with dark slicked back hair, wearing black goggles begins strapping me into the seat. Once the straps are locked in place, a shield slides over the lower half of my body, keeping my legs in place and I feel scared. Looking around at the others, they all look excited and I begin to think this is probably going to be more exciting than scary.

The attendant appears to do some checks before stepping out of the sphere and with another swish the door closes. The quiet whirring begins, it builds up gradually getting louder and the sphere moves round so we are tilted backwards, facing the sky, the whirring is now incredibly loud although, cheers and screams can be heard from the crowd outside. There are some clicks and electrical tones which are only just audible because of the loud external whirs. My hands tighten over the rests of the seat, although I can't see them I know my knuckles are much whiter than they have ever been on any theme park ride.

The countdown has begun outside and rapidly the inside of our small sphere joins in, 5...4...3...2...1! The whirring reaches a loud peak and the sphere feels like it jerks back, before smoothly moving upwards. Starting off slow, the whirring loudening again, moving faster and faster, we can no longer hear the cheering from the crowd below. Gathering speed, there is cheers and screams of joy from the fellow passengers. The hurtling begins and I am stuck to the seat with an extreme force, it crosses my mind this is actually a very bad idea but it's much too late to do anything about that now. The other passengers are now silent in anticipation of what is about to happen. There is a loud bang and a flash, it becomes apparent that we are in the sky, completely free of the tower.

Everyone is silent, perhaps unsure of what is happening, the whirring is less loud and now there is faint intermittent buzzing as we seem to continue upwards. Suddenly, the exterior of the sphere fades and we can see everything, there are several gasps and one squeal from a child. We seem to slow down and spin around so we are sitting up-right, we are in outer space, we can see all around us for miles. The view is truly breath-taking against the deep purple sky, the stars and planets. The beauty is intense, beautiful, bold, sparkling.

We float in space for a while taking in the scenery, I can see a bright green planet in the distance, oval in shape. Out of nowhere, or so it would seem, a spaceship zooms past us at great speed, so fast I am not sure how to describe it, large and metallic. A loud beeping begins and it feels like we are moving down gently. Then I see the planet as we are being pulled back, blue and green, similar to how earth would look under a satellite. I believe it to be some sort of parallel universe and I realise how little we really know about the world, there are so many thoughts running through my mind, I find it hard to process them all.

As we are gently pulled back towards the ground I am amazed by what we can see, there are parts of the land below with tall towers and buildings. We move safely and with ease between these tall buildings, passing effortlessly between flying vehicles and then coming into land. A huge hole has opened in the ground, the exterior has reappeared and we can't see outside anymore. There are a few cranks and clunks before the sphere comes to a stop. With a swish the door opens and attendants quickly come in to help us out of our seats. I notice other people need to be helped and when they come to me after releasing all the straps I stand up but, fall back down again instantly. My legs are like jelly, so wobbly that the kind attendant puts his arm around me and helps me out of the sphere.

We emerge into a steely tunnel where we are led down a ramp by the attendant and at the end we make our way up a set of metal stairs. At the top of the stairs we come out from the dark tunnel and up onto a stage with flashing lights all around us. A pretty woman with pale blue skin, bright red and blue hair is standing there, wearing shades and a silver jumpsuit. We are lined up by the attendant, I look around at everyone, all smiling and laughing together. For a fleeting moment I feel sad that I don't have somebody I am close to, somebody to share this experience with. The lady has a huge microphone in her hand and makes her way along the line.

"Did you enjoy the Skyship!?" She asks the children loudly.

"Yes!" They both scream back at her.

"What about you sir?" She asks an older gentleman standing next to me.

"It was amazing, simply amazing." He states happily, as the crowd lets out cheers and applause.

"This young lady looks speechless." She says as she comes to me. "Did you enjoy the trip?"

"It was fantastic!" I shout and the crowd joins in again. She continues down the row but it all becomes a blur, I am confused and don't really know where to go next and I wonder if that is a result of the after effects of the epic flight. I want to ask somebody if it is normal to feel this way, but I am still fearful and conscious of the fact that they could realise I am essentially an alien to them. I see a small café up ahead and decide to go in and take a seat at one of the booths. The shiny steely theme is continued in this café as a robot slides over to me with no effort.

"Please can I take your order?" It states in a monotone electronic male sounding voice.

"Please may I have some water?" I ask softly.

"Yes, certainly." He responds before zooming off and reappearing as quickly as a flash with a tumbler of water in his metal hand. He lays it on the table and I take a sip, it trickles down my throat so very lovely and refreshing. The robot has disappeared so extremely quickly that I have no idea where he has gone, I look all around, there are a few people sitting in the café. There is a lady standing at a counter looking bored, I decide to drink up and move on, hoping there is nothing to pay.

I go back into the park and walk along the path, past the huge shining tower, disappearing up into the sky, I can hear the faint cheers of the crowd enjoying yet another sphere blasting into outer space. It feels strange that I was one of those lucky people who got to fly in the sphere only a short time ago.

As I continue along I see another huge arena with a silver, flashing sign which reads; "Fly High". Intrigued by the sign I make my way over to the entrance. An attendant rushes out from behind the desk holding a silver vest. She signals at me and holds the vest out in front of her, nods and smiles. I raise my hands above my head and she slides it over, she tightens a strap round my waist to fit the vest comfortably. She then points to a large black door, about 15 feet high. I walk over to the door and push it open, only to be plunged into extreme darkness. There is some gentle music playing quietly and a flashing purple arrow signalling to walk ahead, I make my way down the corridor. There are occasional flashes like a strobe and loud thumps, bangs and crashes. I come to the end of the corridor and there is a wall, I am completely confused and don't know where to go, there are a few kids standing pushing against it.

All of a sudden the ground begins to vibrate, it feels like the building is going to come crashing down, there a rumbles and thuds, crashes and bangs. The floor begins to give way, we try to reach out to try and grab something, afraid that we will fall to our deaths. We float down, there is loud electronic funky music playing, the bass is loud. Everyone laughs as they realise they are flying, one kid does a somersault in the air, another pushes forwards into the arena in front of us. The huge arena is filled with obstacles and there are many Adians having a wonderful time. *I can't believe I am actually flying.*

Some are very experienced, zooming back and forth, round all the poles and obstacles. There is a large seated area hanging from the roof where you can have a seat and something to drink, a viewing area I suppose. Some Adians are up in the seated area, sipping on cups of glowing liquid through straws, acting cool, watching the activities below. There are people like me who are clearly unsure of exactly how to fly and float about gently, slowly figuring out how the dynamics of flying works.

I push my arms forwards and do something similar to a breast stroke which seems to propel me forwards. I realise I look a bit stupid compared to everyone else. I want to go up high, I put all my weight to the back which flips me round so I am lying facing the ceiling, this doesn't seem to work either. I try flapping like a bird and I start to propel upwards, but now I look really stupid. I feel a tap on the shoulder and stop my flapping around, suddenly I am pushed into an upright position.

"Let me show you how." A nice older lady speaks confidently, her hand is on her waist and the other pointing up to the ceiling.

"I want to try going up to the ceiling." I tell her hoping she will show me how.

"Put your left hand on your waist, your right pointing to the ceiling. Bend your right knee a little and keep your left leg straight. Now with your left foot gently flick your heel." She does the motion gently and begins to move up, I copy her actions dutifully, now I start to move up.

"Thank you! This is brilliant." I shout happily as I continue up to the ceiling. As I quickly reach the top I touch it and push myself back down again, I can see the whole arena from up here. I start getting the hang of this flying malarkey and decide to glide all the way over to the viewing area. I get inside and take a seat, watching everyone flying below. I realise that this is a once in a lifetime chance and I should probably be flying, but I want to just sit for a moment and take it all in.

A lady floats towards me with a tray full of glowing drinks, pink, blue, yellow and green. She smiles at me and I smile back.

"Would you like some bug-juice?" She asks cheerfully, I don't know how she can be so cheerful when it sounds so revolting.

"I would love to but I don't have any Barra." I respond shyly.

"It's free! Pick one!" She replies excitedly.

"Ehm, the pink one please." I say nervously as she picks up the neon pink juice and hands the tumbler to me with a long pink straw sticking out the top. "Enjoy!"

I take a sip, to my delight it tastes sweet and lovely. I drink it down quickly enjoying every last drop, watching everyone below I feel energised and ready to fly again. I run off the platform, braver than I have ever felt in my life about to drop hundreds of feet, instantly as I hit the air I know what to do. I correctly position my hand on my waist and bend my knee, flicking my heel and I fly forwards.

I fly to the back of the arena where there are some large objects in a variety of shapes, I can hear lots of laughter as I float gently over. I notice people flying against a huge square on the ground which sends them bouncing up into the air. There is a huge ball in one corner that people try to balance on before bouncing up again. I decide to fly straight for the big square and launch myself against it. It is like a gigantic spongy mattress, sending me flying back up into the air with a big bounce. I spin into the air for a few moments before gaining composure again. I fly towards the huge bouncy ball next and try to balance on it. I start off quite well with exaggerated movements, balancing one leg and hopping on to the other leg as the ball moves around. As my foot comes down again, I hit it with slightly too much force and I am sent tumbling into the air again, giggling as I go.

I have lost track of the time I have been flying around the arena for, part of me really doesn't care I am having so much fun. I haven't forgotten about Kala or Indiara, I feel a little guilty for enjoying myself. I decide to go to the exit, there is a blue door with a platform half way up the back wall, flashing multi-coloured lights illuminate the door. I make my way over to the platform and open the door. As I go out into the corridor I am hit with the sad reality that I can't really fly, I feel the urge to turn back and fly in the huge arena for a while longer but I am ushered out by an attendant. I hand back my vest and realise that the park is closing. *I must have been in there for hours.*

I exit the arena and walk along a path, I look around at all the flashing lights and rides, some more for small children which aren't really that interesting and more shops and stalls. I look straight ahead and I notice a flame red haired young man, from the back wearing a black jumpsuit, he is quite tall with a medium, muscular build. His back is to me, he is talking to a group of people. I feel awe struck as I realise who this could be. I begin to make my way over to him, excited and skipping. *It must be him.*

I raise my hand to tap him on the shoulder, I pause for a moment, feeling incredibly nervous because I believe I have finally found him. The boy I have not stopped thinking about from the very first day I laid eyes on him. I tap him on the shoulder, eager to see his gorgeous face in real life. He turns around and my mouth drops wide open.

"Who are you?" He asks completely aghast and I am utterly mortified that I believed he was actually Kala, from the front he looks nothing like him, blue eyes and quite dark skin.

"I am so, so sorry, I thought you were.... erm, doesn't matter, sorry to have troubled you." I gabble on, my face feels flushed, I am embarrassed by what has happened. He smirks and turns back to his group of friends who proceed to laugh at my stupidity.

I notice the attendants and guards in the park ushering people to the exit and realise it's time for me to leave. There are hundreds of bodies exiting the park, it's dark and I don't know where to go, I feel upset and embarrassed about what just happened with me tapping a random boy on the shoulder. I more than ever need a friend and I now begin to feel that I might need Indiara. I made a stupid mistake arguing with her and going off on my own, I want to cry but I can't. I can't help but feel if she was here she would know what to do. I consider heading out of the city but it is so dark with no street lights, I am frightened that something bad could happen to me. If I go back into the city I have nowhere to go there either and I need food, also I need to sleep. I follow the crowd along the footpath because, I fear if I stand around it will become obvious that I am lost, I can't be noticed in case they reveal my secret. I am unsure where exactly I am going to end up but I have no choice but to keep walking.

Chapter 15

I turn away from the group that are making their way back towards the city. I find the courage to go the opposite way from the crowd and head towards the outskirts, despite the darkness and my tiredness. I could be fearful, but if I am afraid then I will never find Kala, so I know I need to find the courage to keep going. I try my best to stay focused, I take notice of a few houses scattered across the countryside, as I leave Cordovan behind. There is a track which I follow carefully, making my way as fast as I possibly can.

I am struck by the peacefulness of the countryside, not a sound apart from the crunching of my feet against the earth. I walk over small hills, down into dips and back up again, it becomes more and more tiring. I come to a woodland area which looks very dark, I turn back to look at how far I have come and see Cordovan well into the distance, lit up brightly, the same way I looked at it only a few days before, full of anticipation. Now I stand in front of a dark forest, without thinking I decide to go forth into the trees, I have no time to think or I will panic. *I would never do this if I was at home.*

It crosses my mind that there could be wild beasts, or killer cats ready to jump out and kill me. The silence tells me there isn't anything living in here, so far it seems that way. I find a quiet spot, off the beaten track and remember how I sunk into the leaf before and find a large comfy one before settling myself down for the night.

I wake up feeling a weird tickling sensation on my nose, I don't want to open my eyes. I try dusting the feeling away, thinking it must be some kind of insect. The tickling continues and then turns into an itching, I can hear voices, which forces me to open my eyes and jolt into an upright position.

I am stunned to see several little bodies climbing all over me, prodding me with sticks. There is a girl standing on my nose wearing a pink dress with her hand on her hip looking at me strangely. I look down to my shoulder where another girl in a blue dress is jumping up and down, I can hardly feel a thing, just a slight itchy irritation. Normally, when an insect is crawling all over me I would jump or scream, but these little things are cute and seem harmless enough.

"What are you doing here?" The little girl in the pink dress asks whilst pointing and waving a stick frantically at me, I feel my eyes go crossed as I try to focus on her.

"I needed to sleep. I am sorry if I am not supposed to be here." I say apologetically as I try to get up from the leaf, struggling and sliding about as I am still sleepy. The little girl bounces down accompanied by various other tiny people and gather around me on the ground. I look down at them speechless, unsure of what I should do when, out of the blue a little man, dressed in green walks across my shoulder.

"Oi you! You should know you are trespassing on the land of the Tavia. It is a rule you must never step on the land in this side of the forest. You should really know that. We are too small to move you. You must go now or there will be trouble." The little man speaks aggressively.

"I am sorry that I have trespassed. I am not from around these parts and I don't know where to go. Maybe you could help me? I can become one of you." I say, hoping they will be able to help me find my way but, also nervous that I will need to drink the potion to transform.

"Hmmm, you can become one of us you say? That is not possible." The little man barks at me, as the rest of the little people burst out laughing.

"I can, I will make you see. If I prove it will you help me?" I ask feeling braver.

"Ok, go on then, prove it." He says impatiently with his hand on his hip, frowning at me.

"Can I have a minute to prepare?" I ask politely, not wishing to aggravate the Tavia any further.

"What does everyone think? Can she have time to prepare?" He asks the group of little people, who have assembled at my feet.

"Yes. I like her." States the little girl in pink.

"Yes." Follows the little girl in blue. The rest of the little people follow suit and they wait patiently for the green man to confirm the verdict.

"Right, you! You can have your minute, but I expect you to have proven yourself to become one of us. If you're still the same you must leave immediately!" He orders me boldly.

I pick him up as gently as possible and place him on the ground with the rest of his little friends, then they scurry off towards a leafy green tree and turn around to give me some time away from their prying eyes, time which is much appreciated.

I removed the sparkling Tavia potion from my pocket, I stare at it for a moment in awe, the most beautiful potion of them all. I know I don't have much time so rather than hesitate, I open the top and slurp down the potion as quickly as I can. I feel warmth as it slides down into my stomach, different from anything I have tried before. I imagine my body sparkling on the inside, worryingly, nothing is happening.

The little people give up waiting, turn round and march back towards me. They all stand staring, some with hands on their hips, others simply with expressions on their faces which look suspicious, all with an accusatory manner about them. I am powerless as to what I can do, maybe the potion isn't going to work. They can see my discomfort, the little man dressed in green stares at me, making me feel worse, merely an intruder with a stupid notion.

"You aren't one of us." He says pointing and shouting, wings unfold from his back before he floats up to my face. "I didn't think you were telling the truth, you don't have special magic powers. Now leave!" He yells so hard he floats off backwards and upwards, losing control and spinning around facing the opposite direction. The other little people seem to be getting annoyed and stamping their feet, shouting all sorts of what I imagine to be Tavia obscenities, directed at me.

I notice my skin feeling hot and itchy, I feel I might be having an allergic reaction, I want to run but I feel heavy and fused to the spot. The tiny Tavia float upwards to accompany the angry green man. What I am witnessing has become hazy. My body begins to shrink, I stare helplessly at my hands which become gradually smaller. Frightened, I wish I could go back to normal but it's too late now. After a few moments I am aware that my size is considerably smaller and my skin is violet, I look up and the trees and the bushes look impossibly huge. The Tavia turn around only to realise they can't see me, the green man looks down at me and points before zooming down towards me, the rest of the group follow him.

"You were telling the truth! I suppose you can come with us now." The man proclaims seemingly unperturbed by my rapid change of appearance. The other Tavia crowd around me, cheering and smiling. One little lady with pale pink skin, wearing a dress that matches her skin, comes towards me and grabs my arm holding it up against her, she smiles with her eyes wide and sparkling.

"You look pretty." She says softly. I look down and notice I am wearing an outfit that can only be likened to a ballet tutu, with a top that now matches my skin, it feels strange, I want to see myself in a mirror but I have a suspicion I'm not going to find any around here. In fact, all the Tavia wear clothes that matches their own skin, maybe it is in their DNA, I wonder what would happen if they were to try and put on clothes of a different colour. I start to tug at my top and realise it is stuck to me, realising this is really odd. *How can you be permanently stuck in your clothes?*

"Follow me!" The little green man shouts as wings appear from his back, with that all the Tavi arrange themselves behind him ready to go, their wings rapidly appear. I follow behind them and without even having to think,

234

I feel movement in my back, looking behind me, wings have appeared. *How am I going to use these?*

I quickly realise I don't have to think, the wings are attached, it was like I was born with them and I fly without even trying, like knowing how to walk without conscious effort suddenly I just know how to fly, which is strange considering I have ever had wings before. Perhaps the flying arena at the park helped my flying skills but this feels completely natural, effortless. We weave between the trees, there is much giggling and hilarity as they enjoy the journey, flying is so much fun and my face aches from the permanence of my outstretched smile.

We fly up higher and in a fleeting moment I glimpse back to see the trees, the world below looks gigantic, everything is massive compared to my tiny body now that I have shrunk to such a small size, no more than three inches tall. Suddenly, we swoop back down at great speed, I struggle to keep up as we hurtle towards the ground speedily and to my surprise, ever so gracefully.

We land one after the other, following the leader through a village under some bright green bushes. Each Tavi has their very own beautiful glow which I find quite mesmerising. There are several houses and a bubbling pool where some of the Tavia seem to be dangling their feet, the greens and the blues in the shade occasionally catching the sunlight make for a tiny piece of paradise, in the middle of the huge forest, tranquil and peaceful. I can see the Tavia are filled with joy within their serene, glorious existence, in the depths of the magical forest.

Suddenly, they all begin to notice me. They turn to face me, giggling and pointing, some run towards me. Many of the Tavia are dressed in bold bright colours, others are dressed in pastels, all matching their perfect glowing skin. They all begin to gather around me, friendly, smiling and welcoming me into their village. I feel a little awkward standing in the middle of the crowd and I don't really know what to do or say. After a few moments, the crowd of Tavia begin to part, leaving a small gap where a tall man, dressed in black comes towards me, this is in sharp contrast to the brightly coloured other fairies, his presence makes me uneasy. Now he is getting closer I feel completely on edge and I wish Indiara was stood next to me, she would know what to do.

He stands right in front of me, a little too close for comfort, staring straight into my eyes. He then very rudely pokes me in the shoulder which startles me, I step backwards from him. He look suspiciously at me, raises his hand and touches my cheek more gently still looking into my eyes, with his large black eyes staring back at me, he looks like a cartoon character.

"She is not one of us! Where did she come from?" He shouts turning to the group.

"She's ok, give her a chance." One little voice speaks out from the group, I feel slightly relieved.

"Hmmmm, give her a chance you say?" He shouts boldly, grinning whilst twiddling my hair around his finger, looking at me menacingly. "Ok you can have a chance I suppose, I can see you have gone to a lot of effort to look like one of us but, there is no fooling me!"

He steps to the side with an outstretched arm and an open palm, he smiles and the other Tavia step to the side. I smile and step forwards because I think they mean for me to walk ahead but I stop myself because I am unsure, I look back for reassurance.

"Go on." He nods and smiles, signalling for me to continue forwards. I walk past the line of Tavia, they are all smiling and giggling. When I come to the end of the line, a girl smaller than me, dressed in lilac and pink takes my hand and leads me across the dark green grass, then up some stone steps and we stand at the edge of the bubbling pool, glowing blue and green. The girl takes both my hands and turns me around, I feel uneasy turning my back to the pool, still haunted from my experience of near drowning. She lets out a huge laugh and all the Tavia cheer, she pushes me hard.

I feel afraid but there is nothing I can do, I fall backwards into the warm bubbling pool. It isn't very deep and I realise quickly that there is nothing to be scared of, I float up to the top and scrape my soaking hair away from my face. Relaxing music begins to play and I lean back against the side of the pool, looking up to the deep blue sky, through the deep green trees. The trees are humungous in comparison to my tiny self and the little Tavia all around me.

Some of the Tavia have climbed into the pool to join me and we begin splashing around having fun. Right now, I feel like I am in paradise, this place is so peaceful, so magical with the gentle music tinkling away in the background whilst we play in the pool. The beautiful blues and greens, shining and twinkling silver lights around the Tavia village add to the ambience. I don't ever want to leave this place but I know I have to soon, I have to keep looking for Kala and I have realised I want to find Indiara and sort out our differences.

Some Tavia shoot up into the air, doing somersaults and flips, some fly fast down to the pool creating big splashes with everyone cheering. We eat tiny berries that taste juicy and delicious, we dance and play until the night falls. I can see the stars glistening in the sky, as the night air sets in, a little cooler but still warm. All the Tavia people begin to get tired and quiet down for the evening, I make my way over to a smooth looking rock and sit down, breathing in the atmosphere, taking in my surroundings. The girl who pushed me in the pool walks over to me and sits alongside me, crossing her legs.

"Do you need to rest now? I can show you where you can sleep for the night." She whispers sweetly.

"Yes that would be wonderful. I need to leave in the morning, I have to find my friend Kala." I explain to the kind Tavi girl.

"Hold my hand." She says holding her hand out towards me. I take her hand gently and she closes her eyes tightly, I am curious as to what she is doing.

"Hmmm, you have good energy, you will find him." She tells pleasantly.

"I hope so." I say unconvinced by her seemingly psychic ability.

"You will so!" She says brightly before standing up and taking me with her, holding my hand she leads me to a little hut. When we get inside, it is much bigger than it looks on the outside. There is a beautiful, big circular bed, covered in cushions with soft lighting above. She signals for me to get into the bed and stands by the door smiling at me.

"Come and see me before you go, please." She asks caringly, filling me with warmth.

"I will. What is your name?" I ask quietly, beginning to feel sleepy.

"My name is Sariah." She replies melodically, her beautiful, unusual name is like a song to me.

"What a beautiful name." I reply as she turns off the light. The bed is so comfortable and I am so exhausted, I fall straight to sleep.

Chapter 16

I wake gently, feeling well rested in such a large comfortable bed, I look down at myself and still I am tiny, in my Tavia form. I look at the painted ceiling, patterns in the shape of diamonds in pretty purples, blues and bright yellows. I think about what I should do today. I need to start trekking again, I can't stay around here. I have to find Kala. It has been days now and I realise I have no clue where I am and I don't know where I am going. I wonder if there is somebody around here I could ask to point me in the right direction.

I gently roll out of bed and put my feet down on the ground, I stretch out my arms and my legs, letting out a sigh. I stand, then make my way towards the front door and take a look around the village. Some of the Tavia are busying themselves doing different tasks, arranging breakfasts, bathing and some even playing already, they really love to have fun and enjoy themselves. I feel we could learn a lot from them back at home where it's all work and no play.

Sariah appears suddenly and begins to run and then leaps off the ground. She floats speedily towards me and lands right in front of me, smiling with a piece of a green foodstuff in her hands.

"Here, this is for you. You must be hungry." She says thoughtfully handing me the green thing as I bravely take a bite, it tastes sweet and juicy, I gobble the whole lot quickly. "Did you sleep well my friend?"

"I slept very well thank you. You have been so kind to me, it is very much appreciated." I tell her appreciatively.

"Anything I can do to make you welcome, you are one of us now." She speaks, making me feel at home.

"That means a lot, but I am afraid I must begin my travels again, I need to find my friend, Kala, but I don't know where I am going. I have never been in this part of the world before." I say hoping she will be able to help.

"You need to be careful my friend. There are bad people in these parts, big tall scary monsters, they wear black and their eyes red and angry! You should turn back, go to the city, you will be safe there and somebody will help you find your friend I am sure of it."

"I already came that way and I believe my friend came this way. What if the angry monsters have got him and he is in some kind of trouble!? I must keep going into the forest and hopefully I will be ok." I explain concernedly, filled with fear for Kala.

"Come with me." Sariah says very seriously. She leads me to a hut across the way and into a room all decorated in baby blues and pinks. She opens a small box decorated in sparkly gems. Her face lights up with all different colours from a colour changing crystal inside. "This is for you, my Mother gave it to me to keep me safe when she is not around. I think you are going to need it more than me.

"I can't accept this, it is too precious." I say holding the crystal, mesmerised by its beauty.

"You take it please." She says looking me straight in the eyes and closing my hand over the crystal.

"Thank you, it is the most beautiful gift I have ever been given." I say graciously.

"I will take you a little way into the forest, I can't go too far from my family but I will help you go in the right direction." She says sweetly and stretches out her arm towards me with her palm open, wiggling her fingers and smiling. I take her hand and wink at her, placing the crystal safely into my pocket. We then run as fast as we can, leaping into the air and flying between the dark green trees, deep into the forest.

We laugh and giggle as we fly through the air, twisting between the huge trees. I see a huge footpath before us and we slow down. As we land on the ground, I look at the massive trees ahead of us and how the way forward looks considerably darker than before, the shrubs and trees are so thick and close together. I am so small and it crosses my mind that it may take me even longer, now that I am so tiny. I don't know how I get back to my usual size and that begins to bother me.

"Are you sure you want to go that way? You can still change your mind, I could take you back to the outskirts of the city." Sariah offers genuinely.

"I have to go, I have to find him." I say seriously, looking into the distance.

"Your friend means the world to you, you are very brave."

"You have made me so welcome and you have helped me so much. Thank you very much, there are no words to explain how much this means to me. It was wonderful to meet you and the other Tavia, I will cherish our memories forever. Take care Sariah." I say stretching my arms out to give her a cuddle and she wraps her arms back around me.

"You take care too." She replies before flying off into the distance and I begin to make my way slowly forwards on foot to start with. I look back a couple of times, Sariah is so tiny I can no longer see her. After walking for a short while, I begin to run into a leap and fly at greater speeds through the trees, covering more ground than I ever thought I could, I love to fly.

As I zoom at rapid speeds deeper into the forest, weaving and swaying to avoid trees, bushes and various other obstacles in the darkness it becomes harder for me to see my way. Eventually, I have to move more slowly, the last thing I need right now is to injure myself. It also dawns on me, since my transformation I no longer have the potions or the band on my wrist, the realisation of this makes me realise I am completely alone which is worrying to me.

After a few hours or so, I feel myself growing tired, I look behind and I see darkness then I turn to the right, then the left, then back to the front; everywhere around me, all I can see is darkness. The forest is so thick I feel afraid, soon I will need to get some rest and something to eat. I float down to the forest floor and inspect my surroundings for something that looks edible. I spy some growths coming out of the ground that look like dark green mushrooms. I prod one curiously, it feels soft and I decide to pluck it out of the ground, as I do so some orange liquid pours out, neon in stark contrast to the dark surroundings, it looks hot, I am afraid to touch it and watch it ooze along the ground until it comes to a stop. I can't help but wonder what it is, but I am too afraid to touch it just in case it is poisonous.

I begin inspecting the mushroom looking object and consider whether I could eat it. I remember at home that sometimes mushrooms can be poisonous and I am fearful that if I try a piece that I could become unwell. I smell it but I can't really notice anything, perhaps a bit musty but no real scent. So lastly, I pull it apart, ripping the top off, it is all orange inside like the liquid on the ground. I put it to my nose again and this time I notice a sweeter smell, I decide that it smells safe to eat so I will take a chance and chew on it. Only a little bite at first, it tastes crunchy and sweet, not bad at all, I eat the rest of the internal flesh and leave the outer skin. My tiny tummy is full up and I instantly feel sleepy. I find some leaves on the ground to relax and lie down for a short while, before I begin my trek again.

I wake from my nap feeling a little odd, I am not sure how long I have been asleep. I notice the forest doesn't look so tiny anymore. I look down at my body and to my horror, one of my legs is huge and the other one is half the size, my arm on the left side is huge whereas my right arm is again half the size.

"Oh my!" I whisper, upset by what has become of me. Instantly I wiggle all my fingers and toes, everything seems to be working accordingly which brings some relief. I can't understand how this has happened, perhaps there was something weird about that mushroom object. *I knew I shouldn't have eaten it!*

I raise my hand up to touch my head, which feels like it is back to its regular size, this is extremely strange and I am not entirely sure what I should do. I try to stand but immediately fall down, I don't have the ability to balance. Feeling determined, I try again and I almost manage to stand on the big leg, but I topple over still completely unable to balance myself. I sit for a few moments trying to figure out what I should do, I have to come up with something soon because I have probably been here for ages and I need to move faster.

I come to the conclusion that I should try eating another one of the dark green things, maybe it counteracts Tavia potions or something and I didn't eat enough, it's definitely worth a try and I have nothing to lose. Using all my strength I drag myself with the big arm along the ground, it pains me as twigs from the forest floor jab into my hands. I find a large mushroom looking object and pull it out the ground again watching the fluid ooze from the ground slowly. I eat the lot, again, leaving the skin and wait hopeful that something will change.

I wait for maybe ten or fifteen minutes and tiredness sets in, I fall asleep uncomfortably in the dirt. I don't know how long I have been out for when I wake again. I am flat on my back staring up at the dark trees, almost afraid to look down, I wiggle my fingers and toes before I look. Everything feels like it is working normally but I am unable to gauge by my movement whether I am back to normal or not, I have no choice but to raise my head and look.

When I look down, to my disbelief my plan worked, I am in one piece and back to my usual size, I raise my hands up to touch my head and face, it all feels back to normal. I am completely relieved that my idea worked, I laugh out loud, I almost cry with happiness. I am about to stand up to begin my trek when I hear rustling in the bushes. I move quickly backwards trying to hide in bushes, but there is no way I am camouflaged as I am wearing the light coloured all-in-one suit. I just hope it isn't some horrible flesh eating beast with a huge appetite. I cover my face with my hands peeping between my fingers, I hear footsteps coming towards me, I have no choice but to run.

I jump out of the bush and run as fast as I can, jumping over bushes and logs, I hear the footsteps behind me, gaining on me. I breathe faster, I am terrified. The adrenalin flowing through me keeps me going as I sprint. The forest is so thick, it is difficult to manoeuvre but somehow I keep my speed up, desperately running swiftly to get to safety.

Suddenly, my foot gets caught on something and I can't seem to free it up. I am totally rooted to the spot, like one of the large trees in the forest. I grab my leg and tug at it desperately, I look around and I can't hear or see anything but I feel I am not far away from danger. I scramble around trying to free my trapped foot.

I struggle to no avail, I am completely stuck. I look around and panic that I am lost without any hope of finding my way back now, the sprint through the forest has made me disorientated. I have no idea which way I was going or where I have come from, I don't know how to get to the outskirts, I begin to cry feeling utterly hopeless but I still have to free my trapped foot. I fall to the ground and try to examine how my foot has got stuck, it seems to be tangled up in vines which I start trying to rip apart but inevitably become more twisted up and feel increasingly frightened.

I hear footsteps and I can't breathe I am so fearful, they are coming towards me at great speed. I notice through the fear it sounds like human steps, but I am so scared I can't even look around me, I tug desperately hoping I can free myself. I have a very bad feeling as I wipe away sweat beads from my forehead. I shrink down into myself, trying to make myself look small in the hope whatever this thing is doesn't notice me and lastly, I hold my breath.

Two massive strong hands are on my shoulders, I can see the dark outline of fingers, they grip forcefully against my bony shoulders and I let out a little whine. I can't even look I am so petrified, I close my eyes tightly and pray for a miracle. I feel something around my foot and I am forced to open my eyes. A dark figure in a long hooded robe is tending to my trapped leg, pulling the vines apart without struggle. This thing is huge and almost human-like but I fear this character may not be humane at all, I believe I have met one of the *Vultus-Saudades*.

As my foot is freed from the vines I wiggle it, feeling my circulation returning to normal. I don't know if I should be grateful as the terrifying thing looks at me with a grunt, his eyes red and angry. He points to somewhere in the distance and lets out a few grunting noises to the other character who is behind me holding onto my shoulders, he acknowledges the one in front of me with grunting noises and hauls me to face him. He then covers me in a black cloak and I can no longer see anything, which is more frightening as he seemingly picks me up like I weigh nothing.

I feel a great deal of fast movement, but I am completely disorientated, there is little noise from the two tribe members. I struggle for breath in the tightly wrapped sack as I am hauled about like some kind of 'catch of the day', an animal being treated with no respect, I strongly hope they are not planning to eat me for supper tonight.

I am tossed onto the ground and the sack is ripped open and my head dragged through the gap. I am shoved into the corner of the room as the two figures stare at me with their evil red eyes. I look back at them pleadingly but they look soulless, I doubt they care about my fearfulness. I look around and I appear to be in some kind of dingy cell with a hard, dirty floor with no light or windows. The two horrible beasts leave the room and close the door, bolting it form the other side, I realise I am completely trapped. I think about screaming for help, but I imagine I will be wasting my time so I don't bother. I merely sit, cry and shiver, awaiting my impending doom.

It feels like hours have passed as I sit in the complete darkness, waiting to find out what these frightening monsters are planning to do with me. The door begins to unbolt and wobble as I shake uncontrollably with fear. Four figures enter the room and there are various meaningless grunts and noises as each of them grab an arm or a leg, they then lift me as I start to wriggle and struggle in a pathetic bid to free myself without success. I swear some of their noises sound like they are enjoying watching me panic.

I look around their village which is very dark and basic with a huge fire roaring in the middle, I hope with all my heart that isn't where they are taking me. I am thrown down on some kind of caged area with an open top that is too high for me to climb out. A vicious looking creature comes towards me with huge red angry eyes, wearing the same dark robe as the others with the hood, but his robe has two thin red stripes down the front. I suspect he is some kind of leader as he approaches the cage.

His long arm easily stretches into the cage to have a prod at me, he tilts his head and grunts at my cries. He moves me about, pokes at my face, painfully in my eyes, tugs my hair and ears. I am obviously some kind of interesting find for this monster and he wants to toy with me for a while. Finally, he walks away and I am left shivering and terrified as he grunts to some other tribe members. I look around trying to get a hint of where I am, an idea of how I could possibly escape. These creatures are so gigantic and strong that I do not expect I stand a chance.

Again, the four monsters come towards me making their strange noises, hisses and grunts. They lift me roughly out of the cage and remove the sack I have been wearing.

Two of the beasts step away from me as the leader comes towards me, it starts patting me down, perhaps checking for weapons. I hate the way it thinks it's acceptable to put its grubby hands all over me, like some kind of pervert, I have had enough and kick my legs aggressively towards the vile being.

He instantly grabs my legs and grunts much more loudly than before, a terrifying roar, some kind of order to the others as they drag me more roughly than before across the ground, hurting me all over. There is a huge wooden pole which I am pushed up against and I can feel them tying my hands behind the pole and wrapping vines around my feet, tightly so I can't go anywhere. They have tied the vines so tightly it hurts me horribly and I want to cry. I wonder what horrible things these monsters have in store for me. To my surprise they walk away, hissing and grunting as they go.

I am a little relieved I am not being prodded at like some kind of exhibit anymore, yet I fear for what those beasts may be planning to do with me. They can't just leave me tied to this pole for a long time, because I am sure the circulation is being cut off in my hands and feet. The more I wriggle, the tighter the vines become so I have no choice but to stop. I am sweating and panicking, I feel my chest heaving, I fear I will be sick all down myself.

Suddenly, I am drawn to some movement behind one of the huts, it draws my attention. I wonder if it is some kind of forest animal, but I am sure I can see arms and legs moving, I can see hands moving against the hut, they don't look like creepy Vultus-Saudades hands, they look small and dainty. I want to shout for them to come and help but I know the tribesmen will hear me so there is no point, I watch carefully to try and fathom who or what is between the huts.

The figure comes out from the side of the hut, towards me, in a black cloak, I cannot see any red eyes. I am fearful as they approach me, I just hope they don't start man-handling me. To my surprise, the figure is right in front of me, lifting their hands up to their face and tugging at something beneath the hood. Black cloth slides down gently and the face beneath is smiling, I keep a straight face. Inside, I am overjoyed to see Indiara's beautiful smile, I just want to grab her and give her a big cuddle.

She quickly pulls the cloth back over her face and quietly starts cutting the vines with a knife, I pray she doesn't accidentally cut my hand. She begins to crouch to free my feet, but there are grunting sounds and footsteps again.

"Oh no." I whisper sadly.

Indiara casually stands up, she is not as tall as the *Vultus-Saudades* and they may notice something odd. She just stands motionless, staring, as they begin coming towards us both. I fear it is over for us both now, but I know Indiara is a lot stronger and wiser than I, if anyone can save us she can.

We hear some odd mutterings and then they appear to make their way in a different direction, disappearing into a hut. I wink at Indiara, and she proceeds to cut the vines around my feet. Within moments my feet are freed. Tragically, the *Vultus-Saudades* have reappeared and they are coming towards us with great speed. Indiara reacts sharply and removes the grey bottle from the belt, drinking it immediately and as quickly as possible.

Terrified I drop to the ground with my hands above my head as there huge bodies stand tall above us, shadowing us, bright red eyes beaming down frighteningly. Indiara turns to face them, standing strong with her legs in a wide stance, her hands on her hips. There is no fear on her part, she raises her right hand in front of her with a flattened palm, I remember the shield potion and realise that's what she has drunk in order to protect us. The *Vultus-Saudades* try to grab Indiara but their attempts are futile, they push against the invisible force with no success. They continue for some time angrily pushing and punching without any effort, the thuds come down hard, letting out a dull banging noise on our side of the shield. There is nothing to be afraid of, Indiara has such a solid stance, she is so brave I stand behind her and look at them with an evil in my eye that I have never felt before. I don't think I have ever truly hated somebody until this day, but I am disgusted by them.

Eventually, the wicked tribe give up their plight, they accept they cannot break down the shield but they sit and watch, waiting in the hope Indiara falters. If she lets her guard down, perhaps they could get to us both and I can only imagine they will treat us very poorly, our lives are at risk.

"Start moving sideways, follow me!" Indiara instructs forcefully.

"Ok." I oblige and copy her movements in order to get out of this dangerous situation.

The *Vultus-Saudades* clearly begin to get enraged by our apparent will to escape and make a further frightening attempt to stop us leaving by hammering punches down on the shield. Indiara somehow manages to push with all her might and to keep a stable shield around us. We continue to move slowly as she holds her hands out strongly keeping the shield in place, the stress etched across her face as she grimaces and strains.

After a terrifying battle against the angry tribe, I can see Indiara is growing tired from holding the shield. I find it remarkable how brave she is, I wish there was something I could to help, but because she was the one to drink the potion only she can operate the shield. We attempt to continue moving, but the force of the tribe throwing themselves against the shield is causing difficulty and we haven't moved more than a few feet.

"Listen to me!" Indiara shouts in a strained voice. "We have no choice but to drop the shield and run as fast as we can!"

"But, they are faster than us. It is impossible to outrun them in the thick forest, I tried to get away, that's how I was captured." I say apprehensively.

"Just trust me Melody." Indiara instructs loudly.

"I do." I shout in response.

Indiara bravely continues to shield us taking bigger steps, taking risks but attempting to stay strong despite a few wobbles. We make it to a narrow stretch between two of the huts where it becomes harder for the tribe to fight against us. Their large form means they cannot squeeze into the gap so well, we can see their long spindly fingers trying to grab at us.

"Run." Indiara whispers as she drops the shield and we start to sprint out from between the huts, onwards into the forest. I am aware of footsteps behind me but I don't look back, I just follow Indiara as fast as I can. We run for what seems like forever, further into the dark woods, we can hardly see where we are going. After a while, we realise the *Vultus-*

Saudades have given up following us. Indiara begins to slow down and I am able to keep up with her more easily.

"The coast might be clear at the moment but we have to keep moving, they may come looking for us. How are you feeling?" She asks breathlessly.

"I can keep going." I reply, more determined than ever before.

"Good. We have to keep going. Why did you get so angry with me before? You shouldn't have just disappeared like that, anything could have happened to you. I am just glad I had an idea of the path you would take and I was able to track you down." Indiara explains in a genuine tone, as we continue walking onwards at a slower pace.

"I am sorry Indiara, I just lost my temper. I missed you so much and hoped we would find each other again. I would probably be dead if it wasn't for you. Thank you so much for saving my life, I don't know how I can ever repay you." I say gratefully and apologetically in the same breath.

"You don't need to repay me, just help me find my brother." Indiara speaks desperately, tired from the drama and the journey. I know she just wants to find Kala and I really want to also, I hope she knows I feel exactly the same.

"I can certainly do that." I respond positively, trying to make her see how much I want to find Kala so we can finally rest but, I get the feeling she is still upset with me.

We walk for hours through the night, the darkness slows us and I realise we will need to sleep at some point. The forest is less thick and I am sure we are almost at the other side, free from the fear of the wicked tribe, free from the uncertainty for our safety and less scared as we walk out of the darkness into the light.

"Where should we go now Indiara?" I ask quietly, my voice croaky from being dry.

"We will go back to the village, we have done all we can, Kala has given up looking for answers and gone home." Indiara speaks exhaustedly, but still walking briskly.

"What happens if we get home and he isn't there?" I ask troubled by this thought.

"We will rest and then start looking for him again." Indiara responds determinedly.

"But, I have been away for days, I dread to think how worried my poor parents must be. I need to go home." I speak shakily and upset before collapsing to the ground with exhaustion.

"You can't give up now Melody. We should rest for a while before continuing on this journey. We should climb up a big tree to make sure we are safe and get some sleep." Indiara speaks quietly whilst lifting me up, propping my body against hers, she helps me onto my feet. "Do you think you can climb?"

"As long as you're with me Indiara, I can do anything." I say meaningfully, looking into her beautiful green eyes. She pats me on the shoulder and I know our friendship is back on track, we are stronger than ever.

We slowly climb up a large tree until we are high off the ground, safely away from any danger so we can have a restful sleep. It is a struggle as we are both weak from trekking so far. With Indiara's strength we both make it up high, out of the danger of anything below that could hurt us. Snuggling down into a large leaf, we go to sleep, almost instantly, worn out from what we have been through together. I feel safe with Indiara close beside me and I fall asleep soundly.

Chapter 17

I wake up feeling relaxed after a deep sleep as the sun rises through the trees, I look over to see if Indiara is awake but she is still sound asleep. I see some fruit further up the tree and quietly begin to climb up the branches, towards the red fruit. Once I have a handful I make my way back down to

Indiara, she still sleeps soundly on the large branch. I roll over beside her and stroke her hair gently, she opens her eyes slowly and smiles.

"Good morning, sleepy head." I say softly. "I got you some breakfast."

"Wow! I am impressed" Indiara speaks brightly as she sits up and grabs a piece of fruit out of my hand.

"Oh, it was nothing." I respond modestly, before taking a bite out of the little red fruit.

"I mean it Melody. When we started out on this journey you were like a little *parci,* you were nervous and clumsy. Now you have grown up, you are independent. You are brave and strong in a strange world that is not your own. How you have managed to cope is incredible, I am so very proud of you, but also you should be proud of yourself for all you have achieved." Indiara states loudly and passionately, I feel mildly bashful, I am lost for words. "You are amazing Melody."

I smile at Indiara as she throws her arms round me, her first warm embrace. This time it is genuine and comfortable, rather than forced and awkward. I feel proud of Indiara too.

"You are very courageous Melody." Indiara compliments me again and I feel confident enough to respond.

"You know something? I am proud of you too Indiara." I say with a wink and a smile towards Indiara. "I hope we find Kala soon. What are we going to do now?" I change my focus onto my concerns about what options we have left.

"I think we should head back, oh wait, hold on I better answer this." Indiara stops our conversation, her wrist band has begun to beep repeatedly.

"Shalama Mother. Are you ok?" She asks concernedly, turning away from me to concentrate on her call.

"Do not worry about me! Are you ok!? I haven't heard from you in so long!?" I hear her mum yelling down the line.

"We are fine Mother, we have walked for miles but still no sign of Kala I am afraid." Indiara speaks regretfully.

"This is why I am phoning child! He is here! He came home, he is exhausted from searching for answers. He was informed that although there is evidence that other worlds exist that we cannot travel to these worlds, so he gave up trying and came home. I told him that Melody is here looking for him and he is literally in disbelief. You have to come home right now! Where are you?" Her Mother speaks frantically.

"We are still quite far away, if we hurry we might make it home before night time. We will try Mother, please don't worry. Tell Kala that we will be there in no time." Indiara attempts to calm her Mother.

"Please just hurry, I want both my children home now, I am tired of worrying about you both. I love you my child." Her Mother responds lovingly.

"I love you too Mother." Indiara replies softly and the call is ended as she turns back towards me.

"We need to go as quickly as we can, Kala is waiting for you. I am so glad he is safe. Mother is concerned for our welfare, we should make our way home as fast as possible." Indiara instructs me, but I feel she's missing something quite important. I have no choice but to speak up.

"Indiara I won't be able to spend much more time here, my own Mother and Father will be concerned for my safety, I have been gone for days. They must be terribly worried about me." I say almost apologetically, but feeling that she simply must be aware of this concern.

"Well, we will find a way to get you home to your family. You have to see Kala for at least a little while first. This is why we have travelled all this way and he has gone to so much effort to find you. You have been gone for days, what harm is a little longer going to do now?" Indiara speaks boldly.

"Of course I want to see him, I have thought of very little else apart from him." I respond honestly. "I don't suppose it will do any harm to stay here longer."

"I hope that when you go home you will find a way to come back again, I will miss you." Indiara tells me sweetly.

"What if I am not able to go home?" I say filled with dread for my family, my friends and my Bertie.

"There is always a way back, if you could find a way here then you will find your way home, you have nothing to fear. Just remember how brave you have been, you are still stronger than you ever were before. Come on now we have to go." Indiara says encouragingly filling me with a new found strength.

We begin climbing down the tree, which takes a while because we are very high up. As we approach the ground, I realise that we are quite vulnerable and we need to move quickly to get out of the forest which will be safer.

"Indiara." I yelp frozen to the spot, clinging to a branch about two feet from the ground. "I am sure I can see red eyes staring at me. Over there between the bushes." I whisper pointing.

Indiara signals for me to be quiet by raising a finger to her mouth and points in the direction where I think I can see the red eyes, she then holds out her palm flat to me, signalling for me to wait where I am. She gently climbs down to the ground, slowly and silently. She moves in the direction I pointed to, but I start to fear for her safety, if there is a member of the tribe hiding nearby then we could be in grave danger. I know Indiara is strong but the tribe are extremely powerful, and we could be outnumbered. I hold my breath and pray it was just my mind playing tricks on me.

She crouches down, moving slowly sideways looking between the trees and leaves. A noisy bird jumps out from between the bushes and flies up towards the sky startling us both. Indiara composes herself quickly and looks around her, in all directions, examining every inch of the forest. She signals for me to come to her, waving her hand towards herself, still remaining very quiet.

I slowly and deliberately climb down the last few branches, gently steadying myself onto the ground, trying my hardest not to make a sound. I step carefully towards Indiara, focusing on every step I take, to ensure I don't make any noise. I reach Indiara and she holds her hand out towards me, I take her hand in mine and squeeze tightly.

"I can't see anything Melody, but I can't be sure we are not being watched. We need to be careful." Indiara whispers.

"What should we do?" I ask quietly.

"Just follow me." She replies. There is a rustling in the bushes. We both look towards where the rustling is, and the terrifying sight of red eyes and a black figure come towards us.

"Run!" Indiara shouts loudly.

There is no time to think, our lives are on the line, we have to run as fast as we can. Indiara holds my hand, but I can't run as fast as her and I have to let go. All kinds of thoughts rush through my mind, I see myself falling over like I did the day the tribe found me. The thought fills me with fear, I focus hard on running without tripping up and falling over. I can see Indiara ahead and I dare not look back to see if we are being chased, I can feel footsteps behind me. I continue running as the forest becomes less dense, and my fear of falling is growing less of a concern.

We must have been running for a while, it feels like a long time, my legs ache but I cannot. I can see the light brightening and the blue sky as we run, coming closer and closer to the edge of the forest. Indiara finally looks behind, at me, and she slows down. I find the courage to check behind and realise they are not chasing us. Perhaps they didn't bother trying to chase us, I will never know, it certainly felt like they were. I slow down to a walking pace and catch up with Indiara.

"Are you okay?" She asks breathlessly, still walking.

"Yes I am, I got a bit of a scare. We seem to have got away." I respond struggling to speak between heavy breaths.

"We need to keep moving." She tells me in a very serious tone.

"I know we can't risk stopping now." I reply in a strained voice from the exhaustion.

"Stay strong Melody." Indiara advises me positively, flashing me one of her lovely smiles.

We walk at a fast pace for about another thirty minutes or so and we come to the edge of the forest, which is a great relief. We can see deep blue beautiful sky for miles, in all its glory. We walk for maybe another mile, the tiredness is growing and Indiara flings herself rather dramatically onto the ground. Laying flat on her back with her arms and legs spread out like a starfish. I decide it would be extremely rude not to join her.

I roll down beside her and stretch my arms and legs out into a starfish position, turning my head towards Indiara, giggling. She smiles and giggles back at me, she is much more relaxed than before. I love seeing this side of Indiara, I was beginning to wonder if she knew how to have fun because she is so serious, quite a lot of the time, but now I see her enjoying laying down in the lush green field I am certain her life is filled with happiness. I know I need to get back to my parents, but right now I am terrified to leave this beautiful world. My life was so boring, I can barely remember what it is like to be there now. Even when the horrible *Vultus-Saudades* scared me half to death, it was still far more exciting than my boring life back at home, I felt more alive being so close to impending doom than ever before.

"I don't think I want to go home anymore. Maybe I can stay here forever." I say gleefully.

"I am glad you like it here Melody, but you cannot stay here forever. Like you said before, your family will be desperate to find you, they must be worried and scared. You must go home. You know how to get here so you can always visit us. It may be possible for us to visit you and see your world. I do love an adventure." Indiara states enthusiastically whilst looking up at the sapphire sky.

"Yes your right but I do love being here, your world is beautiful. I never told you before but I went into the big theme park on the outskirts of Cordovan. I even tried some of the rides, it was an amazing experience. There is nothing like this where I come from. The only way we fly is on aeroplanes." I explain happily.

"What are aeroplanes?" Indiara asks in an intrigued tone, rolling onto her side to look at me.

"You got to a big place called an airport where all the aeroplanes are. They have large wings and they are very long. They can hold lots of people and fly them to places all over the world." I try my best to describe it, but I fear it doesn't make much sense.

"Will you take me on an aeroplane one day? Your world does sound interesting." Indiara sounds even more interested than before, her eyes light up, I suppose it does sounds exciting when you haven't seen one before.

"Of course I will one day." I promise truthfully.

"What do you eat?" Indiara asks inquisitively.

"Oh we eat all sorts of different things. You can have dinner at my house with my mum and dad one day. We will need to dye your hair a normal colour, like black or brown because if you turn up with blue hair they might think you are a punk rocker or something." I explain joking with Indiara.

"What's a punk rocker?" Indiara asks with a confused expression. Adia doesn't have punk rockers.

"Doesn't matter." I say deciding not to go into detail.

"I don't want to dye my hair black or brown, it will look weird." Indiara tells me honestly.

"Okay you don't have to dye your hair. I love your blue hair anyway, I wouldn't change anything about you. You can even keep your bad temper!" I reply cheekily.

"Good. We should probably start walking again." Indiara states as she stands up, dusting herself down.

"Sure thing." I say as I stand up also, I am immediately struck by a patch of bright red flowers nearby that stand out against the bold green grass. The gorgeous red flowers remind me of Kala and his flame red hair. I want to lay here with him, I imagine what it would be like, one day I believe I will.

We begin walking again, it feels like the beginning of the end of our epic journey, I feel nervous and excited at the same time. I have a slight flutter in my stomach every time I think about seeing Kala for the first time. I wonder what I will say when I see him for the first time, I wonder what I should do. *Should I run up to him and hug him?*

Time passes quickly as we wander through the fields, up and down hills, free in the countryside, further away from the tribe. We reach the top of a high hill and look back over the land as night falls upon us, realising how far we have come I feel a tear in my eye. It is beautiful and for the first time I feel completely overwhelmed by the magnitude of the journey I have been on.

I breathe deeply as the waves of emotion hit me hard. Indiara grabs my arm, as she starts walking down the other side of the hill. There is no sense in stopping now, despite the tiredness growing we can't stop until we get back to the village. I feel myself slowing down, I don't know if it is due to exhaustion or sheer nervousness almost causing me to want to walk backwards. I have wanted nothing more than to meet Kala for the first time, it has turned into a huge event. It will be in front of other people. I hope I can get to a mirror, I have no idea what I look like after everything we have been through. I haven't been able to wash for a while now. He might take one look at me and decide I am completely disgusting and he doesn't even want to be near me. The emotions, thoughts and feelings I am going through verge on inexplicable, I don't understand them myself.

I conclude that all this walking has given me too much time to over-think the situation and I need to try and get my head together. I need to get excited about meeting him and let go of all the worries. There is no reason to fear, I know my concerns are blown out of proportion because of the unusual circumstances I find myself in. I mean it's not every day you smash a mirror into another world and trek for days to find your one true love. There I said it, my one true love, I know and I can admit this is meant to be. You don't put yourself through all of this for nothing, it has to be true love and I can't wait to see him.

"Do we have far to go now?" I ask expectantly.

"Not far now, we can do this if we just keep moving." Indiara speaks determinedly.

"I am tired and thirsty. I need a shower." I realise I sound very whiney.

"We will sort all of that out when we get back to my home." She says in a tone that suggests she can't be bothered with my whingeing.

"You must be thirsty too, what if it's too far for us to go without a drink. Is there nowhere we could at least stop for some rest to freshen up?" I ask hopefully.

"We could go to my Aunt and Uncle's house but it means we would probably need to stop for the night, because it is in the opposite direction to the village." She informs me which gives me hope, I decide to try and persuade her to go there instead of trying to get all the way back to the village tonight.

"We need to rest Indiara, if your Aunt and Uncle's house is closer than the village then we should go there instead. Get something to drink and a shower." I say persuasively.

"Well we shouldn't risk collapsing from thirst." Indiara says coming round to my way of thinking before changing the direction we were walking in.

We walk for what I guess to be around another half a mile, reaching a tiny village with only a few houses. The houses are very grand, like the mansions back at home, they are spaced out, some on higher ground and some lower down with large spaces of land around them. I turn to look behind me and realise the houses are in such an idyllic place. I imagine living here one day, with Kala, happy and in love.

We cross a small bridge that is over what appears to be a moat, running around the village. On the other side of the bridge there is a peer with a small raft tied to a pole on the very end. Indiara climbs down onto the very precarious looking raft and waves at me to join her. I nervously climb down onto the unstable raft as it sinks down into the water under my weight. I freeze to the spot, reaching out towards the peer to try and steady ourselves, I am scared that we go under the water.

"It will move around Melody, don't be afraid, crouch down beside me." Indiara encourages me to find my sea legs.

"Why can't we just walk to your Aunt's house?" I ask grumpily.

"Where is the fun in that!?" she cheekily asks, as I chuckle and slide carefully towards her. I sit with my legs straight out in front of me as Indiara picks up the oar and begins to row along the moat.

It is very dark and I have no idea how she can possibly see where she is going. I try to enjoy the ride despite feeling unsteady, I am looking forward to being back on dry land more than anything else. As we pass the large and very grand houses I know it must be late at night, but there is something quite eerie about how abandoned this place appears to be.

"Indiara, is it normally this quiet?" I ask curiously, looking around at the empty houses.

"No, it's like there is nobody here." She replies quietly, seemingly confused by the lack of activity.

We pull up on a peer further around the moat before Indiara ties the rope onto a pole, then she takes my hand to help me off the raft. I am relieved that we didn't fall into the water but realise there is still an eerie silence to this place, not quite as idyllic as I had initially thought. We wander along a path up towards a big house in front of us, I presume this is her Aunt's house but there is no sign of anyone being inside. There is a large grey monument in the middle of the front lawn with a round base on the bottom and a large voluptuous woman in the middle, looking pensively to the left. The path goes round either side of the monument and Indiara takes the left side, whereas, I take the right and we meet at the other side chuckling.

We walk up some steps to a beautiful house, with white stone and a large black double door. Indiara knocks on the door forcefully and then tries to look through a window to the left, holding her hand up to her forehead. After a few seconds she knocks again, but nobody appears to be at home. It is like the whole village has been abandoned.

"There is nobody here. You wait here whilst I check around the place to see if I can find a way inside." Indiara explains.

"I don't want to wait here by myself, it's kind of spooky here." I say feeling afraid.

"What is spooky?" This is obviously a word they don't use here in Adia.

"Like when ghosts and ghouls jump out and spook you." I try to explain in response.

"What is a ghost?" Indiara asks looking more puzzled and I remember the person passing at the theme park and think to myself perhaps they don't have a concept of ghosts or ghouls, maybe in Adia you don't die, you simply go somewhere else in a different form.

"It doesn't matter, sorry to confuse you. I just meant I am scared." I put to Indiara in a more sensible manner.

"Okay follow me and stay calm." Indiara speaks reassuringly.

We walk back down the steps and round to the side of the large mansion, down a path to the side which is very dark. There is nothing but silence and darkness, only the noises of our movements can be heard. We get to the rear of the mansion which is only a fraction lighter and we can see windows and a large door.

"Look up there Melody." Indiara whispers and points to a small window which is a few feet off the ground.

"I don't know if we could fit through there." I say nervously whilst tilting my head from side-to-side trying to judge whether I could make myself fit.

"Of course you can fit, come here." Indiara stands directly below the window. I walk towards her feeling worried that I won't be able to get through the miniscule gap. She suddenly grabs my legs with all her strength to help me reach the window. I grab hold of the window and open it as wide as it will go. I then grab the sill and pull myself up through the tiny gap. It is very dark inside and I can't really see anything, as I slide through the gap more easily than expected, I realise I am completely disorientated and land inside the house on top of something hard, with a thud and a cloud of dust.

"Are you okay Melody!?" Indiara shouts, worried by my apparent fall.

I dust myself down and cough a few times to clear the dust from my chest. I try to look around me, but I can hardly see a thing. Over to my left I can see a door slightly ajar letting in a little light. I decide I will try and get to the front door to let Indiara in the easy way, rather than tumbling through the tiny window.

"I am fine Indiara, I am going to try and find the door to the front of the house if you want to wait there so I can let you inside." I yell back to her.

"Okay, I will see you there!" She replies loudly.

I slowly step towards the door and open it gently as it creaks eerily, I am immediately in a huge space with large windows but the environment is still extremely dull, I can see very little. I run my hand up the side of the wall to try and find a light switch, but there is nothing so I give up. I walk carefully through the large room trying to navigate my way to where I believe the front of the house to be. Eventually, I find the front door, it doesn't appear to have a lock so I try opening it from the inside by pulling the handle. Indiara is standing right there smiling back at me.

"The door was open the whole time!" I shout angrily. "Why didn't you try the handle? I can't believe you risked my life, launching me through that window, anything could've happened to me!" I shout furiously.

"Well at least were inside now." Indiara comments flatly.

"This is true." I respond in a sarcastic tone, but decide to leave it at that because I don't want to get into any arguments again.

There is a large staircase in the centre of the house and Indiara immediately walks up the stairs. She is looking all around her, investigating her surroundings and has adopted what appears to be a kind of warrior stance. I feel she believes there might be something strange going on and wants to make sure that the house is empty, especially with the door being left unlocked. I immediately follow her carefully, checking all around me, all of the time, just to be sure there is nobody in here. As we come to the top of the dull staircase, I look back to the bottom. I jump out my skin at what I see.

"Indiara!" I bark. "There is somebody down there!"

Indiara immediately turns around and runs to the bottom of the staircase. I feel like crying, I saw the figure of a child in the darkness. I could see the outline of what would perhaps be a seven or an eight year old wearing a dress. I follow Indiara down but I can no longer see the child.

"Maybe my mind is playing tricks on me." I say shakily.

"I knew somebody was in here, I could sense it." Indiara states boldly.

"If there is somebody here, I believe I saw a small child over there." I say pointing to a door over to the left.

Indiara immediately runs over to the door, as she enters the room I hear a high pitched scream and a thud. I go running into the room and there is a small light on, Indiara is holding her arm as if it has been hurt and a small girl is standing in the corner, cowering, holding what appears to be a pan.

"She just hit me." Indiara speaks breathlessly.

"I am sorry Indiara. Who is that?" She speaks in a high pitched voice, she obviously knows Indiara.

"This is my friend Melody. Melody, please meet my cousin Tooteeya." Indiara introduces us, still struggling for breath and holding her arm where she must have been struck with the pan.

"We must have scared you." I say gently. "Are you okay?"

"No, I am most certainly not okay. I have been stuck on my own for five days now. Everybody in the village has fled, I don't know if they will ever come back for me. My Mother and father must not have noticed that I am missing." Tooteeya speaks sadly.

"We are here now, you will come with us." Indiara speaks authoritatively.

"I don't want to leave my home, they said we might never be able to come back. Please don't make me leave, I love my home" Tooteeya cries desperately.

Indiara runs across the room towards her and takes her in her arms as she sobs, clearly something very bad has happened here and Tooteeya has been through some kind of trauma.

"Why did everybody leave?" Indiara asks concernedly, as she strokes her hair.

"The evil red eyes, they kept stealing from us and bothering us, they had to abandon the village in the hope they would leave us alone, but I didn't want to go anywhere. They did say they were coming back, but it has been a long time now with no sign of anyone in the village." Tooteya says determinedly, holding Indiara tightly.

"Lock all the doors and shut any windows now." Indiara says forcefully.

Immediately we all run to doors and windows, checking and double-checking they are closed and locked for our own safety. I am nervous, especially seeing the *Vultus-Saudades* were so interested in me. I dread to think what they would do with me if they caught me again. We all meet in the landing at the bottom of the stairs, panting and leaning over from the frantic running around.

"We need to stay quiet and not draw any attention to ourselves, we cannot leave tonight. We need to keep this place in darkness. We will travel tomorrow in the daylight to be safer. The *Vultus-Saudades* don't tend to leave the forest during the day." Indiara whispers instructively as she takes charge of the situation. "Let's go upstairs, wash up and have some rest before we make our way home."

Tooteya leads us up two flights of stairs, this house must go up at least another two floors, it is absolutely gigantic. I thought that my home was big but, it is small in comparison to this house. It is so dark I feel disorientated, Tooteya knows where she is going. She leads us to a room and flicks a tiny torch light which she must have been carrying with her to show us where to shower, before flicking it off again. We really can't take any chances of being noticed, even although the house is locked down I wouldn't be surprised if the tribe could find a way inside. I have horrible flashbacks at the thought and feel squeamish.

Indiara sets up the shower and directs me towards it, which distracts me from my horrific thoughts. I undress before climbing into the shower cubicle, then I scrub myself thinking about meeting Kala and how I want to look my best to see him properly for the first time. When I come out of the shower, Indiara flashes a light which appears to come from her wrist band so I can see myself in the mirror. I can see for just a moment as Indiara turns off the flash that my hair is back to being brown, I look myself for the first time in ages and I am glad because I was frightened Kala wouldn't like me dressed as an Adian with blue hair.

"How did you do that?" I whisper in the darkness.

"You can set the shower to do many things. I thought you might want to look like you again. We only needed to disguise you for staying in the big city, so nobody decided to abduct you and turn you into some kind of science project." Indiara speaks quietly in a humorous tone.

Tooteya is waiting at the door and leads me a little way down the corridor to a large bedroom and taps the bed to let me know I can sit down. I sit down on the bed wrapped in a towel and realise I have no pyjamas, the thought is fleeting as little Tooteya hands me a nightgown.

"I am going to sleep in here with you tonight, so will Indiara, there are four beds so it is no problem, it's hard to tell with it being so dark in here." She whispers quietly. "I am going to go back for Indiara and you can get changed, make yourself comfortable."

I assume that giving out instructions must be a family trait, as Tooteya leaves the room I drop my towel to the floor and quickly pull on the nightgown before climbing under the covers and shuffling down resting my head into the huge cushions. It feels great to be so comfortable in a bed for a change, I don't think I will have much trouble falling asleep despite being on edge from all the drama today.

I start to doze off comfortably, cosy in the bed. The door opens and it startles me, I am wide awake again. I realise it is just Indiara, trying to quietly get into bed and that's why I felt frightened when she came in, because I never heard her making her way down the hall. I hear her getting into bed and she settles herself down quite quickly. I snuggle into my pillow and start to drift off again, hoping to dream blissfully of seeing Kala.

Chapter 18

I wake up before Indiara, bright and early as the sun rises letting a soft light into the bedroom. I stretch my arms and legs, slowly getting up to go and have a look out of the window. Curious to see where we are staying in the daylight, I look outside at the street below. It looks a lot different in the daylight, there is something eerie about the lack of people. The street looks like a ghost town that was once filled with life and I gaze into the distance, fascinated by this place.

"Get away from there!" I jolt, startled by Indiara snapping at me, I thought she was asleep. I immediately duck down underneath the window facing Indiara looking sorrowful.

"Sorry I was just curious." I whisper.

"You could be seen and get us into trouble." Indiara snaps again as she sits up from the bed.

"I know it was stupid, I won't do it again." I respond feeling really bad for putting us at risk.

"What did you see?" The little voice of Tooteya asks as she pops her head in through the door.

"Nothing, the street looks completely abandoned." I reply quietly.

"That's what I thought." Tooteya says quietly.

"We need to start making our way to the village as quickly as we can. We should have something to eat and then go. Don't worry Tooteya, we will find your parents." Indiara speaks authoritatively yet soothingly, which seems to help little Tooteya relax.

We immediately make our way down the stairs and through to the kitchen to get something to eat. Tooteya presses a button on one of the cupboards and the door slides upwards, revealing a variety of packaged items in brightly coloured packets, she grabs a few and hands them to us. I watch Indiara as she opens her red packet and munches the contents. I gingerly open my packet and examine the contents, looks like a crunchy snack. I start eating and it tastes pretty bland, but I feel full as soon as I have finished the small amount.

"That's weird, there was hardly any food in that packet and I am completely full. I literally couldn't get any more food in my belly!" I enthuse.

"Yes it's clever, it is so lucky we have so many packets of these because I would have been very hungry otherwise. You're not from around here are you?" Tooteya notices which doesn't really take me by surprise.

"No I am new around here, I am from a place very, very far away." I try to explain in a very basic way. "We don't have food like this where I come from."

"Oh I understand, you come from somewhere that only eats food grown in the ground, in the low lands, I have read about this before." Tooteya responds seeming interested.

"Something like that." Indiara chips in, just as I am about to speak. She looks at me and grins, I get the hint, I am sure she probably doesn't want to complicate things further.

"Should we head off now?" I ask in order to change the subject and because I am eager to get going. I can't wait to see Kala after all this time, I have dreamt about this moment for such a long time but now that is exactly what it feels like, a dream. It feels like I have come too far now, that it has to be real, I have to believe we are going to see him today because, I can't have come this far for it not to be real. I can't help but have a niggling feeling that it will never happen, we have struggled so much to get to this point and so many things have gone wrong. *What if I never get to see him at all?*

Indiara ushers us towards the door and Tooteya presses the pad to undo the locks so we can leave. As the door opens the light hits us and I am almost blinded as I blink several times, taking in the surroundings outside. I immediately feel sorry for Tooteya having spent several days now alone, without her family, without a single person to speak to, or to reassure her. I can't help but feel we were meant to find her and take her with us to safety. My Mother always said everything happens for a reason, even if at times we can't get to grips with what that reason may be, we will find out and understand at some point why things will turn out the way they do. Finally, I am starting to understand what my Mother meant when she told me this. We were meant to move to the big house in the middle of nowhere. I had to find that mirror, I was supposed to come here for a number of reasons, not just to find my true love.

Then it dawns on me, even although Kala and I have never met, all this thinking about him and longing to meet him is love. I have fallen in love with this boy and I am so excited that I am finally going to see him. I am so determined to get to him as quickly as possible, so I march off in front of Indiara and Tooteya.

"How do you know which way to go!?" Indiara shouts over to me.

"Sorry I was just guessing, I am eager to get back to meet Kala." I say almost shyly but comfortable that it is truthful, I no longer wish to hide my true feelings.

"Follow me, I know the quickest route." Indiara states taking charge.

Indiara strides ahead whilst Tooteya and I follow speedily behind her, sure to get back to the village as quickly as possible. There is still an intense feeling that we may be followed or even captured by the *Vultus-Saudades*. Especially as they had been bothering the villagers in the area, so, we must make our way as quickly and as quietly as possible so not to draw attention to ourselves. We knowingly march in silence towards the river and cross a wooden bridge to the other side.

As we start walking across the hilly field I think about how far we have come. I realise how much I have changed from being so shy and scared to being a much braver person than I ever was before. I have never had to fight for my life back at home, never been lost or alone, never had to find my way back to safety. Here, in Adia, I have had to do things I never dreamt I would do, I feel more alive than I ever did back at home. I feel like I have grown up from being a scared child into a young and courageous adult. As the light shines over the fields, I am engulfed by the beauty of Adia, it looks different from last night, the darkness has gone and it is a brand new day, filled with exciting new things. No matter what has happened, no matter what is going to happen, this experience has been truly magnificent and once I finally meet Kala, the fear I have faced will be all worthwhile. I wouldn't change anything for a minute, even crossing this field despite it taking such a long time, I wouldn't change a thing. I feel I have a friend for life in Indiara and I am more ready now than ever to meet Kala, all the effort and strife is going to make this moment so much more special than if he had been there on the other side waiting for me.

I can see some trees in the distance and feel that we have gone full circle, I know that Indiara's village is just beyond those trees and that Kala will be waiting for me. I can see some *fuzzles* in the distance, grazing. We must have walked for over an hour and I feel no fear that the *Vultus-Saudades* are chasing us now. We are completely in the open and they seem to like to travel at night, hiding in the darkness of the woods, waiting to prey on the vulnerable. They didn't get us but then I don't see Indiara as a particularly vulnerable person, she is physically strong and determined in nature. I have become a stronger person thanks to her, she has taught me a great deal about life and for that I am truly grateful.

The *fuzzles* are lovely creatures, so cute and chubby, I wish I could take one home. It makes me sad that the *Vultus-Saudades* want to harass these beautiful animals but they don't care about anything, they are pure evil. I wish there was something we could do to help them. As we walk across the fields and hills I think about various ways we could try to stop the *Vultus-Saudades*.

"Is there any way the Vultus-Saudades could be stopped?" I ask Indiara interested to see what she thinks.

"You see Melody, the emperor has tried to stop them but they are so vicious and feared that there is nothing they could do. Some time ago an agreement happened between the leader of the tribe and the emperor that they would stay in the forest and abide by the laws of the land. I don't believe they would abide by the laws and if I hadn't got to you when they took you hostage, anything could've happened to you." Indiara explains clearly.

We come to a high point on a hill and we all turn around to look back, to see how far we have come. The village is far in the distance now, the sleepy place was such an odd experience that I will never forget. Indiara rests a hand on the shoulder of little Tooteya in a supportive way.

"Not far to go now and we will find out exactly what has happened." Indiara speaks protectively.

We make our way towards trees and I realise I am back where I started, back where this whole amazing journey began. I can't believe we are back here, yet I have no idea how long it has been since we were last here. I have completely lost track with days blending into night, blending into days, suddenly a beautiful, colourful, unexpected haze is in my minds-eye as I reminisce over my wonderful experiences here. I picture Stormie in her character drenched house, sitting staring at us, predicting our future in her very own magical way. I see Tikto and his interesting potions and his wonderful vibrant house, I see his smiling face, I feel I am carrying his joy and his enthusiasm with me on my journey, I will forever. I can see Mahari clearly, willing us onwards, her warmth and her caring nature sadly tainted with the pain of never finding her true love. Although there was a large gap between us in age, we truly understood each other and the generation gap was completely closed in our mutual empathy for both knowing the feeling of longing to be with somebody truly special. As sad as I felt for her pain I drew strength from her, after meeting her I knew I had to find Kala.

As we walk deep into the trees, I can see the lake that I nearly drowned in before Indiara saved me and I recognise it straight away, I pause for a moment, oblivious to everything else that is going on around me. I am no longer thinking about getting to the village as quickly as possible. I am lost in a daze, lost in my thoughts almost like I have gone into a sudden shock. I feel like I have evolved into a completely different person, like an outsider reflecting on the life of a person I know longer associate myself with. I was bored, lonely, weak and shy. I didn't believe in myself, I didn't think I was capable of anything worthwhile. I know right at this moment, the reason I have become this way is thanks to Kala and it makes my love for him feel stronger.

I suddenly snap out of my trance and look around to see Indiara and Tooteya up ahead. I run along to catch up as Indiara notices, turning back to look at me and waving me onwards. I still feel apprehensive and perhaps that's why I keep slowing down, deep in thought, taking time to consider everything that is about to happen. I imagine running into Kala's arms, I picture him so handsome on the other side of the mirror. I see how beautiful Indiara is and know that he will be even more gorgeous than I could ever have dreamed. I long for our first kiss, my first kiss. Then I realise I have never kissed a boy before and I really don't know what to do, but the one thing I do know is just how much I want to kiss him even if I don't know what I'm doing.

We walk through the trees, there are various rustlings but I feel no fear. I know that I am stronger than ever before and as long as I am with Indiara we can come through anything. The sky grows darker as we approach evening, the twilight of dusk creates a tranquil atmosphere and the warmth in the air, mixed in with the excitement of meeting Kala fills me with a joy that I can't find the words to describe. I know we are nearly there and my steps begin to quicken as Indiara skips ahead with Tooteya, we are all desperate to get back to the village. We can hardly contain ourselves as we start running.

"Yip! Yip! Yip!" Indiara screeches at the top of her voice in a cheerful way. It sounds like it could be some kind of a call to the villagers, letting them know she is home, safe and well.

Tooteya runs as fast as she can behind and I catch up with her as we approach the outskirts of the village. Despite me going through so many changes, the village has stayed completely the same. We sprint through the village, following Indiara up to the front of her house and we all stop to catch our breaths before going in. The door opens and a bright light is shining, there is a figure of a young man standing there. I stand back trying to work out if it is Kala, but as my eyes adjust to the light I realise it is not him. I feel adrenalin pumping through me, my hands are shaking and I try to control them. I am half excited, half nervous about meeting Kala for the first time. All kinds of questions are invading my mind. *What will I say? What will I do? Will I run up and give him a hug? Should I wait to see if he comes towards me? Will his Mother approve if I do hug him?*

"Daddy!" A little voice shouts breaking my train of thought and it all begins to make sense as Tooteya runs towards the tall, dark haired smiling man. He crouches down and scoops her up into his arms holding her so tight, he simply never wants to let go of her.

Indiara walks into the house and runs to her Mother to give her a hug, I stand and watch like an outsider. I imagined Kala being so excited to see me that he would come running out the door. I feel a pang of sickness as I realise I am just stood here alone after all this time, a sadness drapes over me and I awkwardly look at the ground tapping my feet against the floor.

"Mother!" Indiara shouts. "Where is Kala!?"

"He came home but he couldn't wait for you, he said he had to find Melody. He was going to try the lake where he had seen her for the first time." She replies quickly.

I look up at them and they look back at me, I feel tired and weary but I know I have to go back to the lake. I wonder if we walked passed him, when I think back to all the rustlings I realise perhaps he was one of them and somehow, we just missed each other. I am not upset by this because I know what he wanted to do now. I know he wants to meet me alone for the first time, nobody looking on, just me and him. It will be like us meeting before, but without the mirror between us both. We can talk properly, hold hands, if things go really well, maybe we could even have our first perfect kiss. I turn to face back towards the trees and know I have to go back, but the young man who has put Tooteya down grabs my arm and I turn back to face him.

"Kala will wait for you, please come in and have something to eat with us, you must be starving." He offers in a gentle voice.

My initial reaction is that after all this time, the many miles I have trekked and the danger we have faced that I must go and be with him because I have waited long enough. However, looking into the eyes of this man I can see the concern, I imagine as a father that he wants to ensure that I am safe. He is right in that, after the distance we covered today we must have something to eat. My body will not even carry me to Kala if I don't have some food and that first kiss with him that I long for will be far from the magical experience I dream it to be if I collapse from lack of nourishment.

"Thank you for the kind offer. I am so excited to see Kala after all this time I feel I should go just now but I should probably rest and eat before going to him. Please forgive me for not staying long." I explain carefully.

"I understand why you want to go rushing off but you must eat. Please come inside." He directs me through the door into the house, as soon as I am in the door Indiara's Mother takes me in her arms – her warmth is so calming as I rest my head on her shoulder.

"You must be Melody! I am so glad you both made it back safely. Kala is keen to hear all about your travels but he couldn't wait and I couldn't stop him for going back out. I told him he must not go further than the lake and if it gets late he must come home. He will listen, I am not having my children gone for days again. I know he just wanted to get you back safe an, I couldn't sleep." She bellows rather dramatically. "I will make you something to eat, come sit down in the kitchen."

We all make our way to the kitchen, another lady is standing there with beautiful long golden hair, so bright it is sparkling. She is very pretty and smiling kindly, as soon as Tooteya comes into the room she lets out a scream of sheer joy and runs towards her. Her mum grabs her and holds her tight as she begins to sob into her tiny shoulder.

"Oh Mummy you are being silly." Her Dad says in a giggly voice, trying to lighten the mood.

She puts Tooteya back down, wipes her eyes and smiles sweetly at her beautiful daughter, as she smiles back at her lovely Mother. I am so glad we have all found each other in that moment, a family who was torn apart have found themselves back together again and that is the best feeling of all.

After a short time Indiara's Mother has served up some hot deliciously looking brightly coloured food in a dish. It smells wonderful and as soon as she places the dishes down in front of everyone particularly myself, Indiara and Tooteya begin wolfing the food down as quickly as possible. I am starving but always a little more cautious about tucking into anything because, I am so unfamiliar with the kind of food they eat here. I try a little piece of a mashed up blue coloured food and it tastes scrumptious. I start to wolf my dinner down as quickly as the others do and slurp up some water. I feel much better after having something to eat and I am glad they persuaded me to come inside.

"So what happened at the village Uncle Rollo? Why were all the houses abandoned?" Indiara asks loudly, I can see the disgust on her Mother's face.

"Indiara! Don't ask such things, it is none of your business!" Her Mother shouts angrily.

"It is ok Starzi, I don't mind explaining to Indiara." I think that is the first time I have heard her Mother's name, I was beginning to think she was just called Mother. "The *Vultus-Saudades* had been bothering us for a while. Some of the tribe were even letting themselves into our homes and helping themselves to whatever they could find. We began to get very frightened and the village called a meeting. We decided to flee collectively and left in a mass group at the same time. We felt we would be safer if we stayed together. We walked to various places, making sure that fellow villagers made it safely to close friends or family."

"Why did you leave Tooteya behind? Why didn't you go back for her? She is tiny and was alone for such a long time. Anything could have happened to her." Indiara barks at her uncle, clearly angered at them for seemingly not doing enough to reunite with their daughter.

"Let your uncle speak! Such a rude child!" Starzi shouts again, apparently annoyed and I get the hint very embarrassed at how she would have the audacity to speak to her elders in such a way.

"It's ok. Indiara, you know we wouldn't have intentionally left her behind. I know it is unforgiveable, but we moved in such a rush. We took as much as we could carry and then moved as quickly as possible to get to our various destinations. We were sure Tooteya was in the crowd, there were hundreds of us. I know it isn't an excuse, but as soon as we realised she was missing a rescue operation began. We were advised to stay here with your Mother to avoid any more danger whilst the rescue took place. We were delighted to find out that you had found Tooteya and took her here. Nothing like this will ever happen again, I can assure you." Rollo speaks sincerely.

"No, it definitely won't happen again!" Indiara states firmly.

"That is enough! We all need to get some rest and Melody needs to go to meet Kala." Starzi interjects crossly.

"I should walk you back." Indiara speaks more calmly than before. "For your own safety and to make sure you don't get lost."

"I want to go on my own." I say boldly.

"It isn't safe for you to go on your own Melody!" Indiara says becoming more heated again.

"Let her go, she will find her way." Starzi interrupts, now beginning to sound exasperated with the way Indiara is talking to everyone. She can be very audacious, but I have begun to find this endearing. She has taught me so much, how to be courageous and fight my own corner. I was an anxious feeble little girl before this all started and without Indiara I am certain I would not have come so far.

"Indiara you have taught me well, you have protected me and taught me to look after myself but, it is time to let me go and let me find out if this little bird can fly on her own." I say meaningfully.

"Ok Melody. I trust you will make your way safely to my brother." Indiara speaks before holding her arms out to me. I run towards her and give her the biggest cuddle I have ever given anyone. I know I have to go home, I have been gone for so long now. I don't know if I can even get home but I have to try and the saddest thing is this could be the last time we ever see each other. With all the courage I have learned and for all the boldness Indiara possesses neither of us are able to confront the truth. We just hold each other in a tight embrace, knowing we never want to say goodbye to each other, but for now this may be the last time we see each other for a while; in person at least.

As I walk towards the door I turn back and wave to everyone, feeling a distinct sadness, a heaviness inside that I have never felt before. I would stay here in Adia forever, but I know my family must be worried sick. If I was going to live here I would at least need to go home and tell them that I was leaving first, although I have no idea how I would begin to explain that. As I make my way through the village and back to the trees, I feel a tear roll down my cheek. I quickly wipe it away as I find happiness in knowing I will see my handsome true love for the first time.

I was nervous about the darkness in the trees, but now that I am here I have realised there was nothing to fear. There are various plants and animals that glow in the dark, blues, greens, yellows, oranges and pinks. It looks truly beautiful, a sight of sheer enchantment to behold. I could never have dreamt of anything more beautiful as I walk through the stunning glow. I am inside my very own personal magnificent fairy-tale, feeling more charmed than any of the princesses I have ever read about. I feel on top of the world, I simply can't believe what is happening.

I approach the lake which has a dull, blue glow which appears to become brighter at one central point. I consider whether that must be the way back home but how will I ever be able to jump back in, I am terrified I will drown. I look around but Kala is nowhere to be seen, I feel a shudder, I am so disappointed. I consider that he may have wandered off, not obeying his Mother's instructions. I feel like crying here and now, I am so emotional about meeting him. I manage to keep myself together. I can't have him meeting me for the first time with red puffy eyes and snot running down my chin.

I decide to walk a bit further around the lake, it is warm but I feel shivers from the mixture of emotions running through me. This love thing isn't what I expected it to be. I feel happy, sad and sick all at the same time, not the romantic ideal I had in mind.

I walk in a huge circle, back to the central point with the brightest blue glow and still he is nowhere to be seen. Now I start to feel concerned, I shouldn't have walked so far and perhaps if I had just stayed in the same place I would've finally met him. I can't believe this, I have waited all this time, searched for so long only to be here where he wanted me to be. The perfect moment should've happened at least an hour ago, but it is yet to take place. I sit down, exhausted and emotionally drained by the whole experience.

As I sit, I find some small pebbles and begin throwing them into the lake. I contemplate everything that could've possibly happened. I try to find reasoning with every pebble I throw in. I imagine I have gone wrong somewhere, perhaps even followed the wrong path, although I am sure I was in the right place. I can see the other side of the lake perfectly where we were meant to meet, it isn't far from one side to the other. I am captured by the beauty of the blue glow and the gorgeous surroundings, somehow I have not lost hope or faith, so I begin praying in the hope somebody up there will hear me and bring my true love to me.

I realise I have thrown in all my pebbles and start to look on the ground for more. I see in front of me a rock that is glowing green and I pick it up to inspect it. I close my hands over it and see the bright green light streaming from between my fingers. It reminds me of the crystal I used to smash the mirror to come here. As I open my hands I stand up again and throw it forcefully into the lake creating a big splash.

"Melody?" I hear a gentle voice speak my name and I look up. Stood on the other side of the lake, so near, yet so far is the handsome, flame haired young man I have been longing to see. I am speechless. I just stare at him, captured by his unspeakable attractiveness. Also, I am paralysed by my fear of doing something stupid to ruin this.

"Is that you? It is quite hard to tell in this darkness." He asks sounding a little nervous.

"Yes it is me." I say back.

"What are you doing over there?" He enquires confusedly.

"I was over there, but I thought you would've been here so I went wandering to try and find you. I thought maybe I was waiting in the wrong place." I explain embarrassedly.

"It's ok, I will come to you, hold on." He said as he jumps into the lake to swim to me. For some absurd reason I jump in after him, the water is so deep but I am determined to get to him.

"Why did you jump in!?" He shouts as he swims towards me.

I am unable to respond to his question, I am thinking exactly the same thing. I should've waited, I am struggling to swim in the deep water and I feel almost like I am being sucked under. I am scared and I have no idea what to do, I splash around helplessly trying to stay on the surface.

After what feels like forever but perhaps only minutes of splashing, he grabs my right hand tightly and drags me with all his strength. He gets my head back above water and I look into his beautiful emerald green eyes, lost for a moment, forgetting the danger I had put myself in. I try to catch my breath but seeing him, him holding me in the water, him saving me is too much. I suspect I would have been breathless no matter how we met.

He leans towards me as his lips touch mine, it is all happening so quickly and we kiss our very first kiss. I am swept away by the magic, in the warm water of the lake glowing beautifully and blue underneath. I hope it will last forever, I have never felt this way before, I never want to let him go.

Suddenly, I feel a force pulling me down under the water, I am being dragged. I see fear in Kala's eyes and I know I am slipping from his tight grip. The force dragging me under is much too great for even a strong young man like Kala to fight back against. All the while, all I can think is this cannot be happening to me. I was so happy mere moments ago and I am going to drown, I am going to die.

I am under the water thrashing about as I am being dragged back, Kala held on for as long as he could. He stretches out towards me, but there is nothing he can do. You can see by the shocked, upset expression on his face he is utterly helpless as he floats back to the surface. It is the inexplicably horrible feeling of great force, tearing us apart. I am sucked down deeper and I feel myself running out of air quickly, I black out.

Chapter 19

I wake up laying on the floor of the basement in complete darkness, somehow I am dry. I pad myself down, puzzled by what happened. I thought I had drowned but thankfully I am still alive, although I am sadly separated from Kala. My main concern as I bring myself to my feet is that he won't know that I am okay. I turn to the mirror which has begun to glow blue. I notice immediately it is not broken anymore. It looks like somebody has replaced the mirror, I can see some kind of blurry image gradually becoming clearer.

As the image in the mirror becomes clearer I realise Kala is sitting there drenched from being in the lake with his head in his hands. I frantically start searching around in the basement for the crystal that I threw at the mirror to break it but, I can't see it anywhere. I go through the door and check the chest of drawers to see if it is there, opening all the drawers and padding around in them hoping to feel something. Then I remember the Tavia gave me a crystal, I put my hand in my pocket and sure enough it is still there.

"Kala!" I shout. "Kala!"

He looks up and wipes his face, he is so beautiful and I wish I could be there to wrap my arms around him and tell him everything is going to be okay. His expression reveals he is puzzled and he stretches his arm out in front of him which blurs and seems to disappear.

"Melody, are you okay? I thought you drowned and it was my fault for not rescuing you. I am so happy to hear your voice." He speaks emotionally.

"I am ok, I am at home. We seem to be back where we started." I say sorrowfully. I feel the confidence to tell him exactly how I feel. "I wish I was there with you, that kiss was out of this world, literally."

"I know it was truly magical. I can't believe I lost my grip. It was like some extreme force was pulling you down beneath the water." Kala speaks and my heart jumps.

"Maybe it was meant to be, I have been worried about my parents. I must go and see them Kala, I need to see if they are okay. I need to let them know that I am okay." I say anxiously.

"I understand, you have to go and find your parents, please come back and see me in the morning." Kala speaks and I am delighted, I smile longingly at him.

"I definitely will, I promise." I say before blowing him a kiss and he smiles.

I run through to the basement and run up the stairs, to the kitchen. I struggle with the door at first but then I make it through, swiftly being greeted by my old friend Bertie. He knocks me clean over jumping up onto me, he is so excited we are back together after such a long time and we roll about on the kitchen floor.

"I have missed you so much Bertie, so so much." I say holding him and ruffling up his lovely soft fur that I have missed every day. "You're the best dog ever."

"What's all this commotion?" Dad interrupts and Bertie instantly jumps away from me and runs over to him. I stand up and dust myself down then run over to Dad, wrapping my arms around him. "Are you okay Melody?"

"I am just so glad to see you." I say gleefully.

"I saw you only yesterday. I did think it was a little odd I hadn't seen you all day, but I just thought you were busy doing something." Dad says in a confused tone, frowning at me.

"So I have only been gone for one day?" I ask surprised by his response.

"Gone where? I hope you had permission from your Mother to be going away." Dad speaks grumpily.

"Oh I meant gone for a walk in the garden, sorry Dad, didn't mean to confuse you. Perhaps I am not making sense, I am very tired and need to get some sleep." I say trying to cover up for muttering like I am completely insane.

"Okay Melody, you're a funny little girl." He says ruffling my hair as he walks over and puts the kettle on. "Very funny girl, must get it from her Mother." He whispers, but I hear him perfectly. I don't take any notice as I run upstairs to my bed, nothing has changed in my bedroom, it looks exactly the same. I am in disbelief that really no time has passed and nothing has changed. Perhaps when I was in Adia, time simply stood still. I can't even fathom how that could be possible and right now I am too exhausted to think about it. I climb into my lovely big comfortable bed, fully clothed and fall asleep.

I dream about Kala and our first kiss, I dream of being with him forever but then the horrible moment comes where we are ripped apart. I see the evil eyes of the *Vultus-Saudades* staring at us, laughing at me being dragged away from him. They take extreme delight from my severe pain.

I wake up breathing heavily and I sit straight up, shaken by my own thoughts in my sleep. My Mother comes in and I am so happy to see her, she doesn't speak, she simply sits down on my bed and gives me a cuddle letting me know everything is alright. She pulls away from me and strokes my hair very gently, I didn't realise how much I had missed her.

"Did you have a bad dream my lovely?" Mother asks so sweetly.

"Yes, it was scary." I respond croakily.

"You're okay now. Why don't you come down to the kitchen and I will make you something for breakfast?" She asks and I immediately smile, delighted at the thought of some 'normal' food.

"Yes that would be fantastic!" I say whilst rubbing my eyes.

She leaves the room and I slowly wriggle out from under the covers, get out of bed and put my slippers on, still just where I expected them to be. I don't know why I would've expected anything to change, it is as if no time has passed at all. I can't fathom what the science would be behind this but somehow time has stood still, while time in Adia moved on. I think about what that would mean for myself and Kala.

I ponder my future whilst I make my way down to the kitchen to have breakfast. I think this could be a first for me because I don't believe I have ever worried about the future before, I just lived each day, thinking about the rest of the day with no consideration for next year, not even next week. Now all of a sudden, I am considering the next twenty or thirty years, I conclude growing up is extremely complicated.

I take a seat at the table as Bertie rushes towards me and sniffs around, hoping some food will come his way. I pat him on the head and ruffle his fur as he cheekily, restlessly waits by my feet. I smell the delicious cooked breakfast my Mother has made, I didn't realised how much I missed good home cooking. I wait what seems like an eternity for the magnificent goodies to appear in front of me. My stomach feels surprisingly pained as I am about to delve into my sausage, bacon, scrambled eggs and baked beans. I chew slowly, enjoying every mouthful, savouring the familiar flavours that I haven't sampled for what feels like a lifetime. The pain ebbs away from my stomach and I feel nothing more than a sheer satisfaction from eating greasy, fried, delicious food.

"You're really enjoying that Melody." Mum says cheerfully before sitting down with her own cooked breakfast.

"Oh mum it is fabulous." I reply and she smiles before she begins to eat.

I finish my breakfast and drink down a big glass of orange juice, it tastes like the sweetest, juiciest liquid I have ever tried. I am completely and utterly stuffed full of food, I try desperately to hold in a burp for fear of offending my Mother but suddenly it just comes out.

"Melody! That's not very ladylike." She shouts at me.

"Sorry mum, it just popped out." I say apologetically.

"Don't do it again!" Mother orders disgustedly.

"I promise I won't." I say, but truthfully I feel annoyed that she gets herself so upset about such little things, Indiara was quite partial to the odd burp and never apologised. Sometimes my parents are so up-tight it's just silly. "Where's Dad this morning?" I say swiftly changing the subject.

"He is out visiting the man who used to live here, Stanley I think his name is." She explains.

"Why is he visiting him?" I ask, realising that this is probably the Stanley that Mahari told us about and how she so longed to meet up with him. She thought she would never seem him again but maybe I could make it happen, normally I wouldn't be able to believe such a coincidence but after everything I have been through recently, I am open to believing anything.

"I think he found something sentimental that belonged to him in the attic and wanted to get it to him." Mum explains and it all makes sense.

"Does he live near here?" I ask curious to know if I could find him.

"I think he lives in a village called Newpine, about 20 miles away." Mum explains as I listen intently.

"How do you get there?" I ask without thinking that this might sound a little odd.

"Why are you asking so many questions Melody?" She asks, looking at me suspiciously.

"Oh nothing, I am just curious." I say, hoping she doesn't quiz me further.

"Hmmm. Okay well you can't sit around in your pyjamas all day, go and get washed and dressed." Mum instructs me, so I dash off upstairs to have a shower.

As I step into the boring old shower it seems somewhat mundane compared to the modern technology that the Adians use. I have to work so hard in this shower scrubbing and washing. I close my eyes and at once I am back there, changing my appearance with all the high-tech gadgets that were available. It all just seems like a dream now, opening my eyes I see a very normal, plain off-white cubicle, very old fashioned. It is as if I was never even there. I decide immediately that I must go back to the basement and wait for Kala. I may feel so far away from Adia and from Kala but I have to keep believing I will go back there, I can never give up hope. If I could do it once, I am sure I could go back and visit again. I know he tells me he would like to come visit here, but I am not sure he would like it very much.

I turn off the shower and step out, drying myself on a towel, feeling again like this is an awful lot of hard work and that it isn't even over yet, I will need to brush and dry my hair. *Oh how things are so different back here!*

I feel like my life is so much more complicated than it was only days earlier, I am now torn between too places, my family who I love dearly and my new found love in another world. As I make my way back to my room and dress myself in a pair of black leggings and a baggy purple jumper, I think of Indiara and how much I miss her already. I can hear her loudness, her brashness ordering me around in a sometimes patronising way which is aggravating to me, but, I miss her.

I quickly brush through my thick hair and shake it up so it's even bigger and thicker, much like it was when I had it styled in the Adian shower but less blue, well, not at all blue but never mind. I rush because I need to know I am going to see him again, to make sure this is all real and not some sort of crazy dream.

I rush down the stairs, but I am stopped by Bertie running towards me, he barks and yelps, rubbing up against me like he knows something. I try to push him out of the way but he isn't budging and I am nervous on these stairs that if I push too hard that we may fall.

"What's wrong Bertie?" I ask him rubbing his big head. "Please let me past, I have things I need to do."

Mum comes out of the kitchen and looks at me with a surprised expression on her face. She looks me up and down, seemingly puzzled by my appearance. I awkwardly focus on Bertie, stroking him and pretending not to notice her uncomfortable staring. I know it is only a matter of time before she makes some form of comment as Bertie runs off down the stairs, I begin to follow him slowly. Mum still stares at me without moving, apparently speechless as I head through the door to the kitchen.

"Is there something wrong Mum?" I can no longer ignore her staring so I ask quietly.

"You just don't look yourself Melody, your hair is wild and you look like you're dressed to go to the gym, in the eighties, where did you get those clothes?" She asks aghast.

"Oh just something I found at the back of the wardrobe." I say dismissively.

"Hmm, strange girl, she must get it from her father." She mumbles as she shuffles away in her slippers through to the lounge.

I notice the basement door is slightly ajar, which I am very pleased about because it means I can just sneak down there with no difficulties, without any risk of getting caught doing anything and being called strange. I am starting to get slightly offended of being referred to as strange all the time, my parents are quite bizarre so it isn't really my fault anyway, genetically I didn't stand much chance of being exempt from strangeness.

I shut the door as quietly as possibly, before tip-toeing down the basement stairs, avoiding creaks as best as possible hoping to see that familiar face. Much to my despair there is no blue glow under the door today, it just looks like a normal dark basement. I go into the room and switch the light on. The mirrors and the bright lights dazzle me, going from such darkness to complete brightness is hard on the eyes. It takes a minute for them to adjust as I rub them gently, when I take my hands away it just looks like a gym, the mirror is perfectly intact. I go over to touch it, just to be sure, hoping the portal is there and I can venture through. I don't even care if I have another drowning experience, I just want to go back to Adia and spend the time with Kala that I was so dreadfully robbed of. *Why is life so unfair?*

I turn the light off and close the door, I sit down with my legs crossed and I close my eyes as I begin to reflect over everything that has happened recently. I try to find some clarity as it all seemed to happen so fast, it seems like such a blur so I try to slow things down in my mind and think about everything from beginning to end. Memories of faces and situations are vivid, despite at some points my questioning whether any of this is real, or perhaps I have a really active imagination or maybe even some psychological defect.

"Melody." I hear a faint voice whisper in the distance, a familiar faint voice. I open my eyes and to my delight this is not madness at all, it is real and there she is. My beautiful far-away companion, Indiara.

"Hello!" I yell excitedly. "How are you? Have you been slaying any *jumokee* recently!?"

"Haha! No, but I am good thank you. How are you sweet Melody? I hope you are well, Kala told me what happened to you. He is very upset." She tells me as I feel deeply saddened by the news that he is upset.

"I want to come back Indiara but I am not sure how I can, I suspect I could break the mirror again. Time seems to stand still here when I am with you. I am scared what the future could hold for us, but I know that I want to come back." I explain on the brink of tears.

"I am sure you will and sooner rather than later, my brother is lost without you. So, I decided I should help him and I remember you said you smashed the mirror with the crystal. So I started to think if there was some sort of way of smashing it from this side. I think it could be possible if we swim under with the crystal to try something. What do you think?" She asks and I am extremely interested in her theory.

"I think anything is worth a try. So you mean you and Kala would come here?" I ask curious as to how they would feel about that and whether it would upset their poor worrier of a Mother.

"Yes we want to visit your world. We heard so much about it and we are extremely fascinated." Indiara explains in an enthusiastic tone.

I ponder this, with Indiara's skill, Kala's strength and my big heart maybe we could find Stanley together and take him to Mahari, the way it was always meant to be. I would do anything to make their dream come true and I know after what we have been through we could do absolutely anything.

"When do you want to do this?" I ask keen to know when to expect the most welcome and wonderful visitors.

"Today." She says to my surprise.

"Ok that's great because I really need your help with something." I respond feeling full of hope and with the biggest smile across my face, that has ever been recorded in the history of the world.

The end.

Printed in Great Britain
by Amazon